Faceless Angel

MacCormac Warriors Trilogy
Book One

LuAnn Nies

Scottish and English romances are my favorite genres to read. Faceless Angel is the book of my heart and I have wanted to write it for years. This book is dedicated to my friend and publisher Nancy Schumacher. For without her encouragement and support I would not have had the nerve to write this book.

My hat goes off to those writers who I have had the pleasure to read over the years, they are all extremely talented. I will never be in their league, but I am grateful to have the opportunity to tell this story. I truly hope you enjoy reading it and love the characters as much as I do.

I would also like to thank two wonderful writers and critique partners, Jill Dalton and Elyse Lawrey for their brilliant edits and suggestions during this process.

Scottish Highlands 1690

A land integrated with History, Romance, Beauty, Oppression, and Hatred.

A time and place when women would do anything to survive, and anything to protect those they loved.

One

Castle Corell 1690
Scottish Highlands

Laird Cameron MacCormac, chieftain of Clan MacCormac, ambled out the ancient keep of Castle Corell and drew in a deep breath. The crisp autumn breeze rustling through the nuim trees and mountain ash soothed his tight muscles but did little to alleviate the uneasiness of his forthcoming meeting with the English Baronet, Sir Alexander Boyd. A foreboding sensation hovered in the morning air triggering his senses to full alert. Vigilantly he scanned the inner bailey.

Cam spotted his former brother-in-law, Rory Murdock, and three young recruits standing in the training ring. Scratching his scruffy beard, Cam tossed back his untethered black mane. Taking his time, he trekked down the wide stone steps and strolled toward the fenced in area. There was no reason to hurry; the requested training session wouldn't take long. There were more important matters at hand like the unexpected visit from the Baronet, Sir Alexander, which required his complete concentration.

As Cam approached the training area, he surveyed the four men, determining each man's presumed capabilities. One of the men, more of a lad, cleared his throat and retreated two paces, not unlike a startled young stag preparing to bolt.

Cam snickered.

Hugh MacCormac stepped forward and presented Cam with Cam's double-edged broadsword, which had served Cam well over the years. Holding a wooden targe shield so Cam could slip his arm through the leather straps, Hugh said with an undertone of humor, "Take it easy on the lads. Donae kill them right off."

Cam eyed his cousin and sneered. "I'll go easy on them." Even though he wished this scrimmage was with only his exbrother-in-law, Cam had no plans to grant Rory or Rory's men a scrap of clemency.

Graceful as a red deer, Cam jumped over the wooden rails into the training ring. Steam billowed from between his snarled lips as he slashed the air with his sword and taunted them with barbed insults. "Nay a sorrier bunch of tit-suckers I hae ever seen." He evaluated his four opponents as he edged his way around the training ring. The purpose of Sir Alexander's forthcoming visit loomed in the forefront of his mind. What did the baronet want from him? Cam tilted his head from side to side and rolled his stiff shoulders in hopes of relieving some tension. Nevertheless, the thought of the English Baronet's appending arrival twisted his guts into burning knots.

Cam advanced, singling out two of his four challengers. Both men raised their backswords only to stand frozen in the dirt. The men regarded each other apprehensively, neither aspired to be the first to engage their chieftain, the Black Giant as he'd been labeled over the years.

The third man raised his sword and lunged forward, baring his teeth. Cam growled and advanced. The lad raised his targe to ward off Cam's blow. But Cam's heavy broadsword struck the wooden shield knocking the lad off balance and sending him careening backward. The fourth man, Rory Murdock, Cam's former brother-in-law, took advantage of Cam's position and attacked from the side. Cam whirled out of Rory's reach. Their swords collided; the menacing sound of metal striking metal pierced the air.

Circling each other they fended off the other's lethal strikes. Rory sliced his blade at Cam, missing his mark. Cam lunged forward; his sword slashed across Rory's sword arm. With the tip of his blade, Cam caught the open weaved hilt of Rory's backsword and flung it to the ground. Enraged, Rory pulled his dirk and lunged forward. The strike deflected off Cam's targe. Cam struck Rory in the side of the head with the basket-hilt of his broadsword, dropping the man to the ground. "Mon, yer baby sister was a worthier opponent than yerself," Cam growled at the bleeding man crouching in the dirt like a frightened, wounded dog.

All at once the three other men converged on Cam. Their blades struck his sword and targe; the sound of their skirmish echoed throughout the inner bailey drawing interested onlookers. Within a short time, the three men who'd recently joined the MacCormac garrison were panting and grunting, their sweaty bodies growing weak and weary. Cam easily warded off their unskilled strikes.

Done with this game, Cam delivered several hard blows, sending the men reeling against the rail, leaving them to wonder about their lots in life.

With his opponents momentarily incapacitated, his thoughts returned to Sir Alexander's impending visit. Did the recent raids on the border clans have anything to do with the baronet's reason for venturing so far into the Highlands? A messenger arrived earlier, and merely stated Sir Alexander would arrive today, and wished to speak with Cam on an important matter.

Filling his chest with a long, slow breath of cool air, Cam rose to his full height of six feet four inches and readied his stance for another siege. One of the younger lads leaning against the fence, moaned, and slid to the ground. Cam's cousin and second in command, Hugh MacCormac, and his captain of the guard, Malcolm Haywood, stood beyond the rails of the ring and chuckled at the lad's dejection. Malcolm reached through the rails and patted the defeated lad's shoulder. The other two opponents, dripping sweat and exhausted, exchanged a look. They conceded their defeat, dropped their swords, and sank to the ground beside their friend.

Cam turned to face Rory who'd regained his senses and had retrieved his sword. Blood trickled down the side of the angry man's face and arm. Their eyes locked. The glint in Rory's narrowed eyes pricked Cam's suspicion. The desire to finish the man off, then and there, crept forward from a dark area in the back of Cam's mind.

Recently Cam had heard tales were being spread amongst his clansmen that *he* was no longer capable of leading or holding the MacCormac clan together. No need to wonder who had started those rumors, he thought. Loathing for his former brother-in-law recharged Cam's strength. He needed to abolish these falsehoods before someone managed to divide the clan, pinning brothers against brothers, sons against their fathers.

Rory snarled and lunged forward. Cam raised his targe, deflecting the man's assault. He could smell the man's blood. His sweat. His hatred and determination.

They faced off, scrutinizing each other as they sidestepped around the training ring. Rory lunged forward. Their swords sliced through the tension, jabbing mere inches from the other's body. They fought for several minutes, then Cam heard the pounding of horses' hooves approaching.

Done trifling with Rory, Cam turned his wrist and struck Rory in the jaw with the hilt of his sword. The force of the blow knocked Rory to the ground. Holding his blade out in front of him, Cam stood over the man who lay on his back in the dirt. Leaning forward Cam stated in a quiet growl, "Laird Cameron MacCormac remains yer chieftain. I will continue to hold the clan together. Best heed what I say, mon."

Dismissing the man, Cam turned away and watched sixty riders enter the inner bailey. Dressed in a grand, purple brocade, wide-cuffed coat with matching knee-length breeches, white silk stockings, and low boots, the Baronet, Sir Alexander made a noble and striking presence. His long, curly black wig and wide-brimmed hat bounced in rhythm with his prancing mount.

Cam slid his sword into his belt and hopped over the rails. As he crossed to stand before the Baronet, Hugh stepped to his right, Captain Haywood stepped in line to his left. "Sir Alexander," Cam hailed with a smile. "You couldna hae picked a finer day. Welcome to Castle Corell."

"Laird MacCormac, it is good to see you again." Sir Alexander's sharp eyes shot to the training ring then back to Cam's with a strained expression. "I warrant this is an acceptable time for us to speak?"

"Aye. Just training with some new lads."

Sir Alexander's strained features relaxed. "Thank you for receiving me on this day. We have much to discuss."

"Come inside and wash the dust down from yer long journey with a glass of brandy. I find I enjoy a glass myself after exercising." He shot a glance toward the ring. "No matter how brief."

One of Sir Alexander's thick brows rose, and Cam wondered whether it was due to the mention of his brandy or what he considered mere exercise. The baronet and ten of his guards dismounted, handing their reins over to the approaching groomsmen.

"Yer men can water their horses by the stables, and the ale house is over there." Cam pointed to a building next to the keep.

Sir Alexander nodded his approval and stepped forward. Cam turned and headed toward the keep; though, he quickly adjusted his stride to accommodate the older and shorter man's pace. Hugh, Malcolm, and the ten guards followed a few paces behind them. Sir Alexander studied his surroundings as they walked.

Cam kept a wary eye on the baronet as they ambled toward the stone steps to the keep. What were the man's intentions? Surely, he didn't plan an attack with only sixty-some-odd men? If more men were positioned outside the barmekin, the alarm would have already been raised.

Once inside the great hall, Cam led his guest to the high table on the dais. Sir Alexander slowed his stride as he inspected the enormous fireplaces positioned at each end of the huge hall, the colorful tapestries, and the extraordinary displays of weapons, which covered the ancient stone walls. Cam's chest swelled with pride. He had taken his chieftain's pledge seriously. He'd fought hard to protect what the lairds afore him had built and handed down for his safe keeping.

Cam gestured with a sweep of his hand for Sir Alexander to take a seat at the high table. The baronet's guards settled at one of the trestle tables below. A tall skinny lad with reddish-orange hair advanced and filled their cups with Cam's best brandy, while trenchers heaping with cheese, fruit, bread, and a variety of sliced roasted meats were set before them. Cam glanced at the older man who seemed oblivious to the absences of Cam's second in command and his captain of the guards.

Sir Alexander took a sip of his brandy then set the cup down and turned toward Cam. "I'll get right to the purpose of my visit, Laird MacCormac. Raiders are plaguing border clans again." His black curly wig bounced as he shook his head. "The assaults ceased for quite some time, then last month a band of murdering thieves attacked several of my crofters. They not only burned their fields and homes to the ground, many of my crofters' horses and livestock were either slaughtered or stolen. It's become unmanageable."

Cam nodded as he listened to the man's explanation. He'd heard of a group of vicious thieves, men who supported the cause to see King James returned to the throne. After William of Orangé defeated King James of Scotland in Ireland, James had fled to France. The English, and most likely Sir Alexander, and most of the English borderers, were loyal to their new sovereigns, King William, and Mary II.

Clearing his throat, the baronet continued. "They are not interested in taking prisoners or stock to ransom, they seem intent on killing any living thing they come across. I've lost forty good men." The man's black wig swung from side to side as he shook his head in disgust. He paused to stuff a piece of roasted pheasant into his mouth.

Cam took a drink of his brandy. *So, he's come to request I send my army to defeat this band of thieves, some who are likely kinsmen.*

Settling back in his chair, Cam sighed and gazed out across his servants and clansman who had gathered in the hall. "Do ye ken what you're asking, mon?"

The Baronet turned and pinned Cam with a frustrated stare. "I'm asking a highly respected and powerful highland chief with one of the largest garrisons to put a stop to these murderers. These men have become too reckless, too danger-ous. It has become senseless murder of men and beasts, and destruction of crops." Sir Alexander's gaze locked with Cam's for a few seconds before he turned away and took another drink of his brandy. After a moment, he continued. "I lack a large enough army and the alliances with sizable clans to rise up against this band of killers."

Cam scratched his beard then rubbed at a pain emerging from the back of his neck. If the raiders continued to attack the borderers, the lords would present their grievances before King William. If William and his army marched toward the highlands, it could easily spark more uprisings, which had quieted down considerably over the past couple months.

"Ye ken the cost will not be cheap," Cam exclaimed.

The older man's hand shook as he picked up his cup, taking a sip then setting it down. With his thick grey brows pulled tight together, he added, "I understand. It's a mighty hardship I am asking of you. Nonetheless, I have lost fields of grain that were counted on to feed my people this winter, valuable livestock, and many men. With winter coming, I'm afraid I'm unable to offer you any amount of coin."

Cam pushed to his feet. His chair slid backwards and rocked on its back legs before crashing to the floor. He glared down at Sir Alexander. "Ye expect me to transport my army south, a journey which would take many days, then lead them into a fight for no compensation? Ye've lost yer mind, mon!" The smaller man bolted to his feet; his head snapping back to stare up at Cam. Never turning away, Cam heard Sir Alexander's men clambered to their feet, and a couple dozen heavily armed MacCormac men enter the great hall from various arched doorways. The room fell into an eerie silence, every man waiting to see who would draw his weapon first.

The baronet sighed with irritation. "Not for nothing," he stammered. "I'm willing to offer you my most valued possession, my beautiful daughter, and of course my written allegiance."

Cam glowered at the man. "I hae no need for yer *beautiful* daughter. I donae want a wife." Whatever he had expected the man to offer, a wife was the farthest thing from his mind, and the last thing he wanted.

"Listen to me MacCormac. You are getting older like the rest of us. She's young and obedient. Has beautiful golden locks and eyes the color of the sky on a bright cloudless day. She will give you many strong sons. Strapping, bonnie lads. Lads to carry on the MacCormac name...to lead your clan when you're gone from this world."

Cam leaned forward and scowled at the man. "Ye arenae listening to me, *Alexander*. I said I donae *want* a wife." He turned and began to pace the dais, his heart slamming painfully against his chest. What did he want with another wife when the first had made promises she couldn't keep? He'd almost lost his mind the night his blessed Blair died, taking his son and heir with her.

He shook his head in hopes of clearing the painful memories away. Cam stopped pacing and drew in a ragged breath. Righting his chair, he sat back down. Sir Alexander exhaled a long breath and nodded to his men, who all settled back onto the long benches.

"She comes with a sizable dowry," Sir Alexander added, a hopeful thread in his voice.

Lifting his glass to his dry lips, Cam finished off his brandy in one swallow. Sons, his sons. The idea washed over him like a river of warm healing water, filling his mind with encouraging aspirations. The possibility of a son after already accepting the fact of never having an heir overwhelmed him.

Nonetheless, his past haunted him. The anguish of how it felt to have his heart ripped from his chest. He couldn't go through that again. He considered that this time would be different, he wouldn't love this woman. If she died after giving him a son or two, it wouldn't matter. He would have the heirs he required.

He shot Sir Alexander a quick glance. More importantly, if

he didn't make this alliance and didn't stop this band of murderers, the situation could easily spur the uprisings again, even to the point of a civil war. Too many clansmen had already died in countless battles like Dunkeld and Cromdale. Although those battles were victorious for the cause's army, many clansmen perished in the Battle of Killiecrankie.

King William's troops were many and it was unlikely that James would ever return to the throne and be King of Scotland again. It was only a matter of time before the highland clans would be forced to swear their allegiance to King William or be charged with treason and pay the high price with their lives and the lives of their families and clans. An alliance with Sir Alexander at this time could possibly influence other highland clans to lay down their arms for now and accept William of Orange as their King.

Resigned to his responsibilities as chieftain, Cam turned his attention back to the baronet.. A long gradual breath deserted Cam's body, and he asked, "The lass, she has agreed to this arrangement?"

The baronet threw back his shoulders, his bushy brows dipping deep between his piercing gray eyes. "I stated she's obedient. She will do what she is told," the man replied, insulted by Cam's inquiry.

Cam glanced down at his signet ring and recalled the first time he'd tendered it as his word. Circumstances were different this time. He didn't want to know anything about this girl, not even her name. There would be plenty of time to get to know her after this was all over and settled. Twisting the ring off his finger, he handed it to the baronet. "This is my oath to ye and yer daughter. I will take her for my wife. My men and I will come and retrieve her. From today on you will hae the protection of Clan MacCormac. I will command a hundred and eighty men to escort ye home." He shot a look toward Malcolm who nodded and fled the hall.

The baronet exhaled a sigh of relief and placed the ring in his pocket. Pleased, he reached out his hand and the two clasped arms. The man's expression displayed an air of hesitation, though he nodded and said, "Well done lad."

They finished their meal in silence, Cam having trouble reining in his thoughts. Several minutes later, Cam led his guest and his men out into the inner bailey and watched them mount their horses. Hugh stood next to Cam, they observed the baronet, his men, three supply wagons, and a hundred and eighty heavily armed MacCormac warriors as they rode out the main gate.

Hugh shook his head; his deep chest trembled when he chuckled.

Standing with his hands on his hips, Cam glanced over to his cousin. "What do ye find amusing in the midst of this mess?"

"Did ye not see the mon make the sign of the cross over his chest before ye walked out?"

Cam's hand moved to the hilt of his sword. "No, but little good it will do him if he means to deceive me."

Two

Wiping her wet hands on her apron, Adriana crossed the span of the kitchen to the door leading to the garden. She longed to escape her duties and disappear into the woods. It seemed like such a long time since she'd been able to take a leisurely walk along the river and pick wild-flowers or sit under a tree and read from a favorite book. "I'll fetch those herbs for you, Mrs. Wilson," she said, wanting to get away from the sweltering kitchen and outside in the cool autumn air. "It will only take me a moment." As Adriana reached for the door handle, Penny, the lady's maid burst into the kitchen. With a theatrical flair the young woman waved her arms dramatically in the air and tossed her head from side to side. In her natural Irish accent, she presented her best imitation of Adriana's younger sister, Lynette. "Oh! Which ribbon should I wear this evening? 'Tis so very troublesome. I simply cannot make up my mind. Penny, would you be a lamb and fetch Adriana for me?"

Adriana chuckled at the woman's outlandish performance. However, when Penny noticed her standing at the kitchen door, the woman's face flushed and she stammered, "Sorry, Mistress."

She made a quick curtsy and added, "But her... I mean your sister 'Tis having a wee ribbon crisis. She wishes your self's advice immediately."

Adriana nodded. Today wasn't a good day for Lynette's anticks or any childish crises. She had enough to do without wasting time putting out imaginary fires for everyone. She sighed. "Thank you, Penny. I'll go and take care of her straightaway." Turning, she rushed out of the kitchen. She knew Penny and most of the household servants called Lynette, *Her Highness* behind closed doors. Lynette could not help her behavior. Being barely ten and two and beautiful as her mother had been, their father treated her like a queen, never expecting much from her. She'd become little more than a decoration, an adornment her father pompously paraded around when company visited.

Lifting her skirts, Adriana ran across the landing and up the stone stairs leading to the upper floors where the family's chambers were located. *Why today? Mrs. Wilson has a feast to prepare, and she needs everyone's help.*

She had been busy at her desk posting monthly expenses in the estate ledgers when Mrs. Wilson barged into the small alcove. The cook affirmed her father had returned and ordered her to prepare a feast for this evening's celebration. He had not offered any reason for the event. He'd summoned her, made his announcement, and left. On laundry day, nonetheless. Several weeks earlier her father and a band of his men had departed on a secret journey. When he returned, there were an additional two hundred soldiers with him. Her father appeared extremely happy, about what Adriana had yet to be informed.

She stopped in front of the large wooden door, took a deep breath in hopes of calming her anxiety, then opened the door and entered her sister's chambers. Lynette stood in front of a long mirror admiring herself in her new Cyan blue and ecru yellow silk gown ornamented with gold thread. The new, more modest mantua style with its low waistline was adorned with gold ribbons and bows. Although the fashion normally called for a long flowing train, Lynette's gown merely brushed the thick carpet. A delicate strip of white lace outlined the neckline and elbow-length cuffed sleeves.

"Oh, Adriana! I cannot decide which ribbon looks best with this dress," Lynette cooed when she spotted her sister.

Adriana's long sigh released some of her tension. She could never stay annoyed with her sister for long. "Either one would look fine," Adriana said, walking up behind the girl. "Personally, I favor the cyan ribbon, it brings out the color in your eyes." She took the ribbon with the small pearl pendant from her sister's hand and slipped it around her slender neck. Pushing her sister's long blonde curls to one side, she tied a perfect tiny bow at the nape of her neck. Placing her palms on Lynette's shoulders she gave her a gentle squeeze. "There, you look like a fairy princess."

"You always make the right decision," her sister replied with a wide smile. Lynette's large, round blue eyes, so much like her mother's, sparkled with love and admiration.

Adriana had been ten years old when Lynette was born. Suffering complications from childbirth, her stepmother died six days later. Over the years, Adriana undertook the role of mother, governess, mentor, and confidant to Lynette. Adriana slid her arms around her sister. They both smiled and stared at their warm and loving reflection in the mirror. Adriana admired at how mature her sister looked in her new dress. She was growing up, but it wouldn't be easy. It was time for Lynette to start thinking about her future. She would need to start shouldering some of the responsibilities of the castle. Adriana needed her help. However, she would find a more appropriate time to discuss the subject with Lynette.

"Do you need anything else, Dear?"

Lynette turned and wrapped her arms around Adriana's

waist. "Thank you for helping me. I love you. You know everything."

"I love you, too." Adriana kissed her sister's brow. "But I'm needed in the kitchen. There is much to prepare for this evening's celebration. Do try to keep yourself clean and unwrinkled. We don't want to disappoint or anger father."

"I shall be perched like a statue on the settee in the lady's parlor, finishing the William Shakespeare play, Romeo and Juliet, that you gave me to read."

"Very good. I will see you later for dinner in the great hall. Do not be late."

Adriana rushed out of the room. She quickened her step and headed down the long corridor which led to the huge stone stairs. What did her father have planned for tonight? Why had he commissioned such a fashionable gown for Lynette? She pushed several loose strands of hair back off her face and tucked them behind her ear. Running a hand down the front of her apron, she wondered if her father expected her to wear her best gown this evening or was, he expecting her to stay hidden away with the rest of the servants as usual?

She'd made it halfway down the stairs when she overheard her father speaking to one of his men in the great hall. Slowly she inched down the steps, hoping not to be noticed. Her father despised eavesdropping, and she'd learned at the end of a leather strap what the consequences of listening to private conversations would be. But she had also learned over the years that he intentionally withheld important information from her. So, as she got older, she had mastered the act of eavesdropping without getting caught. She pressed her body up against one of the large stone pillars, so they wouldn't see her as she listened. She recognized her father's man, Balfour when he asked, "And what are you thinking your eldest daughter, Lady Adriana will say about you wedding her younger sister to the MacCormac chieftain?"

Adriana's hand shot up to her throat. *The MacCormac?*

"Adriana?" Her father snorted sarcastically. "No one has ever offered for her. At one and twenty, she's a spinster. Her hair's the color of mud, and she bares the scar of the damned. I doubt any man would receive her as a wife.

"I'm warning you," Balfour persisted, "She is not going to like you marrying Lady Lynette off before her."

"Ha!" She heard the bang of a mug hitting the table. "The selfish child let her mother drowned without doing anything to save her. I require her to stay here and take her mother's place, keep my estate in order. I will never let Adriana leave."

Adriana sank to the cool stone steps. He had found a husband for her sister but planned to keep her to run his castle. Her hand shook as she reached up and brushed her fingers over the long scar just below her hair line. He planned to punish her for her mother's death the rest of her life.

Moreover, why would he choose Laird MacCormac, better known as the Black Giant for her young and impressionable sister, Lynette? The man stood over seven feet tall. He was incredibly old, and he was covered from head to toe with black fur. She had never seen him but heard terrifying tales about how he massacred his enemies. How he could fight ten men at once and kill each one with his bare hands. A shiver streaked up her spine. The man was a barbarian. The thought of her younger sister married to such a beast made Adriana's heart sink to her stomach. Poor Lynette would take one look at the Black Giant and perish straight away. The fear of being married to a man such as he may even drive the fragile thing to take her own life. She twisted her hands in her skirt. She could not let this happen. But feared there was nothing she could do to stop it?

"Oh, there ye be mistress."

Jerking at the sound of Penny's voice behind her, Adriana glanced up. "Yer father has been asking for yourself."

Getting to her feet, Adriana forced a smile. She made a fist with one hand and said, "I dropped something." She pretended to place an object into her pocket. "Thank you, Penny." Adriana watched the woman walk away. Had Penny believed her lie or had she witnessed her listening to her father's conversation? She didn't have time to worry about that now. She ran a hand over the loose strands of her hair and straightened her skirt as she strolled down the remaining steps. Would he reveal his plan to wed Lynette to the MacCormac, or would he lie to her once again? Would he continue with his scheme for her to never marry, and that she was to be a prisoner in Shealoch Castle for the rest of her life? Adriana had dreamed of having a husband and children of her own one day. Along with a husband came a home, security, and maybe even love, most importantly she would no longer be subjected to her father's cruelty. However, had her father been right, no man would ask for her due to her looks. Her hand brushed along the raised scar that ran from the edge of her right brow down her cheek. That horrible day flashed before her.

Oh, mother. I'm sorry I failed you. I miss you, and wish you were here.

Swallowing the tightness in her throat, Adriana squared her shoulders and entered the hall. She bobbed a slight curtsy to her father. "You wanted to see me, Father?"

"There you are." One corner of his mouth turned up slightly in a forced smile. "We celebrate this day in honor of the betrothal of your sister to Laird MacCormac. You are to inform her of this and explain the countless benefits that come with this alliance. Laird MacCormac will be arriving soon to escort her to his home, Castle Corell in the highlands. You will help her pack her trunks."

Her body vibrated with anger and fear. She drew in a deep breath and said, "Father, Lynette is too young and far too innocent to become the wife of a Highland chieftain, much less Laird MacCormac. If she doesn't panic and faint straight away at the sight of him, she will be far too afraid to be a proper wife to him. If he's unhappy or disappointed with her he might hurt, her." She stared at her father hoping he understood her meaning. When he did not respond she added, "Consider her irresponsible and impulsive behavior, she may hurt herself."

"Ha," he growled. "Enough. It is time the foolish chit grows up and stops her silly self-indulgent conduct."

Clutching her hands together, Adriana drew in a ragged breath. "What of me, Father? When will I have a husband?" She waited. Could he say to her face what he so freely said behind her back?

"Well...Well..." he blustered. "You're much too important to me, child. My first born and all. It will take someone quite rich and titled for me to let you go." He smirked like a lad who'd gotten away with the last biscuit.

He pulled something from his pocket, admired it for a moment, then handed it to her. "Here is the MacCormac's signet ring. Pass this on to your sister. It is a symbol of his commitment to her and to me and my holdings."

Adriana stepped forward. Her hand shook as she accepted the item from her father. The heavy ring rolled around on the palm of her hand. It was made of silver and appeared extremely old. Rubies surrounded the MacCormac crest which was engraved on the top. She remembered hearing the MacCormac Clan had lived in the Highlands for centuries and hailed from the Norseman invaders. They were one of the oldest, the largest, and the most powerful clans.

"Adriana." Her head snapped up at the sound of her father's stern voice. "It is your responsibility to make sure Lynette understands what her duties as a wife are." He glanced away and took a swig of his ale.

Duties as a wife? Adriana knew how the running of the household, the accounts and servants went, but she had no idea what a wife's duties to her husband were other than to serve him and have his children.

"I want this taken care of before the feast tonight. Do you hear me and understand what I'm saying?"

She dropped the ring in the pocket of her apron and looked up. "Aye, Father." She would not let him see how his lies wounded her. "I heard you and I understood every word you said." Tilting her chin up, her back straight, Adriana turned and walked out of the hall. With the weight of her task on her shoulders, she plodded up the stone steps in silence.

She trudged past her sister's door and headed to her own room. Life did not mirror the stories writers and poets penned of love and romance. Some people were fortunate and found love in their lifetime while others were destined to go through life unloved and unnoticed. It was the way of the world from the very beginning. Placing her hand on the handle, she turned the latch and pushed open the heavy wooden door. It would be terribly hard to stand at the gates and wave goodbye to her sister as she rode away. Would she even be able to attend Lynette's wedding, or witness her with child, or be present for the child's birth? How could her father do this to her?

Adriana's fate had been sealed. She flopped face down on her bed as her tears came profusely.

Three

Laird MacCormac and forty of his clan warriors were readying their horses for the long trek south to retrieve his betrothed from Shealoch Castle. Cam pulled at the strip of tartan slung over his shoulder and readjusted his brooch. "His *beautiful* daughter. I wonder what the old bog considers beautiful." He grumbled under his breath and jerked his sword belt forward. "I gave my signet ring... Fool! I'll be given the lass something and it willnae be my heart."

Hugh appeared from around the back of Cam's horse. He raised a questioning brow at Cam's declaration, but Cam disregarded him.

Cam rested his hand against his horse's neck. He stilled when a blurry vision of his lovely Blair's face clouded his sight. Och, how he still loved the woman. After five years his heart still ached to feel her touch, to feel her beneath him, to taste her sweet kisses. If he could only hear her laughter once more. How different his life would be if she and his child had lived. He rubbed the heel of his hand across his chest where the muscles had drawn tight. He would never expose his heart like that again. As much as he did not wish to marry this girl, an heir would secure the future of Clan MacCormac and discourage a rebellion from starting up again thus saving countless lives.

One of his men struggled with a strap of leather on his saddle. Cam circled behind his horse and grabbed the piece of leather from the lad's hand. Under his breath, he muttered, "Do it myself... Accursed horse..." He buckled the strap then slipped it through the leather loop and laid it flat against the horse. Turning, he glared down at the lad and snarled, "Weel, mon, ye got it, now?" Cam trekked back to his horse and mounted just as the sun peeked over the horizon. When he turned to yell for his men to mount, he found them all astride and waiting on him.

They rode for several miles before Cam started to relax, though he wouldn't be able to breathe easily until they returned home with his betrothed.

After riding side by side for several miles, Hugh glanced toward Cam and finally asked, "Did ye get any sleep last night?"

Cam glared at his friend and kinsman. "And why would that be any concern of yers, noo?" Hugh didn't try to hide his grin and chuckled at Cam's obvious discomfort. Cam shook his head and sighed. "I shouldnae hae ever agreed to this alliance."

"Weel, 'tis too late to be changing ye mind noo, ye ken. Unless ye be wanting to start the war ye been fighting so hard to prevent."

"Nay. There will be no wars and no dividing of clan MacCormac either."

"So 'tis the idea of a wife that's got yer guts twisted. It might be enjoyable to hae the presence of another *Lady MacCormac* at Castle Corell once again.

"Aye, I will take and wed the lass," he said, nodding his head, then with his eyes as hard as steel, he added. "And if after she bares me a son or two, I donae fancy her, I'll sell her or give her away."

Hugh stared at him, then replied with a sneer, "A war we will be having for sure if ye do."

Ignoring the man, Cam spurred his mount forward. He didn't care if Hugh thought him cruel. He could not look at the situation any other way.

By early afternoon, the trail meandered into a forest littered with a mixture of birch, oak, ash, hazel, and rowan trees. Large ferns grew amongst the thick layer of leaves covering the forest floor. The smell of damp earth, rotting wood, and leaves filled their lungs. The sun filtered through the trees casting dappled shadows across the ground. Squirrels and rabbits watched from safe distances as the troop rode by. After an hour they emerged from the cover of the woods onto a narrow trail that continued south. The grass grew tall along the trail with no trace that the trail had been used recently. They found themselves in a valley between two high grass-covered hills. Every man readied himself, for this would make the perfect place for an ambush. They rode in silence, scanning the countryside for any telling signs of other riders. Before long they came around a rocky hillside to find a lush meadow, which edged alongside a wide calm river.

Cam yelled to halt. There would be plenty of grass and fresh water for their mounts. After nine hours in the saddle, he relished a chance to walk and stretch his legs. Soon his men settled on the ground by the river. They laughed and joked and ate the food that had been packed for them. Cam posted two guards. One to keep an eye to the east and the other to watch for riders from the south.

Stretching out on the ground, the warm sun on his face, Cam filled his lungs with a deep breath then slowly let it escape. His cousin Hugh approached then squatted down beside him. "You seem much calmer than ye were this morning."

Sitting up, Cam leaned back on one arm and casually placed the other upon his bent knee. "I hae convinced myself I hae made the correct decision. The men I sent with Sir Alexander will defeat and capture the thieves, putting an end to their raids and the possibility of any further mayhem."

Hugh shook his head. "Aye, yer actions will keep William in London, and there will be no reason for the rebellion to start up again for noo."

Shaking his head, Cam said, "I pray the clan will recognize this wisdom, and no one will challenge me as chieftain. I will hae a wife, and an heir will strengthen and hold the clan together."

Hugh nodded in agreement. Nonetheless, Cam second-guessed his judgment. *If* he had made the right decision, why did he have such an uneasy feeling about it?

The sound of thunder rumbled from the north, shaking the earth as an army of roughly fifty riders, dressed all in black, their faces smeared with mud, charged toward them. It appeared as if the evils of death were closing in on them. Cam and his men jumped to their feet, pulled their pistols from their belts, and fired at the bandits. After their one shot, their pistols were thrown aside, and they pulled their swords. Cam and his soldiers were pinned against the rock and riverbank. Shouts and orders from Hugh and Malcom could be heard over the pounding hooves as the riders rushed forward.

One rider charged his horse toward Cam. Cam shot but the man leaned forward, low over his horse's neck, and the bullet missed its mark. Cam pulled his sword as the man leapt from his horse and attacked him. Their swords clashed and they fought for several minutes before Cam found himself pinned up against a large rock. Two more bandits joined in making it impossible for Cam to gain any ground. The sound of metal clashing and gun shots filled the small glen. Then a bullet ripped through Cam's leather jack and tartan. The force of the shot drove him back, slamming him against the rocks. His shoulder was on fire. A man charged forward, his sword slashing wildly. His blade struck Cam's right thigh leaving a wide, deep gash across his leg. Cam pushed himself away from the rock, lunged forward, and caught the man's arm forcing him to retreat. Another shot rang out and a bullet grazed the side of Cam's forehead. A sharp crippling pain consumed his whole body and he collapsed to the ground. Cam struggled to his knees, except the pain drove him back down a second time. Unable to move, he closed his eyes and awaited the final strike that would take him from this world forever. Except, he felt the ground tremble, the attackers had mounted their horses and rode off.

Cam could hear Hugh's voice; except he couldn't understand what he was saying. The pain so fierce he couldn't think. Everything started to fade, shrink as if he were walking backwards out of a room. Then everything went black.

~

The next few days passed in a blur. Adriana's mind wandered off to places she would never see or experience while her body trudged through her daily routine. The alliance celebration came and went without any indication that Lynette understood its true purpose. Adriana avoided her sister whenever possible; she couldn't muster up the nerve to relay the news of Lynette's betrothal and upcoming marriage, or that Laird MacCormac would soon be there to collect her. She should be happy for Lynette, but she feared her sister's response when she learned her husband to be, was none other than the nefarious Highland chieftain—The Black Giant.

Adriana kept busy with her regular duties of helping with the gardening, the laundry, and making candles in the kitchen. It hadn't bothered her; the work kept her mind off the task of speaking with Lynette. Adriana punched her fist into the bread dough, flipped it over and pounded it again. Working off her frustration on bread dough all morning made it easier to hold back her anger and her tears. How could their father send Lynette to her doom? He wasn't fond of Lynette, even though he had never shown any hatred for her. Of course, the alliance with Clan MacCormac will be beneficial to them. The men who had been sent back with her father had already fought the thieves as they attacked several of their farmers. A couple thieves were killed and many more injured, but that wasn't reason enough to sacrifice her young sister's wellbeing. In doing so, their father would most assuredly be sending Lynette to her death. If not by Laird MacCormac's hand, then by her own.

"The dough has taken enough abuse for one day, mistress," Mrs. Wilson said, handing Adriana a towel. "I appreciate yer help lass but sit now." Mrs. Wilson gestured toward a stool by the table. "Ye've been working much too hard. Ye have always been a great help to me, even when ye were a wee child."

Adriana accepted the towel and sunk onto the stool, releasing a long renouncing sigh. *Mistress.* They may refer to her as mistress, but she knew she would never be much more than a servant in her own home. A mere prisoner, forced to serve her father for the rest of her life. She dreamed of leaving, but where would she go? No man had ever offered for her and according to her father, no man ever would.

Voices thundering in a heated exchange came from the Great Hall. Tossing the towel on the long preparation table, Adriana headed toward the disturbance. She reached the back entrance to the great hall and hesitated at the sight of a group of MacCormac men standing in a circle, all speaking at once. She clasped her hands in front of herself and authoritatively cleared her throat. The circle quieted and unfolded to reveal three MacCormac men she had never seen before. The man, Cowan, who had returned with her father and had appointed himself spokesperson for the MacCormac men, stepped forward. He bowed and said, "Lady Adrianna, may I introduce our Captain of the Guard, Malcolm Haywood." A tall, handsome, dark-haired man stepped forward and offered a bow. An offensive odor of sweat and dirt mixed with a vile pungent scent of iron assaulted her. Looking closer she noticed the man's filthy clothing was smeared with dried blood.

Instinctively, her hand reached out, and she said, "Captain there is blood on your person. Are you hurt?"

Although his expression appeared grim, his dark eyes flashed with a slight spark of interest. "No, milady. We were ambushed on our way here and Laird MacCormac was severely injured. He is in route back to Castle Corell."

"I'm sorry to hear that. You and your men must be tired and hungry. May I offer you food and drink?"

The other two men who accompanied him shared a look and nodded their appreciation. "Thank you, milady, but I would speak with Sir Alexander at once." He towered over her; one hand resting on the hilt of his sword. His broad frame and wide stance affirmed his strong leadership, and there was a hint of urgency in his eyes.

"I'm sorry, my father isn't here now. He isn't expected back until the day after tomorrow."

An outbreak of whispers were exchanged amongst the group of men who stood behind their stone-faced captain. One muttered, "That might be too late."

Cowan faced his captain. "How badly is he wounded?"

The captain turned to face her. A shadow of sadness and apprehension wafted over his eyes as he replied, "He's been shot twice. His right leg has a severe gash. There is an uncertainty if he weel survive."

Adriana's hand flew to her mouth to stifle her gasp. It was true, she did not want Lynette to have to marry Laird MacCormac, but she would not wish the man ill—or worse, death.

The captain's gaze scanned his men before he turned his

attention back to her. "Milady, are ye aware of the alliance made 'tween yer father and Laird MacCormac?"

Reaching into the pocket of her apron, Adriana nervously played with the ring her father had entrusted her with to pass onto her sister. She pulled her hand out and let the large ring balance on her palm. She glanced at the ring and nodded her head. The men exchanged more whispers and a few confused glances.

When the captain cleared his throat, his voice displayed a gentler note when he spoke. "Do you understand and concur with this agreement?"

Her fingers closed around the ring. No, she didn't agree with Lynette marrying Laird MacCormac even if the poor man were to die from his wounds. At the men's hesitant expressions, she realized they mistook her as the daughter her father had offered to their laird.

"If so," he continued with a note of sensitivity, not unlike a parent would speak to a nervous child. "We would have to make haste. Ye would be expected to marry Laird MacCormac as soon as we arrive to ensure... To ensure his lineage will be carried on."

She drew in a deep breath and pressed her fist against her heart. Did she dare take the chance this opportunity presented to get away from her cruel father? To have a husband and maybe even a child. Then her scar came to mind and reality threatened to sweep away the fantasy. Besides, if he were to die, he would never be aware of it. Her face heated, and she found herself smiling and nodding her head. "Yes, Captain I consent to the agreement.

The captain released a pent-up breath and the deep crevice between his brows relaxed. "We must hurry, milady. 'Tis a long ride. How soon can ye to be ready to travel?"

"I will take only what I must have now. I can send for the rest of my belongings later. Please bring your men in and have something to eat and drink while you wait." Not waiting for his reply, she scurried out of the hall and trotted toward the kitchen. "Mrs. Wilson," she yelled to the cook as she flew around the corner. "Please see to Laird MacCormac's men, give them food and drink." Ignoring the woman and the questions she shouted after her, Adriana dropped the ring back into her pocket, lifted her skirts, and scampered up the servant's stairs to her chambers.

If she were married to the MacCormac before her father arrived to retrieve her, it would be too late for him to protest, the deed would be done. Her head was spinning. If Laird MacCormac died after they were married, her father still would not be able to force her to return to Shealoch Castle. Given the power she would possess as Lady MacCormac, she would send for Lynette. Her sister would come and live with her where she would be safe. Their father would not dare challenge her or the MacCormac Clan. She burst into her room and stopped, not sure what to do first. How fortunate for her Laird MacCormac's men believed it was her he'd agreed to take for his wife. She crossed to the ewer, scooped up a handful of cold water, and washed her face and hands.

Adriana's chamber door opened, and Lynette rushed in. "What is going on Adriana? Who are those men in the inner bailey? What do they want?"

Adriana dried her face and hands with a towel, then turned to the wardrobe and flung the doors open. She must hurry in case her father returned home earlier than expected.

"Lynette, I need you to tell father something for me when he returns from checking on the surviving crofters," she called over her shoulder while extracting a carpet-covered valise from a trunk and tossing it on the bed.

Lynette flopped down next to the bag on the bed. "Why are you packing? Where are you going."

"I need to change. I can't ride in this skirt and apron." She turned to the wardrobe. "I'm going with Laird MacCormac's men. Those men have come here to collect me." Her gaze shot around the room. "I'm going to marry their chieftain."

"You can't leave me. What am I going to do without you here?"

"I will come back to visit you, or you could come to Castle Corell and visit me."

Adriana extracted her best skirt and waistcoat, rolled them up, and stuffed them into the bag. Next her green skirt, which had belonged to her mother. Then she grabbed her tan bodice and a few things from her dressing table. Convinced she had only what she needed she tied the bag shut. Turning to Lynette, she said, "Promise me you will tell father when he comes back. But let him get settled first... Have his meal. When he's rested, you can inform him of where I've gone." Adriana removed her work clothes and changed into her dark blue riding habit. She dropped the MacCormac's signet ring in her pocket and fastened the button closure. Hastily, she removed the ribbon from her hair, twisted the locks into a long rope, then coiled the mass into a knot at the back of her head and secured it with pins. Tossing her hairbrush and comb into her valise, she picked up her riding hat. She tipped the hat at an angle, so the edge covered the scar on her face then fastened it into place. Then she slipped on her riding boots and laced them up.

Her heart pounded with excitement; she glanced around her chamber. She'd packed enough to get her through a couple of weeks; everything else could be sent to her later once she was married. Reaching out her hands, she pulled Lynette up and hugged her. "I must hurry. I will write to you very soon." She grabbed her bag and hooded cloak. Lynette stood by the bed, her eyes brimming with tears.

"Don't be sad, dear. It's much better this way for both of us, I promise." Adriana hurried out the door. She raced toward the stairway, toward her freedom.

Four

The captain of the guard, Malcolm Haywood stood conversing with several of his men when Adriana entered the great hall. One of the man's bushy black brows hiked up revealing his surprise when he spotted her.

"Pardon me for keeping you waiting, Captain Haywood. I am ready now. We should hurry though," she urged. "Get as many miles behind us as we can before it gets too dark, don't you agree?" She felt her face heat up at the captain's unwavering stare.

"Aye, mistress." He offered a slight bow. Crossing to her, he reached for her bag. She handed it to him, and he held the valise out at arm's length, studying it with an air of skepticism.

When he returned his gaze to hers, she grinned sweetly. "It is all that I will need for now. My father will send the rest of my belongings in a few days." He frowned, as if considering her words for a moment. Adriana flung her hooded cloak around her shoulders and headed for the main doors.

Once outside, she stopped and stared at the scene before her. One hundred or so mounted MacCormac warriors waiting to escort her to her new home in the highlands. The vision was unsettling, to say the least. Her heart pounded wildly, and she prayed the captain could not feel her hand trembling on his arm.

Her bag was handed to another man, and she found herself being lifted onto the back of a horse. She abruptly straightened her riding habit over the sidesaddle. She surveyed the MacCormac men closest to her and was pleased to be received with respectful nods. These men would soon be *her* men. The thought warmed her. But apprehension crept into her soul. How quickly would they turn on her if they learned she had deceived them, her father, and their laird this day.

Several days later an exhausted and sore Adriana and one hundred soldiers rode into the inner bailey of Castle Corell. She'd never been this far north before. The skies were gray, and a cold drizzle fell around her. There was a heavy scent of scotch pines in the air, and snow on the mountain peaks which gave the impression of being much closer.

This is the most beautiful place in the world. I wonder if I'll be permitted to take walks outside of the barmekin wall.

Normally she enjoyed riding on a horse, except after such a long journey, every muscle, even the ones she didn't know she had—ached. They passed several large buildings and people came out and cheered. The aroma of someone cooking outdoors or possibly rendering fat for candles, danced on the cool breeze.

Captain Haywood drew his mount to a halt in front of a massive keep. Adriana tilted her head back to see to the top of the stone building. She glanced around. Laird MacCormac's holdings were substantial compared to her father's. "Milady." Captain Haywood stood beside her horse waiting to help her dismount. Placing her reins across the horse's neck, Adriana leaned down and let the captain lift her off the saddle. When she touched the ground, pain shot through her feet and up her legs. Her whole body trembled and for a moment she clutched the sleeves of the captain's leather jack for support.

"Are ye all right, milady?" He gripped her elbows to steady her, his brows dipping low between piercing dark eyes.

"Yes, Captain, I'm fine." She smiled and forced herself to stand alone. Soon she would be Lady MacCormac and she would not complain or show any weakness in front of the laird's men. The thought gave her strength. Elevating her chin, she lifted the hem of her skirt and headed toward the keep. In a couple of strides, Captain Haywood appeared at her side and offered her his arm. Without a word, Adriana placed her hand on his welcoming arm and let him lead her inside.

The captain had been exceedingly kind and considerate to her over their long journey. He'd made sure she'd had whatever she'd desired. He conversed with her and even asked her many questions about her father, his land, and his men, and she had answered him truthfully. However, when he inquired if she had siblings, she'd been forced to lie by saying no. The lie was necessary to protect Lynette for now. Her sister would never have been able to ride the far distance to reach Castle Corell, let alone sleep on a pallet in the corner of a drafty Highland country house along the road.

A tall skinny lad carrying her valise approached her and bowed. "Mistress, if ye would follow me I will show ye to yer chambers."

"Thank you..." When she hesitated, he quickly added, "Kinny."

"Thank you, Kinny." She turned to her escort and said, "Thank you, captain. You have been extremely kind to me, and I appreciate that."

"My pleasure, milady. I leave ye now. Kinny and the housemaid's will see to yer needs." He bowed, then turned and strolled out of the keep.

Adriana followed the lad down a passageway to a wide,

stone, staircase. They climbed three floors before they turned and headed down a long narrow hallway. Adriana couldn't help but marvel at the sheer size of the massive stone castle. There was evidence of the original medieval structure and where several additions had been added over the centuries.

Kinny came to a stop in front of a large wooden door and pushed it open. The room was a lovely chamber. Thick gold curtains hung from the four corners of an enormous canopy bed positioned precisely across from a stone fireplace. The lad placed her bag on the bed then crossed to the hearth. Squatting down he quickly lit the peat. Soon the aroma of smoldering turf floated about the room.

To one side of her, next to two massive wardrobes, stood a full-length mirror and an old trunk. In another corner sat a magnificent harp and a straight-backed chair with a lovely needlepoint seat cover. After unfastening and removing her hat, she tossed it onto the bed. Then she crossed to the harp and ran her hand along the exquisite instrument filling the chamber with an angelic sound. Her mother had played the harp and she'd taught Adriana to play a couple of lullabies, which she performed for Lynette when she was little. She wondered if she would be allowed to play the lovely instrument. When she turned back around, she noticed the lad waiting by the door.

"Someone will bring up food and water for ye," Kinny said shyly. He bowed his head and a clump of red curls bounced forward over his forehead. When he left the room, no sooner did the door close than an older distinguished lady entered. Her lovely black hair was streaked with gray. The long curls were pulled back and fastened with gold pins. An apprehensive smile graced the woman's narrow face while her dark eyes studied Adriana and undoubtedly the scar on her face as she strolled further into the room. "We are verra pleased ye've come so quickly, lass," she said in a chanting rolling burr. The skeleton-thin woman fidgeted with a strand of pearls around her neck and darted a glance back toward the door.

Adriana smiled. "Yes, of course. Captain Haywood stressed we were to arrive as swiftly as we were able."

"And glad we be ye're here. My name is Lady Moira Sinclair. I am Laird Cameron MacCormac's aunt."

Adriana bowed her head and dropped into a graceful curtsy, her leg and back muscles screaming with pain. "It's genuinely nice to meet you, Lady Moira. I am Lady Adriana, daughter of Sir Alexander Boyd of Shealoch Castle on the border. Won't you please sit with me?" Adriana gestured to one of the two high backed chairs positioned in front of the fire. "I am glad you came to see me. I wanted to inquire about Laird MacCormac's wellbeing. I've been told he suffers with several severe injuries."

Lady Moira crossed to the chair and swept her elaborate dress to one side then settled onto the seat. She folded her hands on her lap, and said, "I've just come from the laird's quarters. He's been drifting in and oot of consciousness since they brought him home." Adriana nodded and the older woman continued. "I've been cleaning and bandaging his wounds the best I ken," an expression of repugnance crossed her thin face, "once ye've married, it will be yer responsibility to care for him." Lady Moira pressed her hand against her chest as if she might be ill.

Apparently, Lady Moira assumed the position of chatelaine for her nephew. In hopes of appearing strong and self-assured, Adriana clasped her hands together on her lap. "Yes, of course. Captain Haywood mentioned the wedding would take place soon. Do you know what has been planned?"

Lady Moira casually brushed the front of her gown before glancing back up to Adriana. "The ceremony will take place this evening." Her hand shot up to stroke her long curls before she continued. "I hae questions I'll be needing to ask ye, if ye wouldnae mind, dear. They are most important."

"Yes, of course." Adriana schooled her emotions not to react to the woman's inquiries. She'd learned as a child to keep a tight rein on her reactions and not let her father know her true sentiments, even when he intentionally hurt her feelings or took a leather strap to her.

"Ye no been married 'afore?"

Adriana offered a slight smile and replied, "No."

"Weel, with yer advanced years, and I donae mean to offend ye, lass, but will ye be a maiden?"

Controlling when not to blush had not been one of the things Adriana had managed to master. Heat raced up her body and she figured the woman knew the answer before she could reply. "Yes, Lady Moira I am a maiden, else I doubt I would be here now."

"I donae mean to embarrass ye, lass. I only wonder if ye ken yer way around a man?" She darted another glance toward the door.

Confused on how to respond, Adriana merely stared at the woman.

"Hae ye ever seen... I mean, a grown mon naked 'afore?"

Adriana cleared her throat and licked her dry lips. "I once saw two lads in the river, and I helped Mrs. Wilson our cook stitch wounds on several lads before."

Lady Moira smiled, leaned forward, and placed a trembling hand over Adriana's. "Laird MacCormac is no wee laddie, miss." She paused and wrung her hands. "I'm only asking 'because I fear Cameron will not survive his wounds." She shook her head as her eyes filled with tears. "Without an heir to hold the clan together, the clan will divide and make war against each other fer who will become the chieftain."

A clan war. Adriana leaned back in her chair.

"I tell ye this, lass, so ye understand why the wedding must take place today. Why ye must get with child afore my nephew dies."

Adriana wiped her damp palms across her skirt and straightened in her chair. "How am I to become pregnant when Laird MacCormac is so ill and unconscious? I admit my knowledge is limited in this area, but I'm sure he needs to be healthy enough to at least participate."

The older women's cheeks turned a fetching shade of pink. "Has yer mam never told ye aboot men?"

At the mention of her mother, Adriana winced and stared down at her hands in her lap. "My mother died when I was eight. My father remarried, but my stepmother died soon..." Adriana caught herself before she revealed too much. "Soon after they married."

The older woman's brows squeezed together, and a grimace marred her face. "So ye be saying ye know nothing aboot the workings of a mon's mind and body?"

Adriana fidgeted in her seat. What could there be that someone should have told her before now? "How different from us can men possibly be?"

"Oh, a mon's body works quite different from ours." Moira shook her head. "Most men, especially young fighting men are in a continuous state of rut day and night."

"I've heard our cook and housemaid say as much more than once. But surely you don't presume to mean they can--in their sleep or when they're wounded?"

"Aye." Lady Moira nodded sadly as if men in this state were cursed with this terrible affliction. "Even in their sleep or when ye think them too ill to do much aboot such things."

Adriana caught herself shaking her head in disbelief. "How can this be possible?"

"Lass, ye donae ken a mon's loins has a mind of its own?" The older woman asked suspiciously.

Surely, Lady Moira couldn't be correct in this matter? She

could hardly believe the woman's tale. Did she suffer from a past head wound of her own?

"Ye see lass, with Cameron's severe injuries and being close to death, ye may hae to coax *it* a little to get *it* to pay attention and understand yer intentions."

"What exactly are you referring to when you say—it?"

The woman's cheeks turned crimson, and she struggled with her composure. "Donae be daft, lass." She scoffed, leaned forward, and whispered, "His wee willie."

Suddenly the room felt very warm. Tugging on her waistcoat Adriana wished she'd removed it before she'd sat down. She had no doubt what Lady Moira was referring to, now. "How on earth am I expected to *coax it*?"

"Weel, first ye need to talk to it. Let it know ye're there and willing to..."

Unable to speak, Adriana could only stare at the woman in total mortification. "If that donae work, pet it, or wrap yer fingers around it and squeeze it, gently mind ye. Ye donae want to be hurting him."

Adriana shifted uncomfortably in her chair. This couldn't be happening right now. Could there possibly be anyone else in the keep who could advise her better than Lady Moira about this? Although, as Laird MacCormac's aunt, and how fine she was dressed in a beautiful light green and cream ornate gown, she clearly seemed sane. Besides, she did play the role of lady of the keep.

"If this donae work and his loins donae waken," she interrupted Adriana's thought, "ye may hae to kiss it. It likes that verra much. I am told if ye drink two or three cups of wine or brandy afore, will make the task more enjoyable fer ye." Lady Moira nodded her head encouragingly and continued. "Once it reacts to yer affections and hardens, ye will crawl up..." She shot a hasty glance toward the door. "Ye ken where it goes, dinnae?"

Lord in heaven. "Yes. Aye," Adriana murmured barely above a whisper.

Lady Moira pointed a wrinkled finger at Adriana. "But ye must remember to always be gentle so ye donae harm him."

Adriana slowly stood and began to pace about the room, her heavy legs feeling as if they were made of wood. She shot a glance toward the bed and shivered. With a sigh, she rubbed her hands along her upper arms. There had been a couple of times when she'd entered the kitchen and overheard Mrs. Wilson and Penny whispering about their men. She rubbed her throbbing head. Surely, they couldn't have been speaking of this. Should she believe Lady Moira's words? Adriana squeezed her eyes shut, as the woman's words replayed in her head. She couldn't possibly be so bold as to do the things she'd been instructed to do. She stopped and turned. "Lady Moira, I'm afraid I cannot do any of the things you ask of me."

The old woman stood and took Adriana's hands in hers. "Soon ye will be Lady MacCormac. Lady to the whole MacCormac clan. 'Tis yer duty, lass. Ye must carry on the laird's line to keep peace in the clan." The woman's eyes flashed with desperation. "I will give him a tonic for his pain, it will make him sleep through the night. He will never ken. I will wait outside yer door in case ye need me, and to show the clan proof with the bedding that ye came to the laird as a maiden." She squeezed her hands. "Donae worry, I'll no be letting anyone enter his chamber either. Ye will be shielded from all."

The depths of her seriousness showed clearly on her face and in her dark eyes. The only way to prevent the clan from dividing and war from happening after their laird died, weighed solely on Adriana becoming pregnant with his heir. A shiver slithered up her spine at the thought of what could happen to her if she didn't get with child before he died. She could be sent back to her father or forced to wed the new chieftain of clan MacCormac, whomever that may be.

A knock at the door interrupted Adriana's thoughts. The young lad Kinny entered carrying a tray of food. His eyes and nose crinkled when he grinned, revealing jagged teeth and a missing tooth on one side.

"Water is being warmed and will be brought up to ye soon, along with the tub, milady."

Lady Moira patted Adriana's hand. "I'll leave ye to yer dinner and bath. I will send Bethany in later to help ye dress."

Lady Moira scurried out. Kinny placed the tray on a small table and bowed before leaving the room. Adriana sank onto a chair. What had she gotten herself into? Was this her penance for her deception? What was she to do now? She reached for the cup of wine and ignored the food as she pondered the woman's words. Could she go through with what she'd been instructed? Everything was happening too fast. She hadn't thought this brilliant scheme of hers through.

Tipping the cup up, she took a long drink. She had to be strong. She couldn't return to her father after disobeying him by taking her sister's place. His punishment would be much worse than what was expected of her here. She had no choice in the matter. She'd come this far. No way was she ever going back.

Five

How could I have ever thought it a good idea to marry a man who would soon die?

In a trance-like state, Adriana lumbered down the corridor beside Lady Moira. With hands clasped painfully in front of her, she struggled to name her feelings but came up blank. Though her hands were ice cold, under her dress, liquid fire raced through her veins, and she sensed a strong need to flee. She felt restrained as if her skin were too small, no longer fitting over her flesh. A scream concealed beneath her heart threatened to emerge at any moment.

Earlier a lady's maid appeared at her door and helped Adriana dress in her green and gold wool skirt and waistcoat, then brushed out her hair and fashioned her coiffure with a string of pearls and ribbons. The young woman hesitated for a moment when she saw the scar on the side of Adriana's face. She offered a kind smile then pulled the hair loose from behind Adriana's ear, fashioning it to drape over the scar, then pinned her hair back below her ear. Without a word she nodded and smiled at her achievement in the mirror.

Now, Adriana was being led to her demise as if she were King Henry the VIII's second wife, poor Anne Boleyn.

Pausing at the chapel's threshold, Adriana scanned the small group of people who stood in front of the rows of pews. Some appeared hopeful, others expressed their worry if their laird would survive his wounds or die? She had the same concerns, and yet she couldn't help worrying what Laird MacCormac would think about her marrying him without his knowledge. Mostly, what he would think of her betrayal. Marrying her instead of her beautiful younger sister who'd been pledged to him?

Lady Moira crossed herself when several soldiers entered the chamber. They carried a long wide plank which held the body of a large man. They placed the plank on a low table in front of the altar. The man who she assumed to be Laird MacCormac had been wrapped tightly from his neck down in a white blanket like a swaddled babe. Adriana couldn't see much of his face due to the mass of matted black hair and bloody bandages that covered his head.

The priest, Father Fitzgerald, a small framed, feeble looking man, conversed with a much larger man who stood next to Laird MacCormac. He was dressed in a fine bleached tunic and plaid. They both turned and faced their Laird. While they prayed, the priest sprinkled holy water over the unconscious man, made the sign of the cross, then returned to the pulpit.

As the priest droned on, Adriana's mind swam in thick soup-like fog until she finally settled upon the dancing flame of a large candle upon a tall metal pedestal. The chapel had been filled with an abundance of burning candles. However, between the heat and the suffocating odor of greasy tallow, Adriana felt nauseous. She wondered which she would do first, wretch on the stone floor or faint dead away. At this point either act would be a blessing, and an escape from this unbelievable incident.

Laird MacCormac moaned. She heard him gnash his teeth together. His head swayed from side to side and his face contorted with pain as he teetered on the edge of consciousness. Instinctively, Adriana reached out and lightly rubbed her hand across his chest. She hummed softly and he quieted. Before falling back under the spell of the potion Lady Moira had administered earlier, he murmured something which resembled a name, but she couldn't understand him.

The ceremony lingered on, and she answered the father's questions and repeated the vows when asked. It all felt so surreal to Adriana, as if she were a player on a stage. Then the huge man standing next to Laird MacCormac turned and faced her to speak on his chieftain's behalf. Skepticism appeared in his eyes. He hesitated for a second, then shot a quick glance to the small group of individuals behind her. When he glanced back, his deep voice surprised her as it rumbled through the stale tallowy-air like imminent thunder.

When the ceremony abruptly ended, Adriana released a long breath. Several men stepped forward and retrieved the chieftain. They lifted the makeshift bed and carried him from the chapel. Adriana started to shake, her hand raising to her throat, confused as to what to do next. Soon she found herself being led out of the chapel by Lady Moira. Tears rolled down the older woman's cheeks as she murmured under her breath and patted Adriana's arm. Adriana felt numb to the incident which had taken place in what seemed like merely a flash in time.

There were torches placed in the iron sconces on the walls which lit their way down a long corridor. Old tapestries, some moth-eaten and threadbare, looked as if they had hung in the same place on the stone walls for hundreds of years. Time held no sense of magnitude as she followed Laird MacCormac and the six men who carried him. If one didn't know the way of it, one would think moments ago they'd left the chieftain's funeral not his wedding.

She was led through a doorway into a chamber, not unlike the one she'd been taken to earlier. Except this room held no adornments. A lone chair sat by a table in front of a large hearth. A trunk and wardrobe were placed against one wall, and a huge bed faced the fireplace.

Laird MacCormac groaned as they unceremoniously placed him on the bed. As the men bowed and shuffled out of the room, she noticed the man who spoke the wedding vows for Laird MacCormac had entered the chambers. Dressed in his finest highland kilt, silk stockings and buckled shoes, the use of courtly manors reinforced his position of importance. His piercing gaze washed over her as if measuring her merit or lack thereof. Turning his attention to Lady Moira he asked, "My Lady, is there anything I can assist you with before I take my leave?"

Lady Moira reached out and patted the brawny man's arm. "No. Thank you, Hugh. The fate of us all lies in God's hands, noo."

"Then I'll say, good evening to you, Lady Moira." He turned and faced Adriana. The man's stare easily conveyed his dislike for her. She realized she'd never measure up to what he thought his Laird's Lady should be. Or had he somehow guessed her to be an imposter? "Good evening to you, Lady MacCormac." He bowed with a flourish then turned on his heels and left the room pulling the thick door closed behind him.

Lady Moira strolled to the bed and reached for the blanket laird MacCormac was wrapped in. "I'll show you his injuries and show you how to tend them." She folded the blanket back revealing Laird MacCormac's wide, muscular chest and powerful arms. His exposed skin gleamed a rich golden brown, evidence that he spent a good portion of his time out of doors and not hunched in a chair behind a desk.

"You cannae miss where a shot grazed his forehead," she said. "He also took a led ball in the shoulder." She pointed to the bloody bandage between his heart and left shoulder. "The ball didn't go all the way through his body. One of the lads dug it out and bandaged him the best he could afore they brought him back home." She wrinkled up her nose as if the idea made her ill. "I cleaned and sewed up the wound as best as I could, however, it continues to bleed."

The bandage covering his wounded shoulder was saturated with blood. It was difficult to tell where the long thick, curly black hair on his head and face ended and where the hair on his chest and shoulders began. She wondered if he was covered from head to toe with black curls as she'd heard told.

"Do you not have a healer here in the castle to take care of such things," Adriana blurted out.

Shaking her head, Lady Moira replied, "We had a healer last year, but she left to take care of a sister who took ill, and we haven't found another to take her place. The cook Maddy and I, hae been taking care of any injuries when they happen. Thankfully, we hae no had anything bad until noo."

Circling the bed Lady Moira adjusted the blanket to expose a small towel around his waist and his right leg where a large bandage lay several inches above his knee. Adriana had seen naked men from afar but never up close. This man's arms were as big around as her legs, and his legs resembled tree trunks. His feet were the size of a bear's paw, and his gigantic body covered most of the enormous bed.

Lady Moira cleared her throat and continued with removing the saturated bandage from his upper leg. "When you change the bandages, if the wounds continue to bleed, you might have to add more stitches. He wiggled and jerked so much t'was hard for me to get the stitches tight." She turned and pointed to a table piled high with fresh bandages, and where a needle and thread lay. "There is warm water in the iron pot hanging on the swey by the fire. If yer in need of more, Kinny will fetch ye some."

The poor man's body was covered in dried blood, bruises, old scars, and three serious wounds. It certainly appeared to Adriana that he would die, just how soon was the question. Her heart went out to him at how he must have suffered.

Lady Moira walked over and drew her into a hug. "Noo, let me help ye out of yer dress, then I'll be leaving ye."

Adriana blinked in disbelief. Surely, the woman didn't expect her to crawl in bed next to this man and do as she had instructed? But she let the woman help her undress down to her linen shift. Done with her task, the woman quietly walked to the door. "I will be right outside the door if ye need me lass. Remember yer duty is now to the MacCormac clan. Yer clan, and to the future of the MacCormac's."

Adriana agonized if what the woman told her to do would even work. "Are you sure this is what he truly wished for?

"T'was the agreement he'd made with yer father and what he wants for the clan. Ye would hae their respect my lady, being a maiden and all. I'll be waiting to collect the bloodied sheet as proof." She closed the door behind her when she left. At her age, Adriana knew there would be a question of her having her maidenhead or not, and that the clan would demand proof before the night was over, but the whole idea was outrageous.

She stood before the bed and gazed at the huge man, her husband. A man she would never talk with, never share a meal with, never laugh with. He would forever be a stranger to her.

She lifted his right arm then let it fall to the bed. He didn't move or make a sound. Leaning over him she asked, "Are you awake my lord?" He gave no response. She recalled the vivid instructions the old woman had given her recognizing she couldn't make herself perform such unthinkable acts. There were some things she could do and others she just couldn't—wouldn't do.

His face looked as if an artist had taken liberties and painted him red, green, black, and purple. Though it was hard to tell if the bruising continued under his thick facial hair or stopped where his beard started. His massive chest and arms were severely marred with cuts, scratches, bruises, and old scars. A long thin scar ran just below his dry lips toward his chin but disappeared into his beard.

With care, she reached out and ran her hand over his hairy chest, the soft hair tickled her fingers. She'd never felt anything like the thick black curls that covered his body. Placing the palm of her hand on top of his large bear-like paw, she marveled at the sheer size of the man and his apparent brute strength. Never had she ever seen a man as tall or one with such broad shoulders and such a thick chest. What would it be like to witness this man battle his enemies? She chuckled. No doubt it would be frightening for his opponents. "No wonder everyone is so terrified of you, and why you are deemed, The Black Giant."

With her fingers, Adriana gently combed back the hair on his forehead then peeled the bandage back to reveal a nasty looking gash caused by a bullet that could have so easily killed him. Tilting her head to the side she supposed, if he wasn't so bruised, bloody, and hairy, her husband might be pleasing to look upon. How strange to think of this once commanding man as her husband? "This is not how I had imagined my wedding day and wedding night would be like."

Sorrow overtook her and she sighed. Although she gained a husband and security, she knew she would be losing him within a few days. When he died, his people would lose their leader, their chieftain. The thought filled Adriana's heart with sadness. She replaced the cloth on his forehead and pulled the bedlinens back up and over his shoulders. He didn't appear too terrifying lying there in his bed so close to death. Placing her hand on his arm, she gently patted him. "I'm not a healer, my lord, but I'm here and I will do everything in my power to take care of you and keep you comfortable until the end."

Crossing to the fireplace she placed more peat on the dying coals to warm the cold chamber. Dipping her fingers into the water on the swey, she found it to be warm, so she removed the iron pot, carried it over to the bed and poured half the water into the ewer on the table. As if it were a daily task, she removed the old bandage on his head and gently washed away the remaining dirt and hair from the wound.

Before she had traveled north with the MacCormac army, one of her duties had been to help with the ill and wounded. This was different. She had never been responsible for someone who belonged to her. Though she guessed she now belonged to his clan and him more than he belonged to her. However, under these circumstances, she was responsible for his care until his death. Pausing from her task, Adriana gazed down at her husband. Her heart felt heavy knowing he would die, and she wouldn't get a chance to know him. Shaking off her bout of melancholy, she wiped her hands on a towel.

Spotting a comb next to the ewer, she dipped it in to the water and combed his hair back from his broad forehead, removing the crusted mass of filth and dried blood clinging to his hair. After placing salve and rebandaging the wound, she gently wrapped a long bandage around his head.

Coming back around the large bed she turned her attention to his wounded shoulder. "Well, let's take a look at your shoulder," she whispered, hoping the sound of her own voice would encourage her to continue. Pulling back the blanket, she gently lifted the edge of the bandage and shook her head at the unpleasant wound. The flesh around the bullet hole was bruised, ragged and red with irritation. Whoever removed the bullet made a mess and damaged the tissue around the opening. It was going to take quite a while for this wound to heal. A large bruise covered his shoulder and a large portion of the left side of his chest. Again, she found his chest hair around the jagged wound matted with dirt and blood. Remembering she had seen a washstand, Adriana scurried over to where the washstand stood and found a shaving blade.

Humming to herself, she soaped up her fingers then applied them around the wound as she'd been taught by Mrs. Wilson. Placing the edge of the blade on his skin, she glanced up to look at his face. "Now would not be the best time to awaken, my lord." She chuckled, then carefully drew the blade away from the wound. After repeating this act several times, circling the opening, she cut and pulled out the loose stitches Lady Moira had placed. She rinsed the soap away and flushed out the wound with warm water, then patted the area dry with the towel. Taking the needle and thread in hand, Adriana swallowed hard and glanced at Laird MacCormac's face. As delicately as she could, she stuck the needle through his flesh. She glanced up to see if he reacted or not. His lack of response was all the encouragement she needed to continue stitching the wound as neatly as she could. Pleased with her neat needle work, she washed her bloody hands and wiped them on a clean towel. Tenderly she placed salve across the precise little stitches and rebandaged his wound. "That wasn't too bad now, was it? You're a big strong brave lad to lie still so I can stitch you back together like a tattered old quilt."

Adriana giggled and crossed to the other side of the bed and folded the blanket back to expose his wounded thigh. She shook her head at the old scars covering his massive leg and wondered who had stitched up his wounds in the past.

After gently peeling away the bandage, she washed the extensive wound and with great care shaved a large area around the substantial laceration. However, once she cut the loose running stitch and pulled it free, the wound gaped open exposing just how profound it was, which started it bleeding profusely. A brief glance to his face affirmed he remained unconscious. Sighing, she prayed. "Lord, please keep him still while I clean and stitch this dreadful wound closed."

Biting her lower lip, Adriana flushed out the wound then pinched the skin together and forced the needle through the bruised and tattered flesh, making sure to keep the thread pulled tight, and still loose enough in case it swelled. She was forced to stop several times to blot the blood away, before tying a knot at the end and cutting the thread. By the time Adriana finished, her hands were covered in blood. She reached for the towel, only to find it too soaked to be of any use. Glancing around she found a clean, dry sheet and wiped her hands. The lower portion of her back ached from leaning forward over his body for such a long period of time. She stretched, arching her back, then rubbed the sore areas with both hands. After a moment, she placed salve on his leg, a square piece of cloth over his wound, retrieved two long strips of cloth, and rebandaged his leg.

Satisfied, she readjusted the blanket and covered him. How long could a man live with such wounds, she wondered. She recalled Mrs. Wilson's words and said, "I have been told deep wounds like this can easily become infectious. You are likely to die anyway, but I hope I have slowed the process some. Maybe you will wake long enough to say your goodbyes."

Exhausted and sore, Adriana dumped the filthy water in a bucket, filled the ewer with fresh water, and washed her hands. Once she had finished cleaning up the area, Adriana dried her hands on the sheet and collapsed on the chair. She recalled overhearing a couple kitchen maids talking after one of the younger maids married. The young woman had asked Mrs. Wilson if every woman bled after lying with their husband for the first time. The older woman's explanation gave Adriana an idea. She glanced down at the sheet crumpled on her lap and smiled. She would give the blood-stained sheet to Lady Moira as proof of her virginity in hopes of pacifying her and giving Adriana more time to get used to the idea of what she must do.

Adriana stood, wincing from sore muscles, crossed to the door, and pulled it open. She found Lady Moira sitting on a chair with her back to the door. The older woman got to her feet, but her soft smile turned to a strained expression as her gaze settled on Adriana's shift. "Are ye all right my dear?"

Glancing at the front of her shift, Adriana saw a large blood stain below her left hip. Heat rose from her feet covering her in an embarrassing blush. "I'm fine Lady Moira." She smiled and handed over the sheet.

"Oh, lassie, 'tis a great thing ye've done here this night. Aye, a great thing indeed." Lady Moira's grin widened, and her eyes sparkled with gratitude as she held the sheet as if it were made of pure gold. "Would ye be feeling up to celebrating in the great hall below? I could stay and help ye dress, or send ye a lady's maid?"

"No. But thank you. It's been a trying day. I wish only to crawl back into bed and sleep." She really wanted to change into her night dress and curl up in the big bed waiting for her down the hall.

Concern crossed the woman's face; she reached out a hand and covered Adriana's hands squeezing gently. "Lass, remember ye must continue to wake his wee willie until it will no longer obey. This will insure yer future here and the future of Clan MacCormac."

"Yes, I understand. And I appreciate your words of wisdom and everything you've done to help me today."

The woman smiled and patted her hand. "Good. Good. Yer a sweet lass. I'll leave ye to yer rest noo." Lady Moira peered once again at Adriana's shift and shook her head. "I will return shortly to guard yer door tonight."

Lady Moira scurried down the corridor and moments later Adriana heard the crowd below erupt in a rejoiceful cheer. Even though their laird clung to life, his people celebrated, for they thought he recovered enough to plant the seed of the next generation. An heir to become laird and someday lead the mighty McCormac clan.

As a member of the MacCormac clan, Adriana would be safe from her father's reach and protected as one of their own. Even though Adriana was English she felt she belonged here, where she would be treated as the lady of the keep and not merely the housekeeper.

Tears filled her eyes as she searched for one of her husband's clean shirts. She removed her soiled shift and donned a soft, white shirt, the garment falling well below her knees. She rolled the large garment's sleeves above her elbows then rinsed the blood from her stained shift and hung it on the chair in front of the hearth to dry.

Adriana crawled in next to her husband, his warmth surrounded her as she curled up next to him, a soft sigh on her lips. She figured she'd drift right off to sleep, but the events of the past few days caught up with her and she started to weep. After several moments, exhaustion claimed Adriana's weary soul and she finally drifted off into a deep sleep.

Cam struggled to climb up and out of the darkness. He fought to move but his arms and legs would not function. He couldn't see, couldn't move. Where was he? Was he dead? The sensation of hands moving over his body and a woman's soft cries stirred him. What had happened? The woman, had it been Blair crying over his grave?

He attempted to speak and struggled against his restraints, both to no avail. And then, there she was again. A cool comforting hand rested on his arm and a soft feminine voice murmured incoherently in his ear. The gentleness of her voice and touch soothed his restless soul. He continued to battle his invisible foe, hoping to emerge from the darkness before it pulled him back down. His eyes opened; he drew in a deep breath as if he'd been long under water. Then a sharp stabbing pain seized him, he cried out, and then sunk back into the darkness.

A driana cracked open one eye and took in her surroundings. A small part of her hoped she had merely dreamed about the events of the past few days. Warm and secure, and not wanting to get up, she snuggled deeper into the large bed. Her leg brushed against something warm and hairy. Reality struck like a pail of icy cold river water. "Oh..." She leaped from her warm nest and stood staring at the sleeping man. Her husband. Yes, that was correct. Her husband. She was Lady MacCormac now.

Even though nothing had happened during the night, the idea that she'd spent the whole night in a bed with a man was a little unnerving. Other than her cuddling up next to him and sharing his body heat, he would never know she'd slept beside him. In his current condition, he no longer seemed to be the beast she'd been so afraid of. After a calming moment, a sense of loss washed over Adriana. She would never get to see the color of his eyes or hear his voice. Never receive a kiss from him or spend a night cradled in his strong arms.

The fire in the hearth had dwindled during the night and the chilly air caused her to shiver. After straightening the blankets to make sure he was sufficiently covered, Adriana trotted over to the fireplace and added a few bricks of peat to the dying coals. Not wanting to be caught wearing one of the laird's shirts, she slipped on her stockings and shoes, then removed his robe from the wardrobe, wrapped it around herself and tied the belt. The heavy garment was huge and drug on the floor, the sleeves hanging past her fingertips. The only clothing for her to wear was the dress she'd gotten married in yesterday. She needed to find her room and change into something more suitable.

Without making a sound, she inched her way back to the bed and glanced down at her husband. Memories of the past few days and how her life had changed acted out as a dreadful play in her mind. She sighed. She hadn't been able to save her mother from dying, but could she save her husband? She vowed to do everything in her power to save Laird MacCormac and his clan—her clan.

At first, Adriana had been afraid of traveling so far from her home, coming to this strange place to marry a man she would never know. Her first encounter with her husband and his people had gone well. She liked these people and they seemed to have accepted her.

Nevertheless, she would have to fulfill her wifely duties before it was too late. She gnawed on her lower lip. Could she make herself do the things Lady Moira instructed? Mayhap she needed to only make herself more familiar with the feel and sight of his large warriors' body as she tended to his wounds and applied fresh bandages.

She was checking his shoulder when she heard Lady Moira's voice. "Good morning, dear." Lady Moira strolled into the room. Bethany the lady's maid who had helped Adriana dress for the wedding ceremony followed close on the woman's heels.

"Good morning, Lady Moira," Adriana said with a slight curtsy. Nodding to the maid she smiled and added, "Bethany."

"Morning mistress." Bethany offered a quick bob and a

wide grin, her hands clasped in front of her. The girl's eyes flickered with anticipation.

"How did ye sleep, dear?" Lady Moira crossed to Adriana's side and hugged her shoulder. "Did Cameron's restlessness keep ye awake?"

Adriana smiled. "I slept well. Thank you, Lady Moira. Laird Mac," she hesitated before continuing, "Cameron must have slept comfortably. I don't think he stirred at all during the night."

With a wide smile Moira gave her shoulder another squeeze. "I will sit with him while ye go back to yer chambers and dress. The lads will be up soon with fresh water, some broth for Cameron, and yer breakfast."

Smiling her thanks, Adriana wondered if Moira ever had children. The petite woman would have made a wonderful mother. "Thank you. You are so kind."

"Ye are welcome." Lady Moira presented a small jar from her pocket. "It's more poultice to help take down the swelling from his bruises. It should work better than the salve I have been using on his wounds."

Adriana eyed the small jar before saying, "Oh... That will be a tremendous help. Thank you."

"Ye hurry along now and change. I'll watch over him until ye return."

Adriana hesitated then reluctantly moved away from the bed, collected her garments, and followed Bethany out into the corridor. They walked only a few steps before entering her chamber, which was right next to her husband's. Bethany reached for her gown. "I'll take these and have them cleaned for ye."

"Thank you, Bethany." She quickly removed her husband's robe and placed it across the back of the chair, then crossed to the ewer and washed in the refreshingly cold water. As she patted her face dry with a towel Adriana paused. *Married.* She smiled. She was married. Finally, safely away from her father and his cruelty and hateful words.

"What would ye be wanting to wear this day, mistress?" Bethany's voice interrupted her thought.

"The green petticoat and linen bodice, please."

Bethany retrieved the items and laid them neatly out on the bed. She handed Adriana a clean pair of stockings and her old worn, brown leather slippers. After putting them on she returned to the bed. As the girl dressed her, Adriana admitted, "I'm not used to having help getting dressed, which is why I decline to wear a corset. Normally, I get along with merely wearing a bodice and a waistcoat if I'm cold."

Bethany frowned. "That is because ye are so thin." The woman openly stared at her lack of bosoms. "When yer belongings arrive, I will be dressing ye properly. The Laird will not be having ye looking like a servant, milady."

Adriana wondered how she would be expected to help with the duties of running such a keep while trussed up in fine clothes. "Thank you, but I will not need your help unless it be for a special occasion."

"Lady Moira chose me to be yer lady's maid until yer own arrives, but if ye wish, I could find another to act as yer maid while ye wait," the girl said with a wounded expression.

"There will be no lady's maid coming with my belongings." Adriana placed a hand on Bethany's arm. "I would very much like you to be my lady's maid if Lady Moira can spare you?"

"Ah, that would be fine. Sit noo and I'll fix yer lovely hair."

Adriana forced herself to sit still while Bethany fussed over her wavey brown hair. She wondered how close in age they were and if the girl was married. Though she didn't feel comfortable asking her such personal questions quite yet.

"There, I'm finished," Bethany said, stepping back and admiring her work.

Adriana glanced at herself in the mirror. "It's charming.

You are incredibly talented. My hair has never looked so lovely." Adriana stood, grabbed the laird's robe, and headed toward the door. "I'd better get back to my husband's room. Thank you again." She slipped out and ran the few steps to his chambers.

When she entered her husband's chambers, Lady Moira, the red headed lad, Kinny, and another lad were there. The boys bowed. "Good morning, milady."

Returning their youthful grins, she said, "Good morning."

Kinny stepped forward. "We brought ye fresh water, broth for his lairdship, and a grand breakfast for yerself."

Too excited to eat, Adriana took the bowl of broth off the tray. Turning to Kinny she asked, "Do you think the two of you could raise his *lairdship* a little so I can put a pillow behind him? I would like to try and feed him."

Lady Moira stood by the bed. "Ye hae a lovely hand, Lady MacCormac. His wounds appear better today, and he has no fever." The woman smiled with appreciation.

Lady MacCormac..., Hearing Lady Moira refer to her as such, sounded strangely foreign but warmed her heart. Kinny and the other lad looped their arms through her husband's arms and pulled their laird forward. Adriana quickly packed two pillows around him, so he wouldn't fall over. Adriana turned to retrieve the bowl of broth when Bethany entered the chambers. They exchanged smiles, then Adriana turned and stepped closer to the bed. She dipped the spoon into the broth but hesitated, unsure how to get his mouth open. Shyly, Kinny stepped forward. He took the bowl and held it for her. Adriana tried again, this time placing her left hand under his chin and pinched his lips open. The spoon was much too large, and the broth ran down through his beard onto his chest. With a groan, Adriana quickly wiped it up. "Oh, no this isn't going to work. I need a much smaller spoon." Remembering how she had fed her sister when she was little, she turned toward Kinny and said, "A child-sized spoon would be perfect if you could find one."

"I'll get one for ye." The boy handed her the bowl and dashed for the door. All three women giggled as the long-legged lad disappeared out into the corridor.

Adriana helped Bethany as she began to gather up the dirty rags and rolled them up in a large towel, setting it by the bucket of dirty water for the lads to take back to the kitchen when they left.

It seemed like only seconds had passed when Kinny burst back into the room brandishing a child-sized spoon and a wide satisfied grin. "Here mistress, cook said 'tis the tiniest spoon she has."

Unable to suppress her appreciation, Adriana smirked, took the spoon, and squeezed the young man's arm. "Thank you, Kinny. I think you could run down a stag if you were asked." The room erupted in laughter when the lad blushed, his face almost matching the color of his wild hair and freckles.

Adriana moved back to her husband as Kinny retrieved the bowl. She settled on the side of the bed and carefully scooped up some broth, and like before, gently squeezed his lower jaw until his lips parted, then slowly drizzled the first spoonful into his mouth. Everyone waited to see if he would swallow or choke on the warm liquid. When laird MacCormac automatically swallowed the small amount of broth, Adriana sighed with relief.

Kinny grinned. "Yer idea was verra smart mistress." It warmed her heart that the lad had accepted her and was trying so hard to make her feel welcome. She continued and used encouraging words as if she were feeding a child. After a while, her back started to hurt from leaning forward at such an angle. She stood straight and arched her shoulders back to stretch her sore muscles for only a moment, then sat back down and continued. When she had fed him the whole bowl of broth, she handed the spoon to Kinny. Although her muscles ached, she was overjoyed that she'd accomplished this great feat. She released a long satisfying sigh.

"In a little while I would like to see if I could get some Willow bark tea into him. It has strong healing powers and will help ease his pain." She glanced toward the young lad. Kinny nodded and she added, "Hopefully, it will help him recover more quickly."

When she stood and turned, the huge man from yesterday stood by the door, a stern expression on his face as he closely watched her. Had he learned of her lies? Was he there to drag her out and return her to her father? She glanced away but knew he watched her every move.

His deep voice surprised her as he suddenly appeared at her side. "How is he doing? Do ye feel he'll live?"

As Lady MacCormac she didn't owe this man any explanation of her behavior, though she knew he had taken her husband's place as chieftain, and with doing so, she owed him her respect.

"I'm hopeful," she said in no more than a whisper. "I've cleaned and re-stitched and bandaged his wounds. I also got a sizable bowl of broth into him." Glancing up she met his gaze. "The only thing we can do now is to make him comfortable and pray he is strong enough to recover from his wounds."

Moira hastened to his side and placed a reassuring hand on his arm. "He is in good hands, Hugh. She has done a magnificent job tending to him."

The large man grunted in reply.

She Knew the duties of running a castle and now that Hugh was in command, he was responsible for not only the members of the clan but the land, the many tenants, and all the livestock. It had been another rainy year, and she was sure he worried about their grain crop and how it would affect the price of grain and cattle. A bad grain crop meant there could be a threat of starvation in their country.

With all the confidence she could muster, she added, "I'll do whatever I can to make sure he survives." She retrieved her husband's shaving blade then turned and faced Hugh. "I would like to clean up his face. Could you put an edge on his blade for me?" When he hesitated, she added, "If laird MacCormac appeared better, stronger, as if he were healing, it might give his people hope." He glanced at her plain clothes before his gaze returned to her face. Was he judging her worth as Lady MacCormac? After a moment, he took the blade and walked over to a leather strap tied to the washstand. He slapped the blade several times against the strap, first one way and then the other.

While Hugh sharpened the blade, Adriana turned to Kinny and the other lad. "Do you think you two could carefully hold Laird MacCormac forward with his head tipped slightly back so I can wash the dried blood and dirt from his hair?" Quick to oblige, the two boys stepped forward to do her bidding. Laying several towels along her husband's lower back she washed his hair, his neck and back. After drying him off, the lads gently positioned him back against the pillows.

As he handed her the shaving blade Hugh said, "I will return in the morning to check his progress." He glanced once more toward his kinsman on the bed, then turned and left. Her heart ached for the big man. She had no idea how close the two men were, but she felt his loss at not being able to speak with the person he'd cared so much for. His uncertainty of her abilities was obvious. Though he didn't want to accept it, he'd placed his faith in her to make sure his friend and leader survived and was able to return as laird.

"I also hae things to attend to," Lady Moira said before she hugged Adriana good-by. "I'll look in on ye later. Send for me if ye require anything at all."

Adriana nodded. "I will send for you if he wakes or appears to be in any discomfort."

Placing her hand on Adriana's cheek and with appreciation in her eyes, she said, "Yer a good lass." Then she walked out. Bethany and the other lad also took their leave.

"I'll stay with ye mistress if ye wish," Kinny said hopefully. She had a champion in the lad and the feeling warmed her heart.

Once everyone else left and with Kinny's help, they shaved the laird's mustache and beard off his face and neck. She also applied the poultice Lady Moira made to her husband's many bruises. Taking the blade to his curly hair, she cut off what was dried and tangled, leaving the length just above his shoulders. They also washed the laird's chest, arms, legs, hands, and feet.

When they finished, Adriana covered her husband with a clean sheet and blanket, then stood back. She was surprised at how handsome he looked now that he was cleaned up and his bruises weren't so dark.

"I hae never seen my laird without facial hair," Kinny said, turning his head from side to side. Lifting one brow, he added, "I hope he dinnae mind ye cutting it off?"

She smirked. "I hope he lives to yell at me for shaving his face and cutting his hair." They both laughed.

Sitting cross-legged on the bed, hands clasped in her lap, Adriana watched her husband sleep. She hadn't left his side all day. Now it was late, and she was alone with him. She'd done everything she could think of to help him get well again. But what if he still died? What if he lived?

After their midday meal, Lady Moira divulged the tale of Cameron's wife, and how the poor thing died giving birth to his child. Sheltered from the rituals of marriage, Adriana's knowledge of what happened between a man and woman were limited to what she'd overheard from the staff. Even now possessing all the facts of the deed, thanks to Lady Moira, and knowing it was her duty to get with child, the pretense still wasn't all that clear. Adriana sighed and laid a hand on her husband's chest. She prayed that if he died, he would look down from heaven and see the strong son or daughter she hoped to pass his name and holdings to.

She brushed a curl back from his forehead. He looked better without his long-mangled hair and thick black whiskers. She giggled; his whole body was covered in whiskers. She ran her hand down his arm and marveled at its girth and length. His hands resembled the paws of a great beast she heard told in a story once. She gently lifted his hand and placed her palm against his. She marveled at the sheer dimensions of his fingers that were twice the size of hers.

She'd agonized over her wifely duties most of the day, and now the time had come for her to gather up the nerve to do as she'd been instructed. Reassuring herself that since they were married, what she was about to do was morally acceptable and perfectly proper. She would do this for her future and the future of the clan. Adriana folded the covers back to reveal her husband's body. Taking a deep breath, she reached down and pulled the small towel from around his waist. Gasping, she stared in disbelief at his *wee willie*, as Lady Moira had referred to it. Willie resembled a small, lifeless, furless animal, coiled up in a nest of black curls. Gently she poked at it with her finger. Nothing happened. Lady Moira said his *wee willie* had a mind of its own, that it made no difference if the man attached were awake or not. Mimicking Lady Moira's rolling burr she said, "It only needs to think a woman is nearby lass and it will wake up and stand tall." With no choice but to trust in what she'd been told, Adriana poked it again, and still nothing happened. She placed her hands on her hips and raked her teeth over her lower lip. "I don't think this is going to work. Mayhap there is some-thing wrong with it." Then she remembered that it might take some prompting at first because of the potion he was given for his pain. Her instructions were to not give up. If it didn't respond, she'd been told a wee kiss or two might help. Or to suckle it like a sugar tit. She wasn't sure she could bring herself to do that, but after several minutes of gentle fondling with no response, Adriana was irritated. "This is going to take all night."

Shifting positions, she Knelt between his massive hair-covered thighs. Leaning forward she whispered, "Willie, can you hear me?" Nothing happened. She placed the palms of her hands flat upon his narrow hips, one on each side of his poor little willie. Hoping to build up some courage, she slid her hands up and over the flat plain of his stomach to his chest and back down. Her fingertips grazed the tips of his tiny protruding nipples. His body felt hard as packed earth under her hands, Willie did not stir. She flexed her fingers and gently lifted Willie from his resting place in the nest of black curls. She held him in her hand. It was heavier than it looked, and the skin was soft as silk, which intrigued her to investigate further. Leaning down she pressed Willie to her cheek and rolled him between the palm of her hand and the side of her face. "You're so soft," she whispered. "You smell like soap and honey." Turning her head, she kissed him, and Willie gave a quick jerk. Startled, she'd almost dropped him, but then giggled. "Oh! You are awake now." Once more it jerked. She watched in wonder as it grew longer and harder in her hand and she instinctively squeezed him gently. She kissed him again and licked the rounded tip. Something deep inside Adriana came to life and her most secret place grew damp. Lady Moira hadn't said *her* body would respond this way. She placed her mouth over him and suckled gently. Her body throbbed and a sudden urgency wafted over her like a hot summer breeze. She crawled over him and straddled his hips then slowly lowered herself onto willie. It took several tries before he finally behaved and went where he belonged, and her bottom was flush with her husband's body. The sensation shocked her. Adriana rocked back and forth, the intensity growing with every movement. There was no pain as she had prepared herself for, however, she had an itch she'd never felt before and couldn't quite appease. She continued until Willie withered back to his former self.

Looking down at her husband's large body beneath her, Adriana remembered a time when as a small child she had climbed on to and straddled a fallen tree. She couldn't help but wonder what Laird MacCormac had been like as a child. It saddened her that she would never be able to learn more about him or to know anything of his childhood.

Seven

Something heavy and warm lay across Adriana. She awoke to find herself snuggled up tight against her husband. How she'd managed to sneak between his right arm and his side she couldn't imagine. Although she was surprised at finding herself in such an intimate position, tucked up next to him she felt warm and protected. She allowed herself to linger for several more minutes, listening to his breathing and watching the rise and fall of his chest. She ran the palm of her hand down over the rigidity of his massive chest and his hard stomach. Snuggling closer, she marveled at how soft his hair chest felt against her cheek. After a moment, her sense of responsibility returned, and she reluctantly eased herself away from him and crawled out of the bed.

Her new routine was much like the day before. She dressed, ate her breakfast, then spoon-fed broth into her husband's mouth. Now that his face was no longer covered with a beard and mustache it was much easier to keep his face and neck clean as she drizzled the warm broth into his mouth. After he'd been fed, she changed his bandages and applied more poultice to his bruises. While he slept, she sat before the smoldering peat fire and spent the rest of the morning sewing up his torn trews, and the bullet hole in the left shoulder of his leather jack.

That afternoon, Bethany sat with Laird MacCormac while Lady Moira gave Adriana a tour of the castle and the formal gardens. She met Maddy the cook, the ale maker, and his wife, and several of the servants before returning to his chambers. However, throughout the day, images of what would happen to these people if she didn't get with child flashed through her mind. Would clan members truly turn against each other as they fought over a new leader?

A MacCormac heir would be the saving-grace that would keep this clan together. She released a long-frustrated sigh. If she didn't get with child before he died, she didn't know what the MacCormac clan would do with her. Hopefully, she would be wed to someone who would be kind to her but there were no guarantees. She would do whatever it took to keep from being sent back to her cruel father.

She had been gone for almost two weeks and there hadn't been word from Lynette or her father. She shivered at what his reaction had been when he learned she'd traveled across the country with Laird MacCormac's men with the intent to marry their chieftain.

"He will be furious with me," she muttered to herself.

Adriana clutched her trembling hands together and pressed them against her rolling stomach. She was selfish for worrying about her problems when her young sister was certainly suffering because of her disobedience. She had abandoned Lynette to endure their father's rage alone. Pulling her shawl tighter around her shoulders, Adriana paced the room, her breaths coming in short gasps. *Would he beat poor Lynette for my deception?* She collapsed onto the chair in front of the fire.

"Oh, Lynette I'm so sorry I abandoned you." She pressed her cold fingers to her face and burst into tears. After a few moments she wiped her tears away and wondered if she could ask Lady Moira to send the captain of the guard to fetch Lynette. Would her father allow Lynette to leave, or would he refuse the request? With a band of killers wandering the countryside, it wasn't wise for Lynette to leave the safety of Shealoch Castle right now. What if Lynette suffered at their father's hands and now hated her and refused to come? The thought of her poor sister hurt in any way because of her selfishness tore at Adriana's heart. She'd been so childish to leave without thinking her actions through. Pulling her feet up, she wrapped her shawl around her arms and legs, laid her head on her knees, and sobbed. After a while and utterly exhausted, Adriana's tears subsided, and she drifted off into peaceful sleep.

Cam forced his dry, gritty eyes open. Somewhere close by he heard the soft heart-wrenching weeping of a woman. Though his head throbbed with pain, he twisted his neck and searched the room but found it empty. He tried to speak except his dry mouth longed for a drink of cool water. He spotted a cup to his left on the bedside table. As he stretched out his arm toward the cup a sharp pain shot through his shoulder. With a long sigh, Cam bent his legs and struggled to push himself back against the headboard. Agony instantly seized his right leg sending a wave of overwhelming pain throughout his body. "Bloody Hell."

Intense pain jarred his mind and his memory of being attacked by a group of dark riders came flooding back. Their faces smeared with mud to conceal their identities. By the preciseness of their ambush, the band of men knew exactly which route his army had planned to take. They had been expecting them. So, who were they? Were they the same army who had been attacking the borderers?

Clenching his stomach muscles, Cam struggled to sit up

again. The room whirled above his head forcing him to close his eyes. Groaning, he fell back against the pillows and back into a hole of darkness.

The ancient iron door handle clicked. Cam's eyes snapped open. Was this the same day? How long had he been out? In the light from the fireplace, he watched the small figure of his aunt creep across the room toward his bed.

With a pleased smile, she whispered, "Oh, my boy. 'Tis good to see ye awake. Are ye in much pain?"

"Aunt Moira. I think I am better. Though I could use a drink of water if ye please."

"Of course, dear." She fetched a cup and held it to his lips as he gingerly braced himself on his right elbow.

"I'll make ye a potion out of willow bark to help ease yer pain and help ye sleep," she said, moving away from the bed.

"No, auntie. I would like to stay awake for a while. T's essential I have a clear head. I need to retrace my steps on the day my men and I were attacked."

"Verra weel. Would ye be wanting something to eat? Some broth, mayhap a bowl of hearty stew to help ye get yer strength back?"

"Later. I would speak with Hugh and Malcolm if ye will fetch them to me."

"Ye need yer rest," she protested as she fussed at straightening the coverlet on the bed. "I'll tell Hugh and Malcolm ye wish to speak with them in the morning. The men hae been out searching for the bandits who attacked ye. T's late and they need their rest, too."

Cam took another drink, the cool water soothing his dry throat. As he handed the cup back to his aunt the room began to spin. He moaned and laid back, closing his eyes against the stabbing pain in his head.

"Ye rest noo, dear. In a while I'll bring ye a bowl of stew."

Cam heard her slippers shuffle over the stone floor as she

crossed the room then he heard the door closed and the darkened room fell into total silence again.

The more he forced his mind to recall the day they were attacked, the more it throbbed. There were holes in his memory he could not quite fill. He needed answers but his questions would have to wait till morning. Soon the pain in his head eased, his bruised and battered body relaxed, and he fell back into a deep sleep.

Adriana awoke with a start. It was dark, how long had she slept? Getting to her feet, she stretched to relieve the stiffness that had settled in her back then pulled the shawl over her shoulders. After placing a couple bricks of peat on the fire, she strolled over to the large oak bed where her husband rested.

Flames from the fireplace emitted dancing shadows across his body, licking at his features as he peacefully slumbered. The only sounds came from the crackling fire, fierce wind, and the pelting rain against the thick glass windows. Despite the cold rain there was a warm, cozy, intimacy about the dimly lit bedchamber.

Hours earlier when she'd gone back to her room to bathe and collect herself, Adriana had found a host of presents waiting for her. There was a small basket of rose and lavender scented soaps, an assortment of ribbons and lace for her hair, two pearl hair clips, a beautifully carved wooden cross, and a tray of sweets from the kitchen. If not everyone, at least several of laird MacCormac's clan had accepted her as their lady. She truly felt blessed for the first time since she arrived. She'd spied the lovely harp in her bedchamber and settled herself on the chair. She pulled the harp to her shoulder, placed her fingers on the strings, and opened her heart. The enchanted melody her mother taught her emanated from the harp and had calmed and soothed her troubled heart. Playing the harp offered her a welcoming sense of belonging.

Adriana's thoughts returned to the present and she contemplated her obligations; she knew what she must do. She needed to focus, couldn't lose sight of her responsibilities as Lady MacCormac. Her being here affected not only herself; many others counted on her succeeding and preserving their clan.

Lady Moira's words haunted her. She knew giving birth to his heir would ensure not only her future, but the future of the clan itself. She hadn't believed Lady Moira or her questionable instructions. Nevertheless, last night had proved *Willie* truly had a mind of his own, and he liked her attention.

Her gaze washed over her husband, and she longed to be kissed once by him before he died. She had never been kissed before. *What harm would it do? Just one kiss, he would never know.* Gathering her shift and lifting it above her knees, Adriana crawled onto the bed. She crept toward the massive headboard and the large pillows on which he slept. She brushed her fingers across his bruised brow, then down along his square jaw. He was truly handsome without all that thick facial hair. Though by the dark shadow of what had already grown back, it would be necessary to shave him every day.

Laird MacCormac had drifted in and out of consciousness during their wedding three days before. He hadn't turned and looked at her, or had he? Maybe he had and hadn't like what he saw. He must have guessed he would die so perhaps it hadn't mattered to him what she looked like. He had sent for her... well, actually, he had sent for her lovely sister Lynette. He wanted someone young and beautiful to bear and raise his children. "I will show you," she whispered softly as her hand lightly brushed over his wounded shoulder and down his long muscular arm. "I will be the kindest most understanding and loving mother your child could ever wish for."

The thought of having a child made Adriana smile. "I will

be a good mother to your child. It will grow strong, and all will remember the mighty Laird Cameron MacCormac, Chieftain of the MacCormac Clan for generations to come. I'll make you proud, husband of mine."

She leaned forward and gently pressed her lips against his, then sat back. His full lips were dry, and the kiss lacked the thrill she had expected. His lack of response both saddened and relieved her. She shrugged and released a frustrated sigh, then proceeded to push the bed linens down past his knees.

As she ran her palm over the thick dark curls covering his wide chest, a shiver slithered up her spine and she jerked with delight. It was a terrible shame that this young, handsome, powerful man should have to die. Although she'd heard stories about how terrifying and cruel, he could be, she now wondered if they were all actually true. Her hand drifted lower over the smooth surface of his abdomen. Willie stirred, rising as if inviting her attention. She giggled. "Well, hello there, Wee Willie or should I be calling you My Little Laird? Did you miss me?" She scudded down the bed and gently petted him. She took him in her hand stroking him gently. When he remained placid, she granted him a quick kiss.

"I need you to wake up my little laird. Please," Adriana coaxed.

She slid her hand slowly up and down the length of him while she covered him with tender kisses and delicate licks. A warmth washed over her, and something stirred deep in her core. As her heart pounded wildly, her fingers tightened around him. Her hand continued the up and down motion she knew he liked, and soon Willie increased in size and firmness. She was utterly amazed and marveled at the transformation. Lifting her shift, she crawled over him, straddling his hips. She slowly lowered herself onto Willie. A fulfilling sensation seized her. Instinctively her body tightened around him. Willie hardened, becoming much larger than the night before, it took several tries before Adriana's body finally accepted all of him. Automatically her body began to rock back and forth. This time the sensation felt different. Magnificent. Causing her to dig her fingers deep into the linens at his sides, her hips to rock faster as if she were on top of a runaway horse. Fireflies danced behind her eyelids. The sensation grew, building into a sensualness she couldn't comprehend. The glorious feeling drove her on, she needed more. As if standing on the edge of a cliff, Adriana caught and held her breath. Something inside of her exploded, every muscle tightened as several spasms shook her body. She bit down on her lower lip to stifle her cries. As she drifted back down to earth, her body throbbed with ecstasy, like she'd never experienced before.

Perspiration covered her exhausted body. Spent, she leaned forward and collapsed upon his massive chest. When her head settled on a blanket of dark curls, she could hear a strong steady heartbeat, but wasn't sure if it was his or hers. Her arms and legs were limp, they were so heavy she couldn't move. Breathlessly, she whispered, "That was unbelievable my little lord. I hoped you enjoyed it as much as I."

All of a sudden two giant arms engulfed her, pinning her to his chest as a growl slipped through his lips. "Aye, lass. I did." His broad chest vibrated beneath her as his warm breath floated across her forehead. "And I thank ye," he added with a slight chuckle.

Adriana's heart leapt and stuck in her throat threatening to choke her. She wiggled trying to free herself, but she was trapped in his iron grip, her arms pinned at her sides. "Och, I canna let ye fly off so soon noo, can I?"

She stilled, praying he would fall back to sleep and loosen his hold on her so she could escape. Her brain froze along with the rest of her body, preventing her from thinking of what to say or do.

"Shy, are ye? You werenae a moment ago." His deep voice

rumbled from deep in his chest. It was the deepest, and most ominous sounding voice Adriana had ever heard. "What an angel ye are, lass. Would ye be telling me yer name? 'Tis too dark to see ye lovely face." His fingers combed through her hair, and he lifted a handful to his face and inhaled her scent. "Ye smell of spring flowers and bright sunshine."

She couldn't' breathe, couldn't think. She'd never fainted before, and now would not be a good time to faint dead away in the arms of the Black Giant. Then he relaxed his grip. In a flash, Adriana slipped off the bed, her shift floating back down to her calves.

"Light the candles and show yerself," he whispered weakly. Adriana didn't know what to do, although she felt as if she might swoon. She ran to the door, grabbed the handle, jerked it open and dashed out into the darkened corridor.

ameron was spent. His body felt as if it were tied to the bed. He closed his eyes and tried to gather his thoughts. His head spun; had he been dreaming? He had fought to wake up except his body hungered to investigate the erotic fantasy it was experiencing. An angel had landed on him and with her gentle touch and sweet voice had healed him. He grinned; this angel knew the true magic of healing a man. He loved the sound of her soft voice, the way her hands floated over his body as she healed him. Chinese fireworks he'd witnessed in London once could not compare to the fireworks that had gone off in his head as she rode him to the finish line. He'd fought his way up and out of the intense darkness. The mixture of pain and pleasure threatened his sanity. But if this was what his hell was going to be like, he was willing to die a thousand deaths.

Sometime later Cam awoke. The chamber had grown dark and cold, the blankets rested down below his knees. He twisted to one side and reached for the coverlet, but his fingers couldn't quite reach it. "Bloody Hell." He closed his eyes against the dizziness then tried again. With his good leg he lifted the blanket in hopes of moving it toward his hand. A sharp pain shot through his injured shoulder, nevertheless, he struggled to reach the blanket. If he died, he did not relish being found stripped of his dignity and exposed for all to observe. His fingers grasped the corner of the coverlet, and he pulled it up over himself.

His faceless angel had obtained what she had come for. He chuckled to himself. She would be back for more and when she did, he planned to catch her and never let her go. He smiled as his cock grew hard again. If she were a dream and he fell back to sleep, would she return? Except he couldn't relax, something didn't feel quite right. He wanted answers. Who was she? Why wouldn't she tell him her name? Moreover, why had she run away as if she feared him?

"Quit yer fussing over me, Aunt Moira," Cam said, pushing his aunt's hand away as he struggled to sit up against the head-board. He hadn't slept after his angel had disappeared. The dull throbbing in his head would not cease, and he was going to kill the next person who touched him. There was only one person he wanted fluttering around him. He could still smell her hair and feel her gentle hands roaming over his body. Though one question plagued him. If she had been there to heal him, why was she feckin him? His cock stirred at the mere thought of her warm body stretched out on top of him, and he was forced to bend his left leg to conceal his obvious plight from his aunt's observant eyes.

"Make yerself useful and send for Hugh. I need—"

"Ye need to be staying in bed for a few more days." His aunt glared at him; her fists perched on her narrow hips. "Ye willnae heal if ye dinnae do as yer told."

"I'm weel enough to see to my duties, woman. Am I naw

still Laird here?" He growled, casting his glance toward the window.

She huffed a shallow breath, her eyes sparking with anger. "I willnae be telling ye what yer are, lad. But stubborn and ill-mannered top the long list."

One good thing, Aunt Moira's displeasure with him was working to relax his yearning for his angel's touch. Cam's face and neck started to itch, and the sensation was driving him mad. When he realized what the cause of his discomfort was, he bellowed, "Who the devil shaved my face?"

His aunt glanced around the room as if looking for someone else to blame. She turned her attention back to Cam and replied, "'Tis much easier to spoon broth into yer mouth when a person can see where ye're aiming."

"I'll be feeding myself from now on," he said, glowering at her.

She retrieved a cup from the bedside table and handed it to him. "Drink this. It weel help ye sleep. Ye need yer rest."

"No more of yer dreadful potions, woman. Take yer poison away. I need my wits about me." He waved her off with his left arm and was rewarded for his efforts with excruciating pain.

Cam heard a deep chuckle and knew his salvation had arrived. His cousin Hugh stepped around Moira. The big man slipped his arm around the tiny woman's shoulders. He pulled her close and kissed her cheek. "So, auntie. Is our laird ready for hard work? Fergus could use some help drying the grain that's been harvested."

All traces of Moira's anger slipped away as she smiled and patted Hugh's broad chest. "Ye might as weel drag him out. He'll not listen to reason and stay in bed where he belongs."

Hugh's chest shook when he laughed. "If you wish I could knock him out for a few more days?" He grinned and raised his beefy fist into the air.

"Either that or get him to drink this potion." She set the

cup back on the table. "I'll leave ye to yer business, lads." She turned and walked out of the room.

"Weel? What hae ye learned?" Cam asked, scratching his jaw. "Who were those men, what was their purpose for attacking us?" He hoped his cousin had good news for him, he was in a mood to smash a few heads.

"We followed their tracks to the river then we lost them. Patrols hae been sent out and extra men hae been posted in the towers, along the battlement, and at all the gates."

"What makes ye think that band of thieves would attempt an attack on the castle?"

Hugh's facial expression hardened; Cam knew he wasn't going to like what he was about to say. "When the bullet struck yer head and ye fell to the ground and dinnae move, they grabbed their wounded and fled. T'was plain, they weren't after anything except achieving yer death."

Throwing back the covers Cam eased his body to the side of the bed. He needed to get dressed so he could ride out and hunt down those killers and string them up.

"And where do ye think yer going?" Hugh said. "We hae sent out most of the army, and the men who remain are armed and ready."

Gripping the bedpost Cam pulled himself up. "I need-" The room spun, and he closed his eyes against the stabbing pain.

"Ye need to get ye arse back into that bed. If ye fall and crack yer thick skull on the stone floor, ye'll be no good to anyone."

Cam eased back down. The pain overwhelmed him, but he wanted answers, and he wanted them now. He rubbed his hand around his head hoping to relieve some of the pain. "How many men did we lose?"

"We faired weel. Only a few cuts amongst the men."

"'Tis good. That will show them murderers how strong we be."

"Ye will not be getting stronger if yer donae get back in that bed and do what yer told." Hugh pulled the covers out of Cam's way. He bent over, then jerked to attention. "Och, mon. Where can I find ye a shirt? I donae need yer cock staring me in the face."

Cam chuckled and pointed to his wardrobe. "Ye can find one in there I think."

Hugh crossed the room and flung the wardrobe open. He returned with a shirt and helped Cam slip his left arm into the sleeve before Cam slipped his head and other arm into position and pulled it down to his knees. "There, Cam panted. "Does that appease yer delicate sensibilities?"

"Aye. But I may hae to hae Malcolm pluck my eyes out later," Hugh drawled, his brows pulled down in a fierce scowl. He hesitated for a moment, then leaned down and grabbed Cam's ankles. "Ready, *My Laird*?" When Cam laughed, Hugh hoisted Cam's legs up onto the bed.

Cam fell back against the pillows with a loud huff. "Bloody Hell, mon. Are ye trying to kill me?"

"No. I'll be leaving that to the devils in black who wishes ye dead," he chuckled. "Mayhap, ye should be drinking the potion our sweet auntie left for ye?" Hugh picked up the cup and handed it to Cam.

"Och, no. That wicked potion will knock me out for hours." He waved it away.

"With such wounds, we thought ye would surely die. Auntie Moira saved ye."

Aunt Moira may have cooked up her potions and fed him broth, but Cam knew it hadn't been her boney cold hands that healed not only his body but gave his soul something to live for. Should he ask Hugh if he knew the name of his faceless angel?

"What of the baronet's daughter?" Hugh asked.

Cam rubbed his hands over his face. "I cannae think aboot that noo. We need to find out who this band of killers are and what they're really after." Cam pulled himself up straighter in the bed. "The time isnae right for me to marry. We hae killers running wild, the fields need to be harvested and dried, and I fear if we lose any of the fields, we willnae hae enough to feed everyone throughout the winter. I willnae lose anyone 'cause of a band of thieves and murderers."

"I understand, but Sir Alexander's daughter-" Hugh started again.

"I don't want to hear any more aboot the mon's daughter. We need to fill the smokehouse and the storehouses before the snows come."

"The hunters are taking care of filling the shelves," Hugh said. "Ye need to worry aboot healing, so we donae end up with a war amongst the clan."

"As long as I'm alive, no one will be taking over as laird." He confirmed with a nod of his head.

A soft knock sounded at the door.

"Enter," Cam bellowed.

The door opened slowly, and a tall, skinny, red headed lad entered the room carrying a tray of food. Behind him was a bonnie, little, fair-haired house maid. She carried a tray, which held a bowl of broth and a stack of rolled up bandages.

"What's all of this?" Cam growled.

The two servants stopped and stared as if they had entered the wrong bedchamber.

Hugh laughed and said, "'Tis yer breakfast ye stupid hairy gob."

"Aye." The maid curtsied. "'Tis glad I am to see ye awake, milord." She nodded to the lad, and he bowed. "We weren't sure if ye'd be awake or not, so we brought broth and food." She offered a slight smile. She crossed to the table and set her tray down, the lad followed and placed his tray next to hers. "Can we fetch ye anything else, milord?" She fidgeted with her apron as she waited for his response. The lad stood behind her, his face as white as a cloud, his eyes large and round.

"Nay, lass."

She bobbed then elbowed the lad who bowed. They both fled as if the hounds of Hell were after them.

Hugh crossed to the table and reached for a piece of sliced meat and a chunk of cheese. "I think they dinnae expected to find ye awake," he said, popping the food into his mouth.

"'Tis more likely they thought to find me dead," Cam snarled, staring across the room at the closed door.

Adriana woke in a cold sweat, tangled, and twisted in her blankets. She'd tossed and turned most of the night, until she finally wore herself out and drifted off to sleep. She stared at the gold canopy above her, attempting to unscramble the events from the night before. She was mortified at what she'd done and that he'd awoken while she'd been telling him how wonderful making love to him had been. she kicked free of the covers, crossed to the ewer, and splashed cold water on her weary face. A dull pain throbbed behind her temples. What if he'd seen her face and realized she'd taken her sister's place? Then reality hit her. "Lord. He doesn't even know I'm his wife. Who did he think I was? What did he think I was doing?"

Only a few days ago, Lady Moira had assured her Laird MacCormac wouldn't recover. His wounds were too severe for him to live. Even his men were convinced he would not live for long.

"What must he think of me?"

Placing the towel over her face she shrieked, barely refraining from screaming the rafters down around her. She rubbed her forehead and paced aimlessly around her room. What was she to do now? Besides saving her sister, she had only agreed to marry the MacCormac because he wasn't expected to live.

"Does he remember the wedding ceremony or that he is even married?" she mumbled. "He is bound to find out the truth. What will he do when he finds out he has been tricked into marrying me? If he sees me, my ugly scar before I'm carrying a wee one, he will surely throw me out into the night— or kill me." A shiver shuddered through her body. She wished she were brave enough to go and face him, explain everything, instead she could never go back into his room or let him see her. Adriana crossed to the window and peered out. She could run away, but where would she go? She could never return to her father. She would rather take her chances on her own than to listen to his cruel words or face another one of his beatings. If only there were more time for her to become pregnant. But how could that be possible? She continued to pace, her mind searching for answers. Then she stopped. The only way she could approach him would be to visit him in the darkness of night. She couldn't let him see her face, at least until she knew for sure she carried his heir. Her stomach twisted into painful knots. Why was she such a coward? "I will never get away with this."

There was a soft knock on her door.

Sighing, Adriana reached for her shawl, wrapped it around her shoulders and called out. "Come in."

Bethany poked her head around the door. "Good morning, milady." Entering, she closed the door softly. "We brought yer breakfast tray and a bowl of broth to the laird's chambers," the maid said with a bright smile. "If you dinnae already ken, milaird is awake."

"Yes," Adriana muttered. "He...awoke late last night." Wringing her hands, Adriana strolled back to the window and stared out through the rain. It seemed as if it rained every day in the Highlands.

"'Tis happy am I he's alive and will not die. However, with the way he was acting, I cannae help but wonder if anything is amiss?"

"I'm sure he's trying to figure out what I was doing," Adriana mumbled just above a whisper.

"I bid yer forgiveness, milady," she said, stepping further into the room. "I too am married, and I ken 'tis not always what we expect at first. I'm saying, since ye no family here to talk to... If ye hae questions, be assured I will keep yer confidence safe." There was kindness and understanding in the woman's soft eyes and smile as she shook her head. "The heavens ken men are different from us."

"That is what Lady Moira told me." Adriana dropped into one of the chairs in front of the fire. She pulled her shawl tighter and gestured for Bethany to sit on the other chair.

"Lady Moira?" Bethany rolled her eyes. "And what does her ladyship remember about men?"

"Well, she said the same thing, that men were different from women." Adriana's face grew warm, and her body began to tremble. "I'm so ashamed. I'm too embarrassed to seek out her advice—now." She looked down at her hands clasped together on her lap. "He woke up and caught me... He'll certainly kill me when he finds me."

"Oh dearie. Surely, he guessed at your innocence. I doubt ye displeased him so that he would consider killing ye."

Glancing up Adriana said, "You don't understand. When he finds out what I did, he'll either throw me out, send me back to my father, or kill me." Panic bubbled up in Adriana's chest. She glanced around the room. Her desire to run was strong, but she didn't know where she would go.

Bethany's eyes grew large and round, her mouth gaped open as if Adriana had grown another head. "Mistress?" Her voice low and clear. "What din ye do to the poor man?"

Adriana's gaze shot to the maids, and she anxiously scooted

to the edge of her chair and leaned forward, her eyes pleading for understanding. "I thought he was going to die. Everyone told me he would certainly die. Lady Moira said..." She rung her hands.

Bethany's hand shot up and she crossed herself. "May the Saints save yer soul."

"What? No." Adriana wiped at her tears. "I didn't hurt him. At least I don't think I did. I was gentle as Lady Moira instructed me to be. If I don't get with child before he learns... He's going to have me killed." Her tears started again. "What am I going to do?"

There was a knock at the door.

"Jesus, Mary and Joseph," Bethany huffed, surging to her feet. "Donae fess, mistress. We'll figure this out."

The maid pulled the door open, and Kinny walked in with a tray of food. "Put it on the table there," Bethany said, gesturing to the small table between the two chairs. "Thank you, Kinny for fetching another tray. Now you can go." With both hands she ushered the confused lad toward the door.

"Wait!" Adriana jumped to her feet and strolled over to the boy. "I wish to ask a favor of you, Kinny. Now that Laird MacCormac is feeling better, I would like it if you could bring him his food each day and see to all of his needs? You will also need to clean his wounds and change his bandages like you helped me do the other day. And, oh, he should stay in bed for a few more days, he's not strong enough to try and walk yet."

Kinny's smile revealed how overjoyed he was at being asked to fulfill such an important task. "There is one more important thing you need to remember," she added, stepping closer. "You mustn't mention me to his lordship. Even if he is to ask, you never heard of me and know nothing about me."

With a troubled expression the lad hesitated. "He's milaird, milady..."

"If you utter one word of me to *anyone*, you'll find yourself a scullery maid for your remaining years."

"Aye, milady." He bowed. "I swear I weel never mention ye to himself or anyone."

Adriana pushed her shoulders back in hopes of enforcing her new authority, then nodded once. Kinny bowed again, turned, and fled the room.

Exhaling, Adriana's shoulders relaxed and curled forward, she thought she might faint. Reaching out she searched for Bethany's arm. The woman quickly grabbed Adriana's arm and led her back to her chair.

After easing Adriana back onto the chair, Bethany seated herself. The woman waited three whole breaths before saying, "Milady, ye better tell me everything. Then we'll come up with... With... A solution," she added and nodded her head.

A long overwhelming sigh slipped from Adriana's lips. She glanced up and met Bethany's eyes. "I'm not sure where to start."

"Best start at the beginning, my mum always says." She nodded encouragingly.

Adriana told her about the arrangement made between her father and Laird MacCormac. "My sister is far too young to marry a man like The MacCormac. I couldn't let her marry him. Then that nice captain of the guards arrived. He informed me and his men who'd returned with my father, that Laird MacCormac had been gravely wounded and his clan feared he would soon die. Lynette is too young to be a wife let-a-lone a widow."

Adriana glanced around the room, too ashamed to continue. She hesitated. "I still had his ring in my pocket. The captain assumed I was his Laird's betrothed. I *should* have told him the truth right then, but I... I couldn't. He was going to die." She glared at Bethany, then rubbed her throbbing temples.

"Once I arrived here everything happened so fast. The

wedding ceremony had already been planned for the same day. Then Lady Moira appeared. She told me it was my obligation to the clan and as his wife to get with child before he died. I doubt I'm with child. I might not have done everything correctly."

"What do ye think ye did wrong?" Bethany frowned with concern.

"I didn't understand how the deed was supposed to happen while he continued to be unconscious or asleep. But Lady Moira explained his wee willie had a mind of its own. She said it wouldn't make any difference if he were unconscious. It would respond if I did everything exactly as she instructed. I'm quite sure I understood..." Adriana shook her head slowly.

Bethany's hand shot out and covered Adriana's. "Jesus, Mary, and Joseph. What did ye do, lass?"

Adriana licked her dry lips. She explained in detail everything Lady Moira had told her to do to his willie, and the lack of its response at first. Adriana waited for the woman's reaction, though Bethany just gnawed on her lower lip. Bethany's eyes grew as Adriana conveyed the events of the night before to her.

When Adriana explained the part where her body shuddered and she collapsed onto his chest, and how his arms came up and trapped her to him, little squeaky noises escaped the woman. Adriana continued, "I laid real still hoping he'd fall back to sleep, but he didn't." Panic boiled up from the depths of her soul, her gaze shot around the room. "Then once he loosened his hold on me, I panicked. I jumped off of him and ran out of the room."

Bethany sat quietly for several seconds, then fell back into her chair and roared with laughter.

Offended, Adriana crossed her arms and leaned back in her chair. Bethany continued to howl, and soon Adriana found herself chuckling right along with her. "You shouldn't laugh at the *Lady of the castle*," she said in a forced stern voice. Bethany opened her eyes, chuckled, then started laughing again.

"Not very lady-like of me, was it?" Adriana confessed with a frown. She pounded a fist against her knee.

After a few moments Bethany said, "My apologies, milady. This explains the way he behaved earlier. So, he donae ken who ye are, or that yer his wife?"

"No. But now that he's awake he'll find out he married me." She pulled back her hair to reveal the long scar along her cheek. "And not my beautiful sister who was promised to him." She wiped fresh tears from her cheeks. "How am I to lie with him without him discovering who I am and what I've done, or what I look like? He cannot see me until I know I'm carrying his heir."

Bethany's expression turned solemn. She stood and walked behind her chair, one finger tapping her lower lip. She paused for a few moments, then smiled. "I've got an idea."

Nine

"Quit crowding me, lad." Cam threw the book he'd been reading onto the bed and crossed his arms. The lad, Kinny, had taken it upon himself to become Cam's personal attendant and bodyguard. He eagerly fetched anything he asked for. Had gone as far as stopping and questioning anyone who attempted to enter his chambers. He was like a giant red-headed horsefly buzzing around Cam's bed.

Kinny placed two jars of poultice and a bundle of new bandages next to Cam's leg, then proceeded to remove the old bandage from Cam's shoulder. He appeared to know what he was doing. "Ye say, ye and my aunt hae been the only ones tending me," Cam said intently watching the boy.

"Aye," Kinny replied concentrating on his job.

"And ye be healing quite nicely, milord." The lad beamed with pride as he wiped a generous amount of the poultice across the wound. He wrapped the long bandage under Cam's arm, then up and around his neck to hold it in place.

"And how din ye come to be a healer, lad? Who taught ye how to tend to such wounds?"

"T'was Lady Moira. I paid verra close attention." He grinned and tucked the end of the bandage under the wrap. "And now that yer awake, she thought 'tis best... Proper I tend yer needs, myself." The boy slipped the shirt back over Cam's head and guided his wounded arm into the sleeve.

Cam pushed his good arm into the other sleeve and pulled the shirt down over his chest and back. "She did... And there's been no one else helping ye?" Keeping a wary eye on the lad. Although his shoulder pained him, he crossed his arms across his chest again.

"Aye." Kinny circled around the bed and drew back the covers to expose Cam's right leg. As the boy worked, Cam marveled at the lad's gentle and precise touch. It surely seemed he had done the task afore. "I'm told ye cannae leave yer chambers for a few more days."

Cam stared at the boy. "I cannae leave? I'm laird of this castle. I will not be kept prisoner in my own chambers." The lad flinched when Cam bellowed but quickly continued to place a fresh bandage on his leg. It didn't really bother Cam to stay in his bed chamber. Hugh seemed to have everything under control, plus it had been two days since he'd seen Angel, as he started thinking of the lovely young woman he'd awaken to in his arms. He hoped if he stayed put in his chambers, she would come to him, and he didn't want to take the chance of missing her.

Cameron had become infatuated with the woman and couldn't get her out of his mind. He needed to find out who she was. He had a feeling she'd been the one who tended to him. Besides, Aunt Moira's surprised reaction at how well his wounds looked, and how well he was healing, divulged the fact that she couldn't have been the person who'd pulled him back from the devil's grasp.

"Damnation, lad, are ye almost done pestering me," Cam

glowered at the boy as he tucked the covers around him. "Don't ye hae other chores that need tending to?"

Kinney collected the dirty bandages and with a toothy grin said, "Naw, milord. My sole job is to tend to ye. Can I fetch ye something to drink or eat? Might ye wish to take a nap?"

What Cam wished for was to know the identity of his angel, and to know why she had run from his room as if the devil's hounds were at her heels. Cam threw back the blankets, scooted to the edge of the bed and dropped his legs over.

Kinny rushed to his side. "Yer lordship ye're to stay in bed," the boy persisted.

Pulling his arm away from the lad's reach, Cam barked, "I'll be getting oot of this bed if I wish. There is a walking stick in the back corner of my wardrobe—fetch it."

The boy ran to the cabinet, swung the doors open and quickly returned with the long, carved walking stick. Cam grabbed it from the lad and elbowed his hands away when he offered his help. Cam banged the cane on the floor as he tried to stand, and the walking stick slipped on the stones. A sharp pain stabbed at his wounded leg making him pitch to the side and grab the bed post.

"Ye must be patient, milord," Kinny said, hovering close behind him. "'Tis going to take a while afore yer leg is strong enough to hold yer weight."

"I'm not going to get my strength back by lying in bed all day." Cam took another step and stumbled into the bedside table knocking the pitcher of water onto the floor. Leaning over, he braced his hand on the table and closed his eyes. Although his dizziness seemed to be diminishing considerably each time he stood, it wasn't disappearing quick enough for Cam.

"Milord, 'tis going to take time," Kinny repeated as he slipped his arm around Cam's waist. "Ye need to be patient."

Patience and kindness were two virtues Cameron MacCormac was well aware he had been born without.

~

Two nights later, newly shaved with his hair tied back with a leather thong, Cam departed his room. Dressed in his best waistcoat, belted plaid and broques, his cravat tied neatly around his neck, he lumbered his way down the stone steps to the great hall for his dinner. His nursemaid and protector, Kinny, proudly followed at his heels. Although Cam found the lad overprotective, he realized it was simpler to tolerate the lad's presence than it would be to try and escape him.

Several clansmen were already present and seated at the trestle tables when Cam entered the great hall. He passed under the stone arched entrance and limped toward the dais and the high table. At the sight of their laird, the crowd quieted and came to their feet. Cam scanned the room hoping to catch the eye of the woman who dominated his every waking thought and haunted his dreams.

Once seated, he studied the unfamiliar occupants, then fixed his gaze on the house maid he'd met the previous morning. If he remembered correctly, she had stated her name as Bethany. She stood off to the side and conversed with another woman. When he caught her eye, she said something to the woman who then scurried toward the back stairs, which led to the kitchen. He motioned Bethany forward. She twisted her hands in the front of her apron and hesitantly approached him. Stepping up onto the dais, she crept to his side and bobbed a curtsy. Avoiding his gaze and appeared to be examining the stones of the floor beneath them.

Cam cleared his throat. "The woman ye were speaking to, what's her name?"

"Aunna, milord," she replied, clasping her hands together. "She'd be the new kitchen maid."

Nodding, he waved the lass away. Hadn't he passed Aunna moments ago in the corridor before entering the hall? A lad appeared and filled his glass with wine then hurried away. Cam studied the boy but couldn't conjure up his name. As Cam's gaze washed over the hall, he became aware that he had either forgotten the names of his servants, or they had all been replaced over the past few years.

As laird of the MacCormac clan and all the responsibilities that went with his title, was he also expected to memorize the names of all who served him? Then a thought crossed his mind. Had he once known them by name? What had changed? Why were they scurrying away as if they feared him?

"Who might ye be scowling at," Hugh asked as he and Malcolm found their seats beside Cam and sat down. Cam turned and pinned his cousin with a deep frown. Before he could respond, the lad with the wine stepped forward and filled Hugh's and Malcolm's glasses then swiftly retreated.

"What is the matter with everyone around here?" Cam growled. "They act as if they fear I will bite their heads off if they get too close to me."

Hugh chuckled. "Look at yer hands, mon." Cam glanced down at his clenched fists positioned on the table. "Ye look ready to bash someone's head in as we speak."

Cam flexed his fingers and wiped his damp palms across his plaid.

"Ye've been unbearable to live with these past years," Hugh added. "Yer clansmen and servants hae had good reason to keep their distance from ye."

Malcolm drained his glass and said, "At least with yer face shaved and yer wild hair trimmed short, ye no longer resemble a great beast from the forest. Mayhap children will not cry and run to hide behind their mum's skirts when ye pass by." Malcolm and Hugh both chuckled at the statement.

The time after his wife Blair's death was still a blur to Cam. Had he become a monster? His men *had* been forced to lock him away as if he were. A violent shiver raced up his spine as a flashback of the weeks he'd spent locked in the makeshift dungeon in the lower-level storeroom assaulted him. He had convinced himself he'd come to terms with his loss, but it appeared he had only fooled himself. No wonder Angel and his clansmen ran from him; they feared him. Would Angel return to him if he could somehow prove he wouldn't hurt her? How was he to do that—not knowing who she was? He needed answers, but to get them he would have to gentle his ways, be amiable to everyone. He could do that...couldn't he?

Several servants approached him and placed trenchers with roasted pheasant, vegetables, fresh warm bread, and berry tarts before him. He thanked each of them as they passed and received queer looks for his efforts. After Cam finished his wine, he sighed, leaned back in his chair, and ran his bear-like paw over his full belly, though it was hard and flat under his heavy plaid. The lad who served the high table poured Cam his customary, after dinner brandy, which he hadn't enjoyed since he'd been injured.

Several moments later, the empty brandy glass sat on the table. Cam turned to speak to his cousin Hugh, but when he opened his mouth, nothing came out. As Cam tried to focus on Hugh's face, a dark curtain drew before his eyes, and everything went black as he slumped forward, his head banging against the table.

∼

Adriana glanced at the bottle of brandy in her hand, then lifted her skirts and dashed toward the dais. Gnawing her lower lip, she prayed Bethany's plan had worked and he had only passed out, and that the brandy hadn't killed her husband who lay sprawled face down across the high table.

Hugh and Malcolm scrambled to their feet sending their chairs tumbling backwards, crashing to the floor. Hugh grabbed a handful of Cameron's hair and pulled his head back. "He's passed out cold."

"How much did ye give him," Bethany whispered, appearing beside Adriana with a perplexed expression on her face.

"With him being so large I wasn't sure how much to put in the bottle." Adriana met Bethany's gaze. "It must have been a tinge too much I'm thinking." She shoved the bottle into Bethany's hands, only to have the woman thrust the decanter back into her own hands again.

A deep voice broke into Adriana's thoughts. "What din ye put in the brandy?" Hugh towered over Adriana with his hands fisted on his hips; his brows set in a heavy scowl.

Fear shot through Adriana. She swallowed hard and forced herself to stand firm before the enormous angry man. "The potion was to help him relax. Though, I might have added a little more than was needed." She clutched the bottle to her breast.

"Why would ye do such a thing?"

His hot breath swept over her face. "I assure you my goal wasn't to harm him. I only hoped to persuade him to return to his room and not linger in the hall over long. He needs his rest."

The two brawny men exchanged a long look. Hugh's stern expression didn't waver, but Malcolm struggled to suppress a snicker and came to her rescue. "If his wounds dinnae end his wretched life," he grinned, "a sound sleep shouldnae kill him."

Adriana sighed, thankful, the captain accepted her reasoning as the truth. Handing the bottle to Bethany, she placed her hands on her hips, and with all the false bravado she could muster said, "Would you please carry *my* husband up to his room? I will tend to him there." She whirled around and ran straight into Kinny. Tilting her head back, she peered down her nose at the stunned boy until he abruptly bowed and scrambled out of her way.

Although her legs trembled and threatened to give out, Adriana led the men through the castle and up to her husband's bedchambers. She heard them mumbling under their breaths behind her. What must they be thinking? She prayed they wouldn't dispose of her or imprison her for trying to murder their laird.

Each of the two huge men clutched one of her husband's lifeless arms while Kinny struggled with both of his feet as they maneuvered up the stone stairs and down the corridor. Adriana opened the bed chamber door as the men carried their chieftain across the threshold and deposited their cumbersome load onto the bed. Jetting out her chin, Adriana announced, "Thank you. You may go. I can handle it from here."

She prayed they still considered her their mistress even though she was dressed as a kitchen maid. The two men exchanged another telling look. Hugh's bow was curt, then he turned and marched out of the room. Captain Haywood stepped toward Adriana and bowed. When he rose, he wore a slight smirk and he winked at her. She drew in a sharp breath, then heard the man's roar of laughter as he proceeded down the hall.

Kinny busied himself with unlacing and removing Cam's shoes and stockings. "I shall stay and help ye ready him for bed," he said, placing the discarded shoes neatly in the wardrobe.

"I appreciate your help, Kinny. I'm sure you must be wondering..."

He shook his head. "I donae think nor question ye. I'm yer

loyal and obedient servant, milady." He turned and bowed to her.

Nothing else was said. Soon they had their chieftain stripped of his fine waistcoat, cravat, and belted plaid. Left in only his shirt, Kinny covered Cam with the heavy coverlet. With everything put away, Kinny turned to Adriana. "Will that be all for tonight, milady?"

"Yes. Thank you, Kinny."

"My pleasure." He bowed graciously, strolled across the room, and quietly pulled the door closed behind him as he left.

Alone in the cool chamber, Adriana listened to her husband's slow even breaths. Standing back from the bed, was still amazed and a little frightened at the sheer size of the man. When he strolled into the Great Hall courtly dressed as Chieftain of the MacCormac Clan, she couldn't believe how tall and regal he appeared. Yes, he had seemed large lying on the bed, but now it was obvious why her husband had been called the Black Giant. He truly was a giant amongst men.

He'd entered the great hall resplendently dressed. When his lovely blue eyes scanned over her, she'd almost melted right where she stood. She had never seen eyes so intense or such a piercing bright blue before. Even though he looked straight at her, he hadn't truly seen her. Adriana sighed. "If I hadn't this scar and were beautiful, you would have noticed me."

She tucked a lose strand of hair behind her ear and inched closer to his bed. She had watched him consume his evening meal and thought, if he continued to eat as he had tonight, it wouldn't be long before he regained all his strength. The thought caused her whole body to quiver. She rejoiced at the thought of him making a full recovery from his wounds. However, that meant he would be returning to his duties as Laird and Chieftain, which would make hiding from him during the day much harder. And what about the nights? If she continued to go to him at night, would he demand and take control, force her to show herself to him? She stepped to the edge of the bed and brushed back a silky black curl from his brow.

Could she ignore her conscience and continue to give him the potion each night? No, she couldn't do such a thing to him again. Not after watching his head smack against the table the way, it had. She brushed her hand along his cheek. A look of utter relaxation had softened his features. With his face freshly shaved, she marveled at the handsome man lying there before her.

Adriana took her time removing her clothes, placing each item neatly across the back of the chair. Then she lifted the coverlet and crawled in next to her husband's warm body.

Ten

Cam awoke. His leaden eyelids felt as if they were covered with sand. He stared at the narrow strip of morning light streaming in through the window and across the ceiling, trying to recollect the events of the night before. A heavy fog clouded his mind while a bitter taste coated the inside of his dry mouth. He had dined in the Great Hall the night before; except he couldn't remember how he came to be in his bedchambers or how he'd become undressed. He didn't think he had consumed enough strong spirits to render him unconscious, though that is what he feared happened. The thought that someone might have drugged him crept into his mind. But who would do such a thing, and to what purpose?

Throwing the covers back, he stretched and gingerly swung his legs over the edge of the bed. Scratching himself he wondered if his faceless angel had visited him during the night, and if she were connected to the attacks against him? Anger burned a painful path from his chest to his throat.

It makes no difference who is behind these assaults, I will find them, and they will be severely dealt with. They will pay the price for what they hae done.

I am chieftain of clan MacCormac. If these killers are one of my own who wish to see me dead, they will not be happy to learn I hae no plans to relinquish my leadership to anyone soon.

Hours later, dressed in his finest again, and having finished his evening meal, Cam sat in his chair in the Great Hall striving to appear relaxed. His gaze washed over the crowded hall. Who wanted him dead, and would they be so bold as to attempt to dispatch him again tonight?

Cam had kept busy while he waited for this evening. First, he'd spent two hours in the steward's office going over accounts with the elderly steward, Pembroke. He couldn't remember the last time he'd spoken to the man. He'd been surprised he had actually remembered the man's name. After the midday meal, Cam settled a disagreement over the ownership of five yearling beeves, then resolved a fight between two brothers over the affections of a bonnie lass, which filled his mind with thoughts of Angel and her heavenly touch. In the afternoon, he'd wandered around the castle hoping Angel would present herself to him. When that didn't happen, he decided to head out to the garrison. However, due to the cold driving rain, his aunt Moira had barred his way, forbidding him access to the elements. She emphatically argued that he was not healed enough and would catch his death if he ventured out into the harsh weather. With nothing interesting to occupy his time, Cam returned to the great hall and attend to a pile of correspondence which lay scattered across the high table.

A commotion by the main entrance jerked Cam away from his meandering thoughts. Hugh, Malcolm, and five guards strolled in. The men laughed and their jovial voices filled the reticent chamber. When they noticed Cam's expression, their laughter quieted, and Hugh and Malcolm climbed onto the dais and settled into their chairs on either side of Cam.

Hugh cleared his throat. Leaning forward he placed his elbows on the table and proceeded to report on the condition of the fields due to the constant rain to Cam. Cam listened intently to his cousin, nodding in agreement to his suggestions of digging more drainage ditches and to extra fires to help dry the grains. Once they finish discussing clan business, and Cam was convinced nothing out of the ordinary accrued during the night, Cam placed his correspondences back into the small wooden box and the evening meal was served.

As Cam twisted the crystal glass of brandy between his fingers and admired the amber liquid, he thought about what he'd accomplished that day, but felt disappointed Angel hadn't come forward and made herself known to him.

Lifting his glass, Cam downed half of his favorite brandy. The liquid soothed his agitated disposition, and after a moment the tightness in his neck and shoulders relaxed. Then the unmistakable bitter taste he had awoken with that morning returned. A taste that had never followed his favorite brandy before.

Cam schooled his expression, not wanting to alert whoever placed the potion in his brandy. *So, the elixir which caused him to sleep through the night had been placed in his brandy*. Servants hurried about, appearing tense, and ignoring each other. What did they expect to happen? Glancing out of the corner of his eye, Cam witnessed Hugh's gaze skim vigilantly over the crowded room. The notion his cousin Hugh could be behind the attacks on his life caused a disheartening pain in his chest and a sour taste emerged in the back of his throat.

His thoughts shifted and a plan started to form as Cam toyed with his glass. Turning toward his cousin, Cam knocked his glass over spilling most of what was left onto the table. Grumbling, he quickly righted his glass and drank the last few remaining drops. No one seemed to notice what happened, though Cam observed a suspicious exchange between Hugh and Malcolm. Several moments later, Cam feigned dizziness. Rubbing his hands over his face, he stooped forward and dropped his head onto his arm.

"Good Lord! Not again!" exclaimed Hugh, lurching to his feet, his chair sliding across the floor.

"How many times are we going to hae to do this?" Malcolm grumbled as he grabbed Cam's right arm and draped it around his neck. The hall fell into murmurs. Cam listened as his two-most-trusted-men whispered while they hoisted his limp body to his feet.

"D'ye ken what he's going to do to us when he finds out what we've done?" Malcolm murmured as they hauled Cam's lifeless body from the hall.

"Donae ye think I huvnae thought aboot what my last days on this earth are going to entail?" Hugh grunted. "Where is that lad when ye need him?"

"He must weigh close to twenty-five stones," Malcolm protested as they shuffled along the hallway. "D'ye ken we'll be tortured when he learns the truth of it?"

"I donna fancy being brutalized," Hugh grumbled as he wrestled for a better hold on his laird. "I'll be praying for a quick and merciful death."

"It's aboot time, lad." The young lad, Kinny who had appointed himself Cam's guardian joined the pair of conspirators. Cam heard the lad groan as his feet were lifted off the ground.

The trio moaned, grumbled, and cursed their way up the stone steps and down the long corridor to Cam's bedchamber. Once inside they flopped his lifeless body upon his bed. "Ye got him from here, lad?" Hugh asked, letting Cam's arm fall to the bed.

"Aye. I shouldnae hae any trouble readying him for bed," Kinny said. "He will sleep like a babe again tae night."

"I donna wish to be here if he wakes early," Hugh murmured.

The room grew silent except for the men's labored breathing. Cam longed to jump to his feet and confront his *loyal* men, but he had a feeling this was only the small fragment of a much-larger conspiracy. Then Cam heard the chamber door click shut with Hugh and Malcolm's departure, and relaxed. His relaxing moment was just that. The next thing he knew, the tall skinny lad, Kinny crawled onto the bed and straddled him. The boy wrestled with Cam until he had finally removed all of his clothing. By the time Kinny had finished, the poor boy was huffing and puffing like an old plow horse. After tending to his clothes, the lad poked around in the fire, blew out the candles, then quietly pulled the bedchamber door closed.

Cam released a long pent-up breath. "Bloody Hell? What was that all aboot? He dinnae leave me as much as a stocking to cover myself with." He never would have guessed the skinny lad would have been so strong. As he lies alone in the darkened room listening to the howling wind and the rain pelting against the windowpanes, Cam wondered what part in this deceitful plot Hugh and Malcolm played. Who could he trust? If he could only remember what had happened the night before he might be able to know what to expect tonight. Except whoever came to kill him tonight would not find him unprepared or unarmed.

Adriana stared out the window into perpetual darkness. Everything seemed larger and more intense in the Highlands than in the lowlands where she had grown up. The giant pine trees stretched high into the sky as if they longed to touch the clouds. The fields and meadows extended for miles over rolling hills and down lush green glens. Even the storms were more intense as if God were going to split the sky wide open at any moment.

The fire had burned low, and Adriana's room had grown cold. Rubbing her arms, she contemplated what she'd done.

She'd meant no harm. Hadn't thought she'd put much of the potion into the brandy tonight, except she'd caused her husband to once again pass out. She bit her fingernails as she shuffled aimlessly around her chambers. *Should I go and check to make sure he's all right?*

Last night had been an utter disappointment. No matter what she tried, Willie refused to rouse and cooperate. Dare she hope he would respond tonight since she added less potion? More than anything she needed to relax. She hoped the weather would clear so she could go out of the castle tomorrow for a long walk. Then out of the corner of her eye she spotted the lovely harp. Crossing the room, she settled onto the chair and pulled the hard back against her shoulder. Drawing in a deep breath she exhaled and relaxed, and let her fingers skim along the strings. She smiled at the enchanting sound, then played an old lullaby her mother had taught her. The melody calmed her, taking her to a place where she felt safe, warm, and loved. Her mother's smiling face appeared in her mind, her eyes conveying adoration and tenderness. A warmth washed over her and soon she had the strength to do what had to be done. Except the feeling quickly vanished like the last of the ashes in the fireplace, which turned white and quickly dwindled away.

Adriana stood and removed the blanket from the back of the chair. She pulled it up over her head and crossed to her door. Her hand shook as she held the iron handle. She wished she weren't such a coward. She knew she couldn't drug him with the sleeping potion again or risk the chance of him catching her and finding out what she had done. Although she'd married him under the pretense he was expected to die, she was now glad for his recovery and that he would live. She hadn't been able to save her mother from drowning in the river when she was young, but she had learned enough over the years to save the MacCormac chieftain. This gave her pride and the determination to go to her husband's bed one more time.

Taking a deep breath, Adriana opened the door and peeked out. The corridor stood empty with only one torch at the far end to light the long passageway. She tiptoed down the cold dimly lit hallway to her husband's bedchambers. Slowly, she slid the iron door handle back and pushed against it. The door opened without a sound. Drawing in a deep breath, she entered his chambers and gently closed the door behind her.

Veiled in darkness, Adriana pressed her back against the door. Her heart pounding in her ears as she waited several seconds for her eyes to adjust to the lack of light.

"I wasnae sure ye would visit me tonight." A deep rumbling male voice drifted across the room to her, sending a wave of shivers up her spine. Startled, Adriana reached for the door handle behind her but paused. She had expected to find him once again unconscious. The deepness of his voice both thrilled and frightened her, filling her with anxious anticipation. She wanted to go to him, longed to converse with him, learn everything about this great warrior and chieftain. There was so much to discover about him, except she couldn't risk him restraining her and ascertaining who she was, what she looked like, or what she'd done. Frozen with fear, Adriana's grip tightened on the blanket which concealed her. There was only one thing she could do—turn and run.

Eleven

"Dinnae leave lass," Cam whispered, hoping he didn't sound as desperate as he felt. He wished he could stand and go to her without scaring her away. But he knew she would panic and fly off the moment he began to move. "I wondered if ye'd come to me on this cold rainy eve." The dark blanket wrapped around her small frame sheltered her face from the light. She stood so still Cam feared she would change her mind and flee. He couldn't rush her; he needed to take things slow.

"I've come to see if you need anything, milord." Her soft Irish accent quaked with fear and cold when she spoke.

"I appreciate yer concern, but I'm fine, lass. Come near so I might see yer lovely face." She took one hesitant step closer to the bed then stopped. "Ye're shaking like ye've just crawled out of the river."

"My chamber is near freezing," she whispered. He thought he heard her teeth click together when she spoke.

"Yer welcome to warm yourself under my blankets, if ye wish."

"You're too kind, milord." She hesitated then took another step toward the large bed.

Cameron scooted to the far side and pulled back the covers to allow her room to crawl in beside him.

She took a couple more steps and stopped halfway across the room. Her voice trembled with false bravado. "I won't have you restraining me, milord. I will leave when I wish to."

Cameron smiled at her brave attempt to make demands on the laird of Corell Castle. Aware that if he tried to hold her against her wishes, she would take flight and he'd never see her again, which was quite the opposite of what he desired. He wished he had light to see her. "As ye wish, lass."

She quickened her steps. When she reached the bed, she dropped the blanket and dove under the heavy covers. She snuggled close against his side, placing her head on his shoulder. His cock hardened. He wanted her more than his next breath, however he'd learned long ago that all could be lost if one did not learn to master the art of restraint.

Pulling her close, he felt the chill of her thin body through her shift. "Yer as cold as ice. Was there no wood nor peat in yer hearth?"

She hid her face from his and paused for a moment. "I've been busy with my chores today. I hadn't a chance to fill my wood-box." The log in the hearth snapped and crackled. A flame rose and the fire light danced across the auburn streaks in her dark hair that fanned across his chest and shoulder.

Wrapping his arms around her, he inhaled her flowery scent. He would have her wood-box filled for her from now on. No, on second thought, maybe he wouldn't. As his hand wandered over her slender back her body stilled. "What's the matter lass, ye hae not changed ye're mind hae ye?"

"No..." She paused. "But... I wish for you to lie still, let me touch you."

"I cannae move? I'm not sure that's possible." He chuckled and glanced down, but her face was concealed against his chest.

"If you restrain me or forbid my freedom," she whispered. Her warm breath brushed feather-light across his flesh. "I will leave and never return."

"What sort of game are ye playing here lass? Why do ye sneak into my chambers each night then hide yerself from me?" When she didn't respond he asked, "Are ye married then?"

She swallowed hard, and in a slight whisper, only a single word slipped through her lips. "Aye."

"Humm." Cam contemplated her response for a few moments. "Is yer mon a MacCormac?"

Several seconds passed before she murmured timidly, "Aye."

"Is he older than ye?"

"Much older."

"I see. So, t'was not a love match?

A low soft chuckle escaped her. "Definitely not. I had never even met him before the moment I entered the chapel, and we were wed."

"I donae understand. Is he witless enough to be unwilling or mayhap he's unable to be a proper husband to ye?"

Her head nodded twice. "Weel, I'm not sorry, lass. It appears yer elderly husband's loss is my good fortune."

She sighed and her body once again relaxed against him. Soon her small hand drew a path across his chest before venturing lower. She had the touch of an angel. He was certain she'd been the one who tended his wounds, drew him back from the dark edge of death. Not the long-limbed-lad who'd stripped him bare earlier.

Easing his hand up her back to the curve of her shoulder her hand stilled, and her body became rigid again. He halted, not wanting to frighten her. *Is she truly naive or is this just a game she's playing?*

"I assure you milord," she whispered. "My intent is not to cause you harm. I only wish to bring us both pleasure."

Cam chuckled. "Weel, if that be yer case little one, I leave ye to yer admirable task." He dropped his arms to his sides on the bed. He'd play along, see what the lass was about. He would encourage her mettle, give her the freedom to do as she pleased with him. He appreciated the lass's bravery, her confidence in thinking she could have total control over him. Besides, he didn't feel she would harm him, not after nursing him back to health. The least he could do was give her this small reward for saving his life.

"You must lie still, let me have control," she said firmly. Brushing her hair aside, she placed a gentle kiss against his injured shoulder.

"My aspiration is to gain yer trust, little one. But ye must tell me yer name, lass. I cannot continue calling ye Angel."

"Angel?" The endearment slipped from her lips softly as her now warm hand hesitantly slid across his chest.

"Aye, lass. For 'tis an Angel ye are. Ye healed more than my severe injuries. Ye restored my soul with hope for the future." A chuckle rumbled from his chest. "Ye hae even melted the thick ice which surrounded my frozen heart for years and made me feel again."

Her hand slid over his stomach and around his waist. She hugged him and placed a trail of light kisses along his side. "I have never been called anything close to resembling an Angel before." She swirled her fingers through the thick hair on his chest. "It's quite lovely. You may call me Angel—

if it pleases you, milord."

Her body shook when he chuckled at her response. "Then it's Angel, lass. That is until ye trust me enough to reveal yer true self to me and share yer name." Her hand paused. He feared she felt cornered and quickly added, "I trust ye will share yer secrets with me in yer own time."

She couldn't hide from him for long. He would make inquiries, learn who she was and the name of the gob she had married.

The small amount of coals glowing in the hearth crackled and the room seemed to plunge into darkness, their bodies mere shadows on the massive bed. The lack of light encouraged the confidence Adriana needed to proceed. She reminded herself that it was her duty as his wife and the clan's mistress to secure an heir. She must hurry before he learned of her deception.

Pushing her fear aside, Adriana whispered, "You must trust I will not harm you, milord as I must trust you will not restrain me." She feathered light kisses across his chest and shoulder. "We must trust each other, or I cannot... Will not come to you."

"If I cannae keep ye here all to myself, then I must let ye hae yer way so ye would be returning to me." She pressed her lips to his cheek, smiled, and then kissed the corner of his lips. "Do as ye wish, my Angel."

Brushing her hand across his forehead, she asked, "I have one request milord, if I please."

Cam chuckled at how young she sounded, at how inexperienced she seemed to be at flirting and manipulating. "Aye, and what might that wish be, lass?"

She dropped her forehead, resting it against his chest for a moment, then looked up and answered, "A proper kiss. I kissed you before when you were asleep. But I do not count that one as a real kiss."

Her voice trailed off as if suddenly struck with shyness. "Ye hae not been kissed?" He forced his hands to stay at his sides when he truly wanted to gather her in his arms and thoroughly kiss her.

"Oh! Aye, I have." She rushed to answer. "I only meant not a proper kiss from you, milord."

He wanted to ask how old she was, but remembered she was married, so old enough to know certain things. "If that is yer wish," he said. She was quiet for a few moments, then he felt her inch closer, and her soft lips briefly brushed his. When she moved away, Cam said, "Och, that wasnae a proper kiss." His hands slid up her arms and he pulled her closer to him. His lips found hers and her body stiffened. When she made no attempt to protest or pull away, Cam deepened the kiss. Soon Angel melted against him, her fingers sliding into his hair. Cam wanted to roll her over, bury himself deep inside her until she screamed his name when she peaked with passion. He slipped his tongue between her lips. She hesitated only a moment before her tongue danced with his, then finally caught his tongue and gently suckled it. The action set Cam's blood to boil.

After a few moments Angel broke the kiss, panting as she pushed herself up. "Aye, milord that was most definitely a proper kiss," sounding quite pleased.

Cam's heart pounded, slamming almost painfully into his ribs. Although her body now lay a top of his and he craved the feel of her soft curves, he forced his hands back to his sides. His cock swelled, rose-up and brushed along the inside of her thigh as if begging for her attention.

Glancing down, Angel giggled. "Oh! Willie! Don't fret my little lord, I have not forgotten about you." She placed a trail of soft kisses across his chest and stomach as she slid down Cam's body.

Willie? My little lord? What's this foolishness, Cam thought? He watched as Angel focused on his manhood, which stood straight and proud waiting for its mistress's attention.

"So, you have missed me, have you?" she asked, slipping her fingers around his cock. "I have missed you, too." She placed a gentle kiss on the tip, then giggled when it jerked in her hand. Cam's arms braced against the bed as he grabbed two handfuls of the bedsheet in his fists. Trying to focus in the darkness, he watched, fascinated as she kissed, licked, and stroked him. Then without warning, she took him into her mouth and suckled him. With her free hand she reached down and gently squeezed his sack. Cam pressed his head back into the pillow as lights flashed behind his eyes. When he thought he would explode, Angel straddled him, pressing his manhood against his stomach as she rubbed herself along the length of him. When she found the right spot, she gasped and rubbed harder. The intensity was so great, Cam thought he'd go up in flames.

Rising up on her knees Angel stroked his cock a few times, and said, "You're so big and strong milord. So much larger than before." Cam clenched his butt cheeks together, praying he wouldn't lose control and embarrass himself. Angel slid onto him, taking all of him until she sat on his hips. Her body shook with one furious spasm. Leaning forward, she licked first one of his hard nipples then the other. Every muscle in Cam's body tightened, his hips jerked toward the ceiling twice.

"Oh!" A gasp slipped through her lips. She giggled, then her body clamped around him. "Are you getting impatient milord?" Raking her fingernails gently down his chest, she began to rock her hips forward then backward. *For this, she can call my cock and any other part of my anatomy whatever she wishes*, Cam thought.

He had never experienced anything like this before. Couldn't even remember the last time he'd been with a woman but figured it had been several years. His wife Blair had been young and shy when it came to their lovemaking. And she had such difficulties with her pregnancy that Cam couldn't recall doing more than holding her in his arms.

One thing he knew for sure; Angel's husband was an old fool for neglecting such a passionate woman.

Twelve

Cam awoke early and alone. He'd struggled to stay awake and not fall asleep. He wanted to see Angel's face in the morning light, except she had flown away sometime during the early hours. A frustrated sigh slipped from his lips. Had he truly expected to find her lounging in his bed when he awoke? Who was she? What was she after? He'd heard someone playing the harp, and wanted to ask her if she'd wandered into the wrong room and played the haunting lullaby. However, his little Angel had interrupted his thoughts with her own intensions. Recalling how she felt in his arm made him smile.

Scratching his head, he drew in a deep breath then exhaled slowly. Why had he been drugged? Who was trying to kill him? Mostly, what roles were Hugh and Malcolm playing in all of this? Until he learned who was behind the attacks against him, he couldn't trust even his own men. He would address his troops, put an end to the rumors that he wasn't healthy and strong enough to continue as chieftain of Clan MacCormac. He rubbed his temples as a loud pounding hammered in his ears. Grumbling, Cam threw back the coverlet, determined to dress himself before the red headed, long legged heron, who had so roughly stripped him naked the night before showed and got his hands on him.

He slid on his black tews and boots, strode to the wardrobe and retrieved a clean shirt and slipped it over his head. As he downed his black leather jack and pulled the ties on his shirt tight, he noticed the bullet hole in the left shoulder had been neatly repaired with small even stitching like his wounds. Although his wounds no longer confined him to his bed, Cam realized how close to death he had come. If he wished to live much longer, he needed answers now.

Cam had finished dressing when there was a soft knock at his door. "Enter," he bellowed as he ran his fingers through his unruly hair. Gathering the thick strands, he pulled it all back, then tied it into place with a leather thong.

"Oh! Cameron, I see yer up and dressed." Lady Moira said as she breezed into the room. "I hae come to see aboot ye, and to inform ye I will be heading north today." She crossed to the hearth and rubbed her hands together.

"Ye leave so soon auntie? 'Tis barely autumn."

She pulled her shawl tight around her shoulders and shivered. "All this rain makes me feel as if winter will make an early appearance this year. I would like to reach Sinclair Castle before it becomes much colder, and the snow starts to fall."

"Weel, 'tis quite sudden, but I will hae Malcolm gather a group of warriors to escort ye. Shouldnae take more than an hour or two to make ready a couple of wagons."

She waved a dismissive hand his way. "No need dear, my brother-in-law's men arrived early this morn, and are now packing my trunks in the wagons they brought with them. We will be ready to leave within the hour." She scurried to his side, reached up and kissed his cheek. Her small, wrinkled hand cupped his other cheek. "I'm leaving ye in good hands. Just donae be overly anxious to open your wounds or find yerself with additional ones." Wrapping her thin arms around him she pulled him to her and hugged him tight. "I will write when I arrive, so ye know all is weel." Like a small ferret, his aunt scurried out the door barely missing the tall, skinny, red-headed lad who toted a large tray of food.

Kinny's eyes were large and round. The lad stepped back and offered a slight bow that Lady Moira most assuredly never witnessed.

"Milord, ye shouldnae be out of bed yet, and surely not dressed."

Cam grunted as Kinny placed the tray on the table with a thud. The food smelled most inviting, but Cam had too many things on his mind to eat.

"I need to clean and rebandage ye wounds, milord."

Examining the lad's expression, Cam couldn't remember ever seeing the boy before he'd been injured. He certainly had no idea how the lad became his personal nursemaid and nanny. The raw concern in the boy's eyes led Cam to believe the boy would be unable to hurt anyone let alone his laird.

"Ye must eat to get yer strength back milord. And ye need to rest, so yer wounds will heal." Cam crossed his arms over his chest and glanced at the food with suspicion. Kinny pulled the chair away from the table. "I ended my fast as cook filled a tray for ye and 'tis quite tasty." When Cam didn't reply, the boy offered a toothy grin and said, "If ye wish I can taste it for ye to prove it has not been poisoned."

It was clear the lad took his responsibility seriously and wasn't going to give up until Cam sat down and ate. Crossing the room Cam lowered himself onto the chair and began eating. The lad sighed with relief, nodded approvingly then approached the bed and pulled the linens tight. He placed the pillows against the head of the bed and continued to tidy up the chamber. Cam relaxed against the back of his chair and forced himself to enjoy his meal, which actually was quite tasty.

Besides, the lad was right, he hadn't regained all of his strength. Not only did he need to convince his men he was strong enough to lead them, but he needed his strength to hunt down the killers roaming the countryside. They had to be stopped before King William presumed the murderers were Scots from certain clans wanting to rekindle the rebellion and sent troops north to wipe out those clans. Too many Scots had already died at the hands of the English. The plan to prevent a civil war from starting preceded any other concerns at the moment. Except, Cam had a strong feeling the attack on his life and the attacks along the border were somehow connected.

Moments later Cam buckled his sword belt around his waist as Kinny exited the chamber with the tray of empty dishes. Hugh skirted out of the lad's way as he entered.

"What's yer report?" Cam demanded without greeting his cousin in his customary amiable way.

Hugh stammered before saying, "Eighty soldiers arrived this morning set by Laird Sinclair to fetch Lady Moira."

Cam positioned his bonnet at a slight angle then turned and faced Hugh and growled, "Tell me something I donae already know. Is there any news on the band of cut-throats who tried to kill me?"

Hugh shuffled his feet over the stone floor. "'Tis as if they hae vanished. We hae not been able to find them or where they may hae camped."

"Men on horseback cannae vanish into thin air. Are there still patrols out searching for them? Hae ye doubled the watch?"

"Aye, milaird..." Hugh's normal relaxed stance wavered then stiffened, he watched Cam closely.

Suspicion flooded Cam with questions after hearing Hugh and Malcolm's whispered conversation the night they thought him unconscious and hauled him up to his room. He required answers, yet if he questioned Hugh now and Hugh pulled his sword, would he in his current condition be able to defend himself against his cousin? He would wait to question them, today he needed to insure his men understood he was still capable of upholding his responsibilities.

~

Adriana had spent the day helping with harvesting the vegetables from the garden and packing them away in winter storage. The work was familiar and easy, and it made her feel right at home. However, the best part of the day was when she was fortunate enough to accompany one of the kitchen maids to the storehouse to deliver a tray of food to two other maid counting empty crocks. The sun had warmed the air and felt heavenly on her face. She found being English, it hadn't been hard for the servants to ignore her and not address her as their mistress. Until she became pregnant, she didn't want to draw any attention to herself. It was much easier to hide from her husband if she were dressed and treated the same as a servant. She had even taken to adding an Irish lilt to her voice when she spoke.

She entered her bedchambers and sunk down onto a chair. She was tired from working and felt a little homesick. Her sister had crossed her mind several times during the day, and she wondered if Lynette had been forced to take her place since she wasn't there to help with the chores. Besides, if everything continued to go well between her and her husband it wouldn't be long, and Lynette could come to live with them here in Castle Corell.

She had only been in her room for a few moments when Kinny and two lads she didn't know showed up with a tray of food and several buckets of hot water to fill her tub. Before Kinny left, he pulled a small skin of wine and a cup from his pockets, handed them to Adriana, then smiled and left. Now with her stomach full and sipping from her second mug of wine, she closed her eyes and relaxed. She sunk lower into the hot water and steam billowed up from the water like mist rising off the lake.

No matter how hard she'd worked or if she'd been alone or working with a group of people, the only thing Adriana could think about was crawling back into her husband's warm bed and lying next to him all night. Her husband seemed satisfied with her, which pleased her, nevertheless she feared he would see her face before she became pregnant. It would be the end of her dream of a normal life as wife and mother. It possibly could be the end of her life.

"Then I must do whatever it takes to make him happy and get with child—his heir."

Several moments later Adriana sat before the large mirror and tended to her hair. She anticipated spending the night with her husband. When Bethany arrived and offered to help her dress for the evening, Adriana turned her away. She explained she was tired from working all day and was going to go to bed early. Bethany bobbed a curtsy, turned, and left. Adriana suspected by the woman's smirk that Bethany had been well aware of her real intentions for the evening. But she didn't care. Crossing to where the harp stood, she sat and made herself comfortable in the small chair. Placing the harp against her shoulder she started to play. Although she hadn't played in years, hadn't really taken the time to play, the music flowed from her fingers to the strings as if she had played each day.

Cam entered his room after supper and found a hot bath waiting for him. He'd spent the day amongst his men. He'd joked with some and gave a short speech to a group in the barracks. As he left the barracks, he decided he would call the clan leaders together to prove he was far from dead and to request their support in finding these men. He spoke to the hunters to confirm the storerooms were properly filled for the winter. He'd even stopped by the stables to check on the well-being of his horse. In all areas he believed he'd been well received, and he felt confident in his position as chieftain. Hopefully, he'd put an end to any foolish rumors concerning his leadership.

The faint hum of harp music drifted into his room. Cam smiled then poured himself a glass of brandy and downed the warm amber liquid. The soft arrangement drifted through the air like a mystical being, transporting him to another time and place. The melody reminded him of autumn leaves floating on a warm breeze and the trickling of a tranquil little brook in the forest. His wife Blair had never played the harp with such compassion and interpretation. An overwhelming urge to know everything about his faceless angel washed over him.

His body trembled with anticipation of her next visit. Any soreness he may have had from being outside walking all day melted away. Cam poured another brandy then blew out the candles. He'd purposely let the fire in the hearth burn low, then added small pieces of wood at each end of the glowing embers so they would burn slowly, but still generate heat. He returned to his bed, drank the remaining brandy, removed his robe, and placed it over the back of his chair.

Cam crawled into his bed and welcomed the bewitching tune. Closing his eyes, he could almost feel the warm humid air of summer, the smell of lush green grass, and the sound of birds and insects buzzing around. He must have drifted off to sleep because he awoke to a soft touch on his arm and the voice of an angel. "You must be tired from all the walking and visiting you did today. Hope you haven't overtaxed yourself, milord. You really need your rest if you hope to regain all of your strength."

The soft lilt of her Irish accent caused his body to prickle with goose flesh. Only the ghostly silhouette of her form and her feather light touch on his arm confirmed she wasn't a creation from his dreams. He slid over and pulled the covers back so she could lie where the sheets retained his warmth. She removed her robe and shift and crawled in. Glancing up she whispered, "kiss me."

He found her soft lips in the dark, and lightly brushed his lips across hers. In protest her fingers slipped into his hair, she pulled him closer and deepened their kiss. His arms slid around her thin frame, and he pulled her onto his chest.

Her hands lowered to his face, and he felt her smile against his lips. Pulling back, she rubbed her cheek against his as her fingertips traced the tips of his ears.

"Ye are the one who shaved my face and cut my hair off," he said lightly as to not frighten her.

She kissed his neck and said, "You are more handsome now that you no longer resemble a big hairy hound." He chuckled at her choice of comparison.

"Ye are the one who healed me," he said as his hand slid down her back and rested on her left hip. "Saved my life. Ye pulled me back from the edge of Hell when I teetered on the brink of death, dinnae lass?"

She stilled then lowered her head to his chest, her fingers playing with his dark curls. "Everyone believed you were going to die. I could not let that happen, milord."

"I thank ye for all yer efforts." He ran his hand slowly along her back feeling the bony terrain of her spine. "For everything ye done for me, I am grateful." When she didn't respond he added, "Where did ye learn to play the harp so lovely? Ye play like an angel."

She didn't reply and Cam figured it would take a while before she trusted him enough to confide in him. "Ye hae a talent for the harp, which isnae easy to play. Yer mum must be verra proud of ye lass." After a moment he heard her sniffle.

Reaching down he wiped a tear from her cheek. "No, lass. Donae cry. Tell me what troubles ye so."

"I miss her." She sniffled again. "I may have helped save you, but I could not save her." When she paused for a moment, Cam continued to stroke her back hoping she would continue, reveal more of herself to him. "The river was too deep and fast. I was too little." She drew in a shallow breath. Her voice no more than a whisper, she continued, "There was nothing I could do... I was just too little."

Cam pulled her close, kissed her brow and continued to rub her back to console her. "Wasnae yer fault lass. Donae blame yerself. I too know loss." Surprised when his chest didn't tighten up as it always did when he thought of the loss of his family. "What 'tis like to feel helpless. Unable to do anything to prevent the unthinkable from happening. Took years afore I accepted I wasnae to blame for their deaths."

"Your wife and child?"

"My bonnie sweet Blair... And my son." The pain had always lingered just under the layers of his skin waiting for the slightest memory to cut through the surface and bleed out his confined misery. Except now there had been no heartache, only a sense of peace.

Her fingers danced across Cam's chest and brushed across his nipples, starting a fire deep inside of him. She kissed his shoulder, then asked, "How is your shoulder feeling?" She ran a finger across the ridge of his new scar. "Does it give you much pain, milord?"

His discomfort wasn't from his healing wounds, but from his engorged cock, which ached to be inside of her. He was unable to answer as she found his mouth and drew his lower lip into her mouth and suckled it gently. Her warm lips unleashed a passion so strong Cam thought he would burst into flames at any moment. Nevertheless, he was determined to take his time.

He had let her have her way before, this time he desired to feel more than a fist full of linins.

"I don't wish to cause you more pain," she said, running her hand down his side and back up. "I saw more soldiers ride out the gate today. What will you do with the men who tried to kill you when you find them?"

He sighed. "They are no doubt persistent sympathizers to a lost cause. Scots, neighbors, friends, and maybe even family. But they hae gone past the old traditions of raiding cattle and horses, which hae been fattened on summer grazing, and taking prisoners for ransom to murdering tenant farmers, their live-stock, and burning fields of grain. Reiver groups of old could number in the hundreds. They wore brigandines of jacks of plate, and metal helmets called burgonets. The small swift band of men who attack me wore all black, even their faces were covered with mud so not to be recognized. They hae betrayed all Scots and show no loyalty to any one clan. As laird of the MacCormac clan, I willnae tolerate this type of behavior from anyone. When I catch them, they will definitely hang for their deeds."

When her hands stopped their roaming and her body stiff-ened, Cam realized how gruff he must have sounded. Pulling her close he whispered, "I'm sorry, lass. I ken ye dinnae come to my bed to hear clan business." Tipping her chin up his mouth found her lips in the dark and covered them with a tender kiss, she relaxed against him.

When she deepened the kiss Cam cupped one of her breasts, kneading it gently, testing her response to him touching her. At first, she gasped, her body stilled, but soon she melted into his tender caress with a gratifying moan. He slid his tongue into her mouth as he eased her onto her back. Her nails sank into his hair scraping his skull--pulling him closer. Cam slid his hand down her slender side. He pressed a knee between her knees to keep his weight from crushing her. Ending the kiss, he trailed kisses along her jaw and down her neck. Drawing her small pert breast into his mouth, he flicked his tongue against the tiny bud until it hardened. She gasped; her head rolled to the side as she moaned with pleasure. He couldn't get enough of her.

"Milord!" She panted and arched her back. He showered her ribs, stomach, and hips with kisses. Moving lower he kissed her thighs before finding the sensitive folds of her womanhood. "What? Oh!" She squirmed trying to get away, but he indulged himself until she thrashed and bucked beneath him. Her moans of pleasure turned to cries of passion.

Cam rolled over, lifted her up and placed her limp body on his engorged manhood. She drew in a deep breath and tightened around him. She rode him slowly, letting her desire rebuild. When she reached her peak, she cried out, her body shook with violent spasms. He would burst if he didn't find relief. Pressing her hips down against him, he surged upward to his release--total surrender.

Angel collapsed onto his chest. Their hearts beat wildly for several moments until they melded into one rhythm. He didn't want to move, content to lie here forever with the woman who floated into his life and healed his heart and soul. He could feel again. His fingers coiled in her long thick hair which draped over his shoulder, and he lifted it to his face. She smelled like fresh air and flowers. Wishing it wasn't so dark in his room, he wondered at the color of her hair. What color were her eyes, were they round and innocent or slanted and full of mischief? Was her skin as perfect and unblemished as it felt?

"Angel," he whispered into her hair, "show yourself to me." Her limp body stiffened, and he sensed she considered bolting. He stroked her back again trying to make her relax, to stay with him, to trust him. "You have no reason to be afraid of me, Angel. I wish only to know all of you."

She released a small breath, which stirred the hairs on his chest. "I cannot."

"What is it that you fear, lass?"

"You say I play the harp and sing like an angel. You even call me Angel, milord, but I'm afraid you will be disappointed when you see for yourself that I am nothing of the sort."

He cupped her warm soft bottom and pulled her close. "You have nothing to worry about, lass." His senses roused, ready and anxious for her again.

He kissed her lips and nuzzled her neck. "I'm feeling generous. I'll give you until dinner tomorrow to work up the courage to show yourself to me. I expect ye to join me in the great hall for our evening meal. Whatever yer fears, I assure ye can be resolved."

Thirteen

Adriana's toes peeked out from under the heavy cream-colored coverlet as she leisurely stretched. The chilly air in her chambers caused her to pull her foot back under the covers. She hugged her pillow, nuzzling her face deep into its soft goose down. Her dreams had seemed so real she forced herself to come fully awake to examine them. If it weren't for the soreness between her thighs, she might have been convinced last night had all been a glorious dream. However, it had been real. It had been the most glorious night of her life. She thought back to snippets of conversations she'd overheard between Mrs. Wilson and Penny about coupling and how different it could be from time to time. She never understood there could be a difference between mating and making love, although last night in her husband's arms she learned there definitely was a difference between the two.

A soft knock sounded at the door before it opened slowly. "Ye awake, milady?" Bethany peered around the door. "'Tis late. Do ye wish to sleep the day away?" Glancing toward the windows Adriana saw the sun had risen high enough to cast a wide beam of light through the window and across the floor.

She smiled. "I just might at that, Bethany." She heard the woman giggle as she entered and closed the door behind her. "I feel as if I'm floating on a cloud, and I'm afraid if I move, I'll fall to the ground and shatter the illusion of how perfect my life could actually become."

Bethany tsked her tongue teasingly. "Ye seem quite pleased with yer husband this morn, milady."

"Yes, I am. Oh, Bethany, I never dreamed being married could be this way," Adriana replied as she felt heat rise up her body. But she didn't care. She never thought she would be able to converse with Cameron, let alone be held in his arms and whispered to as she had last night. The thought of being with him again caused a little shiver to tickle her spine, and she giggled. Adriana rolled onto her back and stared at the cream and gold canape above her. "It was heavenly. When he held me in his arms, I felt safe and loved, as if nothing nor anyone could ever hurt me again."

"That is wonderful." Bethany chuckled as she continued to straighten up the chamber and place more peat on the fire.

Adriana sat up and scooted to the edge of the bed. "Do you know what today is, Bethany?"

"I'm not sure, mistress. Do ye wish me to go and find out for ye?"

"No. Silly." Adriana laughed as she stood and slipped on her robe. "I have decided that today is the perfect day to face Cameron." She wasn't used to referring to her husband by his Christian name. She liked it. She crossed to the ewer and proceeded to wash herself. "I want to show myself to him, tell him everything. I'm tired of agonizing over him learning my identity and deception from someone else. I fear he will feel I deliberately deceived him. He deserves to know the truth from me."

"Ye wish to reveal yerself to him today?" Bethany paused in her duties.

"After last night I believe he will be able to look past my appearance," she ran her fingers over the old scar by her temple, "and accept me as I am. Except I don't wish to explain myself in front of everyone to why I needed to take my sister's place. I think it would be best if I describe the situation to him in private." She turned to face Bethany and asked, "Don't you agree that would be better?"

Bethany sailed to Adriana's side. "I am overjoyed for ye, and I think 'tis a grand idea. Moreover, ye may already be with child." Thrilled with the notion, Adriana placed her hand on her stomach. It would be wonderful if she were carrying his child, his heir. "Ye cannot be going to him in yer servants' clothes though. I will dress ye in yer best skirts and do yer hair just so." She coiled Adriana's hair into a long plait then placed it on top of her head. Standing back and admiring her work, then added, "Poor mon 'twill be so pleased he won't be able to keep his hands to himself."

Retrieving what she needed, Bethany ushered Adriana into the chair positioned in front of the hearth. Adriana hoped her husband would understand her situation and realize her sister was not mature enough to be a wife. That she would not be able to cope with seeing his bruised and battered body, nor be able to clean and dress his wounds. Lynette would be too distraught to even go to him.

It may not be easy, but Adriana would make her husband recognize she only deceived everyone in order to get far away from her cruel controlling father.

With a grimace, Cam rolled his sore, stiff shoulders hoping to loosen up the tension. As he dressed, he reminisced over their enthusiastic love making last night, which caused him to wake this morning with more aching muscles than he cared to think about. He grinned at the unrestrained passion Angel generously offered in response to his every touch. She made him feel alive again and there wasn't a moment she didn't invade his thoughts. However, the fact that she belonged to someone else irritated him. He would discover who her husband was, perhaps some arrangement could be made. The man obviously refused to or was unable to see to her needs. Maybe he would accept a handsome sum of gold coins to step aside and go on his way? Tonight, when Angel joined him for dinner, he would learn both her and her husband's names. Then she would be his. Confident his life was back on the correct path, Cam settled into the chair behind his desk and proceeded to pen messages to each of the clan chiefs for which he held alliances with. He would prove the rumors concerning his lack of leadership were false and gain their support by hunting down these murdering thieves. Several moments later he folded and sealed each note with the MacCormac crest in hot wax.

Cam stood and tucked the notes in his belt. Then the sound of boots approaching in the corridor triggered Cam's thoughts to shift to the assault on his life. Unaware of who was trying to kill him, his only defense was to remain suspicious and cautious of everyone. Then the foot falls stopped directly outside his door.

A heavy knock sounded. "Enter," Cam said, stepping back from the entrance, his hand resting on the hilt of his sword. He positioned himself so he'd be prepared for whoever stood on the other side of the access. The heavy door swung open, his cousin Hugh strode in closely followed by his other cousin, Malcolm Haywood. Both men were quite imposing standing straight with their shoulders pulled back. Cam eyed them suspiciously before asking, "What is yer report today?"

Hugh cleared his throat. "There has been another attack. This one is within a half days ride from here. Four farmers were killed, and two fields were set afire."

Cam shot Malcolm a questioning look and the man replied, "I have dispatched more troops to comb the area for any sign of the thieving murderers."

"This is outrageous! Why can't we locate these men?" Cam's booming voice reverberated off the stone walls.

"They attack with no pattern or reason," Malcolm said. "Then simply disappear without a trace."

"I fairly doubt 'tis that *simple*, or there is no trace of them to be found. There must be hoof-prints to follow, places where they camped for the night." Cam hastened toward Malcolm, scowled down at the man, and growled, "Or are ye telling me their horses sprouted wings and flew away without a single soul noticing?"

Both men's eyes were downcast, Hugh shifted his weight from one foot to the other. The notion they knew more than they were telling had Cam ready to cut off their ears. "What is it yer keeping from me?" He roared. When Hugh turned his head and glanced at Malcolm, Cam drew in a deep breath letting it out between his clenched teeth. He leaned toward both men, his voice once more controlled. "Does this hae anything to do with me being drugged and what I overheard the two of ye whispering aboot the night ye carried me from the great hall up to my room?" When neither man offered an answer but continued to stare at the floor, Cam continued his interrogation. "What was afoot that night? Why was I drugged?" He fisted his hands and placed them on his hips. "Who wanted me out of the way and why? Cousins or not, ye best answer afore I run ye both through."

When Hugh glanced up, he focused on something behind Cam and said, "From the severity of ye wounds we all thought ye wouldnae mend, let alone live." Hugh's gaze met Cam's eyes. "To protect the clan and to keep yer people from dividing and turning against each other, I made the decision to go through with yer agreement to wed Sir Alexander's daughter."

"Ye did what?" Cam turned away from his men and slammed his fist down on the table. "Why would ye do such a thing to me and then not inform me of this when I awoke?"

"Ye were planning on marrying the lass already," Malcolm's voice trembled when he answered.

"I truly believed 'twas the best for the clan," Hugh persisted.

Cam turned and glared at his cousins. "And Father Fitzgerald accepted yer word on the matter without question?"

"We all feared ye were going to die." Malcolm added.

"There were murmurs the clan would possibly divide if ye died to decide who would take over as Laird," Hugh added.

Cam thought about the clan, his people, but couldn't believe they would war amongst themselves. They were all true to him, but would they automatically accept Hugh as their next chieftain? "Ye were so close to death, there was no time to waste," Hugh said. "The wedding took place within an hour of the baronet's daughters' arrival."

Cam scratched his jaw as he paced around the room. "Who brought the lass here?"

Malcolm cleared his throat. "I took a troop of soldiers to fetch her."

Rubbing the tension at the back of his neck, Cam asked, "So, after traveling for days the first thing ye do when the lass arrives is to marry the poor thing off to an unconscious, dying man. Did she not protest?"

Avoiding Cam's glare, Hugh glanced toward the door as if he wished to flee.

"The poor child must have been terrified at the sight of me." Cam crossed the room, rested his arm on the mantel and recalled Sir Alexander's description of his young daughter. No wonder she hasn't made herself known to me, he thought. She must be too frightened. Seeing me shot, my leg sliced open, covered with dirt and bruises, and blood-stained bandages. The sight must have been too much for her young sensibilities. How she must have dreaded ever facing me again. The thought made him sad and angry. Though he no longer wanted a wife, neither did he relish the idea of being the things nightmares were made of. Nor did he want to be blamed if the poor lass decided to take her own life. He couldn't handle the guilt caused by the death of another wife. She would be safer and much happier if he sent her back to her father.

Cam turned to face the two men, once again his left hand landed on the hilt of his sword. He scowled. "'Tis unconceivable ye would go behind my back and deceive me so." His voice rose with each word until he was yelling like a raving lunatic. "The last thing I need right now, is a sniveling, mouse of a wife, too cowardice to come forward and face me. I donae want her. Damnation, I dinnae want her in the first place. I hae no use for a wife." He waved his hand dismissively. "Return her to her father immediately. There is no place for her here." He'd send her back to her father and the people who would care for her. Moreover, she would be safer in more comfortable in familiar surroundings.

He faced his two cousins, pulled the sealed messages from his belt, and handed them to Malcolm. "Send our messengers out today. These must be delivered as soon as they possibly can." Malcolm bowed and turned on his heels to leave. Cam's gaze met Hugh's and he snarled, "Ye are both dismissed."

Once the door closed behind both men Cam strode to the hearth and dropped into the chair. His heart ached with disappointment. That wasn't a twelve-year-old child who spoke softly to him as she washed the filth from his body and cared for his wounds. Definitely not a child who'd been coming to him each night. He had feelings for his faceless angel even though he was unable or mayhap unwilling at this point to give those feelings a name.

He sighed as he felt the tension slip from his body. Tonight,

Angel would present herself to him at dinner, and all would be as it should be.

～

Adriana froze when she heard the iron door latch to her husband's bedchamber move. Terrified at being caught eavesdropping, she turned, lifted her skirt, and dashed back to her room. Closing the door as quietly as she could. Her knees shook as she leaned back against it as if that would keep the inevitable from happening.

"Milady, what has happened?" Bethany crossed the room toward her. Adriana's chest rose and fell with each anxious breath. Her mind spun with confusion. She heard the anger and frustration in Cam's declarations as they passed through the wooden door as if it were made of mere parchment. What had happened? He no longer wanted her. How could he be so cruel as to toss her aside like a camp follower after the wonderful night they'd shared? Her chest tightened with such pain she thought she might die.

"Come sit by the fire," Bethany pleaded as she grasped one of Adriana's arms and gently pulled her to the chair by the hearth. "Would you like for me to fetch ye some tea?" The woman fussed with a blanket tucking it around Adriana's shoulders. She patted her shoulder then stood waiting, wringing her hands.

Adriana felt sick. How was she supposed to return to her father after defying his order to ready her sister for Cameron's arrival? The beating he would bestow on her would be far worse than any other she'd ever received. Her hands went protectively to her stomach though she doubted she'd spent enough time alone with her husband to be with child. The right thing to do would be to go to Cam and explain herself, except she knew her heart couldn't take the look of disappointment from those blue eyes. Nor could she hear his voice, which had only last night whispered soft words of love to her, declare his rejection and disapproval of her. A gasp slipped between her lips. Adriana slouched against the back of her chair in anguish.

"Oh, mistress," Bethany said as she knelt before Adriana. "Please, tell me what I can do for ye. Tell me what happened."

A persistent knock sounded at the door. Bethany glanced at the door then turned back to Adriana and squeezed her hands. "I'll tell whoever 'tis yer resting, milady."

"No. It's alright." Adriana drew in a ragged breath. "Let him in." She suspected who stood on the other side of her door and guessed what his orders were. The sooner all of this was over, and she was gone from here the better. For whom she was not sure.

Bethany opened the door and the captain of the guards stepped in. Gone was his quick stride and bright smile. An air of melancholy surrounded him as he avoided her eyes and stared at the wall behind her.

Adriana's knees shook as she stood to face him, forcing her to reach for the back of the chair for support. She cleared her throat and said, "Good morning, Captain."

The man came to attention. "Good morning, milady." His glance seemed forced when he turned toward her. "I am here to inform ye his lordship wishes, for yer safety, ye return to yer father. I will escort ye as soon as ye can make ready."

The man struggled with his emotions as he stood before her and lied. She knew full well her husband was not concerned for her safety, but no longer wished to have her here. Pulling her shoulders back, Adriana nodded her head. "There is no need for you to accompany me, Captain. A small troop of soldiers will do."

"I cannae let ye go without my protection, milady. I will see ye there safely, and I pledge to stay at yer side until I'm struck down in death."

Adriana blinked at the captain's promise, which in reality would only last until he was called back to serve his laird. "Very well. It will not take me long to pack my belongings. Please send Kinny up to fetch my valise."

The captain bowed his head and turned. But before he reached the door Bethany said, "milady, if ye please, may I accompany ye? My husband is one of the soldiers sent back with yer father, and I hae no seen him in weeks."

Adriana glanced at the captain to perceive his reaction. She smiled when one corner of his mouth hiked up and he bowed slightly, and said, "Very good, milady." She admired the young captain of the guards who had been so kind to her on her journey to Castle Corell. He had kept her company by the fire and spoke of how different her life would soon be. Since she had been here nothing had gone at all as she had expected. Her husband hadn't died as predicted, and she doubted she'd been here long enough to get pregnant. But worst of all, she had fallen in love with her husband who was discarding her as if she were the contents of a chamber pot.

Adriana's stomach tightened, as a wave of nausea washed over her. She was returning to her father a failure. He'd view her no less than untrustworthy, and she would surely be punished for disobeying his command.

Fourteen

C am poked the log fire in his hearth. The orange, yellow, and red flames snapped and danced merrily, unaware of his discontentment. Dressed in his finest belted-plaid, stockings, and polished brogues, he'd lingered in the great hall after the evening meal hoping Angel would appear and join him, but she never showed. For that matter, no one even glanced his way or attempted to speak to him. After serving his food and drink, the servants scurried away.

How dare she ignore her laird's request.

Raising his brandy glass to his lips, Cam took a long drink. The smooth amber spirits coated his throat and warmed his soul, soothing his aggravation. Sighing, he forced himself to relax, though patience was not one of his strongest virtues.

Mayhap she feared her husband's retribution for humiliating him in public. She may have decided to wait and come to him later when she could safely get away from her husband. The notion that the man might strike her or harm her in any way, caused Cam's chest to tighten. She'd felt so thin and delicate in his arms, even the slightest slap could do substantial damage to her. If she appeared with even a scratch or red mark on her person, he'd hunt the man down, beat him, and then throw what was left in the dungeon to rot. He surged to his feet, pulled the thong from his hair, then raked his fingers through the long strands.

She'd healed him and never recoiled at his scarred, broken, bruised body. She'd given him the gift of life and hope. A promise that his life could be as it once was. His lust was powerful, unlike anything he'd ever experienced before. However, he struggled with the heartbreaking realization that she belonged to another. A man who overlooked her gentle and caring soul. A bloke too foolish to realize what a treasure he possessed.

Cam crossed to the window and peered out into the darkness. *Where is she? She must have known he'd married; she couldn't have been intimidated by his child bride.* He'd give anything if only he'd never agreed to take the baronet's young daughter to wife. His rash behavior may have cost him Angel.

Earlier his cousin informed him that Malcolm would be escorting Sir Alexander's daughter back to her father and would stay and guard her until the killers who were running across the Highlands were captured. Cam had watched from his window as Malcom, two wagons, one hundred of his warriors, and his child bride rode out through the gate.

Cam turned away from the window and returned to his chair by the hearth. Why would a man want a slip of a girl when he could have a woman like Angel? He didn't care who she was or what her reasons were for not showing herself to him. He longed for only her. The pendulum clock on the bookcase ticked softly, showing the passing of time and the unlikelihood she would show. Suddenly Cam's stomach clenched, and he thought he may cast-up what little he had eaten earlier. He clutched his chest. *Am I becoming ill?* His head ached and he had difficulty swallowing. Leaning back in the chair he rubbed his temples hoping to ease his pain. He knew if he went looking for her, he'd scare her off and she'd never come back to him.

Besides, he had no idea where to start looking or who he'd be looking for. The only thing he could do was wait and pray she would come to him.

Turning his thoughts to the men who attacked him, Cam tried to recall what they were wearing, and if there was anything that would reveal their identities. However, his thoughts kept returning to Angel and how she'd saved him from an eternity in a cold dark grave.

By midnight, Cam resigned himself to the fact that she was not going to present herself. She would either have been detained by her husband or she'd chosen to never reveal herself to him. He burnished the heel of his hand over the tight muscles in his chest. What if she never came to him again?

The thought wrenched his heart.

After a week of traveling, Adriana, Captain Haywood, and their entourage neared the gates of Shealoch Castle, which somehow now appeared diminutive compared to the distinguishing Corell Castle. Even though Adriana had spent only a brief time there, her perspective had changed. Despite the fact that every muscle and joint in her body ached, she forced her shoulders back and kept her chin up, hoping to appear confident and worthy of her new station in life as Lady MacCormac. The first thing she would do was apologize to her sister for leaving her here to face their father alone. She had prayed he hadn't beaten Lynette for *her* deceitfulness. Each day of their journey Adriana agonized over what her father's reaction would be when he learned she'd been discarded by her husband. He would gloat in the fact that he'd been right that no man would ever want her.

A wave of dizziness washed over Adriana causing her fingers to tighten over the edge of the wagon seat. She closed her eyes, and as usual, her thoughts reverted back to the last night she'd spent with her husband. A long sigh slipped from her lips. Cam had lavished her with warm kisses, tender strokes, and words of adoration. Allowing her to experience the wonderment of making love. She had readily relinquished control for the first time, granting him complete power over her. However, in doing so, he seduced her and then the next day cruelly rejected her and ordered Captain Haywood to return her to her father. Her back stiffened and she made a pledged to herself not to ever let another man have control over her again.

How dare he use me then toss me aside as if I were nobody.

Malcolm and nine guards led the way through the portcullis into the outer bailey of Shealoch Castle. The two wagons which carried Adriana, Bethany, their tents, and additional supplies rattled along behind them. The remaining soldiers entered, then fanned out in a half circle around them. Their caravan of intrepid Scot warriors dressed in kilts and covered in a variety of weapons were imposing to say the least.

Adriana studied the keeps wooden door and small glass windows. Shealoch Castle, although not as ancient as Corell Castle, could not compare to its history, grand size, or the magnificent strength it exemplified.

"Milady... Lady MacCormac?"

Pulled from her thoughts, Adriana turned to find the captain of the guards, Malcolm Haywood, standing next to the wagon, waiting to help her get down. She smiled, stood, and placed her hand in his to assist her, off the wagon. "Are ye feeling ill, milady? Ye appear quite pale. And if I may, ye hae not eaten much, or slept much since we left," he said, steering her away from the muddy wagon wheel.

"I appreciate your concern, Captain, but I assure you I am only tired from traveling. I am sure I will feel better after I have a long nap in my old bed," Adriana reassured him.

"If ye require anything, milady, ye only need to send for me. I'll be here faster than a hare with a fox on its tail."

"Thank you, Captain. You have been so tolerant and kind to me. I do not know how I will ever repay you. I am afraid I will always be indebted to you." She grinned. "However, I promise to find a way to reward your benevolence. Thank you."

The captain bowed, then turned, and helped Bethany from the wagon. Suddenly, a giant of a man with bright blue eyes and flaming orange hair rushed forward and snatched Bethany from Malcolm. "Alec," Bethany shrieked as her husband lifted her into the air and spun her around in a circle. When he stopped, Bethany's feet were three feet off the ground, and she giggled until he silenced her with a crushing kiss. Surprised at the couple's openness, Adriana's gaze shot to the captain. He grinned and winked, then they both laughed at the couple's joy of seeing each other after being apart for so long.

Adriana's heart soon grew heavy as she realized she would never share that kind of love with her husband. She needed to put him out of her mind and concentrate on how she was going to deal with her father.

Hearing a squeal coming from the keep, Adriana turned and saw a young woman in a day dress and apron running toward her. As she drew closer, she recognized it was her sister. Lynette wrapped her arms around Adriana's neck and hugged her close.

"I can't believe you're here," Lynette said enthusiastically. She stepped back from her embrace; her brows dipped together, and a frown marred her pretty face. "You have lost weight since you left. There is hardly any meat on your bones."

As her sister stood back and examined her, Adriana took the moment to observe the changes in her sister as well. Lynette's hair no longer hung in golden childish ringlets around her shoulders but had been pulled back into a neat bun. Her skin held a golden hue no doubt from hours working in the garden. She looked so different, so grown up.

"You must be hungry after your long journey," Lynette said.

"Come with me, I'm sure Mrs. Wilson will fix you one of your favorite dishes."

Adriana's hand cupped her sister's cheek. The helpless little girl she'd left behind had with in a short period of time, grown into a responsible young woman. But before she could follow her into the keep, she needed to know if their father was lying in wait for her. She wanted to collect herself and be prepared before she faced him. "Is Father inside?" Her voice came out as a soft whisper.

With concern showing in her large blue eyes, Lynette replied, "No, but he should be back for dinner."

Relief engulfed Adriana. She would have time to prepare herself for her father's onslaught of insults and accusations, which would be served at dinner with a side dish of mocking sneers.

"Well, let's get you out of this cold breeze and into the warmth where I can find you something warm to eat." Lynette slipped her arm around Adriana's shoulder and gave her a loving squeeze.

"Oh, Lynette, this is my lady's maid, Bethany." Both women smiled at each other as Bethany continued to shoo her husband away. "Bethany will need a room, too. Preferably, close to my room," Adriana said.

"That won't be a problem at all." Lynette propelled Adriana toward the keep. "She can have my old room. I have moved my belongings into our mother's chambers. I hope you do not mind, but I went through everything Father had stored in there and separated what belonged to my mother and yours. I placed *your* things in your room." When Adriana could only stare, Lynette added, "Your mother had so many beautiful gowns and slippers. And wait until you see her amazing jewelry box! It is filled with beautiful necklaces and broaches. You are going to love them."

Adriana had been unaware of what had happened to her

mother's belongings. She figured her father had given them to Lynette's mother when they married. However, they hadn't been married long before she became pregnant with Lynette, only to die a couple of days after giving birth. Her father had her room closed up and the door locked. She shot her sister a sideways glance and wondered how she was able to get the key from their father to get into the room.

They entered the keep, and it seemed as if nothing had changed since she'd left. Nevertheless, everything about Adriana had changed. How was she supposed to slip back into her old life when she was no longer that person? Lynette chatted on about servants and house accounts, but Adriana drifted in a daze as she crossed to the stone steps and ascended to the fourth floor which housed their private chambers.

With a wide grin on her face Lynette swung the door to Adriana's old room open. Adriana entered the room and instantly noticed numerous gowns hanging from the wardrobe doors. More gowns hung inside, and the bottom of the wardrobe was filled with slippers. She crossed to an ornate box on her dressing table. It was trimmed in gold, with four ornate gold feet and matching latch. The background was painted pink, and the cover and sides were decorated with gold roses. It was filled to overflowing with ear bobs, necklaces, rings, bracelets, and broaches. Each piece was incrusted with tiny diamonds, rubies, emeralds, or pearls. As she inspected each item, she realized everything was real, not one gem seemed to be made of paste.

Lynette sat on the edge of the bed and asked, "Have you ever wondered what your life would have been like if your mother wouldn't have died?"

Adriana had pondered that same thought many times. She had wondered if her father would have treated her differently. Even loved her. With a tight rein on her emotions, Adriana replied, "Yes. But if my mother would have lived, father would not have married your mother and we would not have been graced with you, my dear."

There was a knock at the door. Bethany pulled the door open to find the servant who was delivering their carpet bags.

Lynette stood. "Thank you, Duncan. Leave this one here and deliver those two to my old room." She had crossed to him and pointed to the room down the hall.

"Yes, Mistress," he said, bowing. After placing Adriana's bag on the bed, he turned and left.

Adriana shook her head. "I can't believe how well you've adjusted to the role of mistress. I am so very proud of you." She pulled Lynette into a hug. "I can't wait to see what else you've done around here."

Since Lynette had taken over the role of mistress, would Adriana be expected to return to her duties in the kitchen and garden? Surely, her father wouldn't accept her as Lady MacCormac, wife to Laird Cameron MacCormac!

Fifteen

Frustration cloaked Cam like a wet wool blanket as he abandoned his bed. Readying himself for the day, he stumbled around his chambers, cursing under his breath as he dressed. Retrieving his broadsword and belt from his trunk he buckled it around his waist. His head pounded like the remains of a three-day drunk. His neck and shoulder ached from a night tossing and turning in hopes of finding a comfortable position and a moment's sleep.

He needed to put Angel out of his mind and focus all his energy on locating the band of thieving murderers roaming about terrorizing and destroying the countryside. The last thing he wanted was for them to stir up a hornet's nest. The Highlands did not need more of King William's troops or even himself marching north and inciting a civil war.

There was a knock on the door.

"Enter," he called as he positioned his bonnet on his head.

The door swung open and the tall, skinny, redheaded lad, Kinny entered and bowed. "Good morning, milord."

"Och, whit d'ye want," Cam snarled.

"Forgive me, milord. I was wondering if ye needed my help

with anything this morning. Can I bring ye food and drink to break yer fast?"

Cam snorted, "I donae need yer help, Pup. Now get out of my way before I throw ye through a window."

"Milord. I...I must protest," Kinny stammered. He struggled to hold his ground and not flee. Though the boy's body shook with trepidation, Cam recognized the lad's bravery at standing up to his laird. Genuine concern for his chieftain's condition was evident in his bright blue eyes. One day Kinny would grow into a man to be revered, and when that time came, Cam would not forget to reward him for his ardent loyalty.

A long sigh slipped from Cam's lips. "I appreciate yer concern, lad. And because of yer care, I assure ye I am whole again."

Kinny's brows pulled into a deep frown. Before the lad could protest, Cam stepped around him to exit the room, except his escape was prevented when he encountered Hugh in the doorway.

Hugh stopped, coming to attention. "I'm sorry to report that two of our fields have been set on fire. I've dispatched all the accessible men and women to tend to the fires. Hopefully, we willnae lose both fields."

Cam turned to Kinny. "Inform me the moment any patrols return."

Kinny stood a little taller his shoulders pulled back as he replied, "Aye, milord." With a curt nod, the lad fled the room.

"We shall help in the fields to extinguish the fires, however when the first patrol returns, I will accompany them on their next search."

Hugh's brows lifted. "Ye think yer healed enough to undertake such a strenuous journey? Are ye fit to fight?"

"Fit enough. I wouldnae want to be the mon to stand in my way and try to stop me."

His intention to join his warriors in the search for the

thieves was delayed when he received a message that clan chieftains and their men were filing into the inner bailey.

Exhausted, Adriana dropped onto the chair. Her feet and back hurt from organizing her room and finding places for all of her mother's things. Bethany moved about the room as if they hadn't worked all day at finding places to hang dozens of gowns and stuffing drawers and trunks with boots and slippers. Hopefully, each item was in its rightful place and wouldn't be difficult to find when needed.

"Bethany, I truly appreciate you helping me to put everything away. It has been many years since my mother passed, yet I can remember her wearing some of those gowns. I just didn't realize she had so many."

"I told ye I dinnae really need yer help, milady. Ye should be resting. Yer going to need yer strength when ye face yer father tonight," Bethany replied, her eyes soft with concern. "At least crawl onto the bed and rest back with yer feet up."

"Oh, that does sound wonderful." Getting to her feet Adriana crossed to the large, canopy bed. After kicking off her slippers she crawled onto the bed and settled in the center. With a sigh, she leaned back against the pillows and closed her eyes. Soon she felt the weight and comfort of a thick blanket as it was placed over her. Adriana didn't need to open her eyes to know who covered her. "Not only are you the best lady's maid, Bethany, I have come to consider you as a dear friend and companion. I'm sincerely grateful for your support and the kindness you have shown me. Even though it's only been a few months, it feels as if we have been friends and cohorts for several years."

Bethany chuckled. "Weel, milady, it has been quite the adventure right from the beginning. Ye are easy to like, and I am honored to be considered yer friend and accomplice when ye need one. Ye rest and I'll finish this up."

Smiling Adriana snuggled deeper under the heavy blanket, then said, "If this didn't feel so lovely, I truly would get up and help you."

"Donae ye worry aboot anything milady except for resting before dinner."

Dinner. "I don't look forward to facing my father this evening." She drew her lower lip into her mouth and gently raked her teeth over it as her fears grew. Then she sighed.

"Do ye wish for me to send yer regrets? I could say ye arenae feeling up to it after yer long journey?"

Adriana sat up and placed her hands on her lap. "As much as I would like that, I have to face him eventually. He is going to get such joy when he learns my husband sent me away." She picked at a thread on the blanket. "I fear my life will be as before if not worse."

"Milady, even though we are no longer at Castle Corell, ye are still Lady MacCormac, prestigious wife of the mighty MacCormac himself. Yer father would be a fool no to recognize the importance of yer prominent position. And donae forget ye hae three hundred and eighty MacCormac warriors at yer disposal. Yer father would be foolish to dare misspeak or mistreat ye."

After exchanging smiles, Adriana retreated into her thoughts. *If need be, I will not hesitate to remind Father of his station, which is now below mine. I will never let him, or any other man control me or treat me as anything other than what I deserve as Lady MacCormac. I am done with serving any man.*

Yes, it was easy to think these things and act accordingly, but the child within her remembered her father's cruelty. Not only did his strap hurt, but his words hurt just as bad if not more-so.

A shiver shot through her body. If only Cameron were here.

Even though he no longer wanted her, Adriana's heart ached to see him, to be held in his arms. As much as she wished she didn't, she still loved him. Once again, her world had shifted, turning her dreams and her life upside down. As a result, she now had to learn to live alone without her husband.

There was a soft knock, her door opened, and Lynette entered. Adriana forced a smile and patted the bed for her sister to come and sit with her.

Crawling onto the bed she said, "Father has finally returned from whatever adventure had taken him away this time. I have been sent to tell you that dinner will be at eight o'clock, and that he's looking forward to seeing you again after your long absence." She shrugged her shoulders at Adriana.

Bethany bobbed her head to Lynette in acknowledgement. Then turning to Adriana said, "I will go and fetch water for yer bath, milady."

"Thank you, Bethany."

Once the door closed, Lynette studied Adriana. "As far back as I can remember you have always been so kind and considerate to the housemaids. It is hard sometimes, but I've tried to remember that. I strive to be like you, so I do the same when I can remember." Lynette forced a smile, which was quickly replaced with a frown.

Adriana took her sister's hand in hers and squeezed it tight. "It's not hard to remember to be nice to the servants when you have been treated as a servant yourself."

"I suppose you are correct." Lynette scooted closer and laid her head against Adriana's shoulder.

"I'm so sorry for leaving you here with Father." Adriana ran her hand over her sister's blonde curls. "I did plan to send for you as soon as I was able. But Laird MacCormac had been injured and everyone thought he would not live. I spent most of my time cleaning and dressing his wounds." She giggled and added, "I even shaved off his beard and mustache so I could feed him broth with a tiny spoon like I used to do for you."

Lynette sat up and smiled. "Did you really? How did he like that?"

"I'm afraid he was unconscious at the time, so I didn't care what he might have thought." They both laughed.

"You know Father was rather upset when he returned and found that Laird MacCormac had sent men to retrieve you, and that you were already gone."

"Did he hurt you, Lynette?"

"No. Father has never mistreated me as he did you. Though he wasn't pleased with me when he learned I'd stepped forward and took over your duties."

"I'm so proud of you." Adriana brushed a few loose strands of hair back from Lynette's cheek. "You have grown up so much in the short time that I have been away."

"I had to." Lynette sat up a little straighter. "I wanted to prove to Father that I could oversee your responsibilities. And as a result, from me standing up to him, he no longer treats me like a child."

"You're a clever one, aren't you?" Adriana felt her heart swell with pride.

"Well, I was lucky I had you there to take care of me when I was a baby after my mother died, and to teach me everything I needed to know as I was growing up. I appreciate everything you've done for me over the years. I know taking care of me hasn't always been an easy job," Lynette said, her eyes filling with tears.

A lump formed in the back of Adriana's throat, and it took several seconds before she was able to say, "It has never been a job to me. I loved you from the first moment I saw you, and enjoyed watching you grow up. Soon Father will make a match for you, and you will marry and have children of your own. Beautiful blonde babies with big blue eyes."

"What about you? Will you be having children soon? When is your husband coming for you? I so want to meet him."

Adriana closed her eyes and shook her head. "I'm not sure if he will come for me or not. Things didn't end well between us before I let Corell Castle."

"Do you *want* him to come for you? Do you *love* him?"

Adriana's eyes filled with tears, and she could not swallow. She nodded her head then said, "Yes. Yes, I do love him. I thought he loved me too, but it turned out he really didn't want a wife. Now I'm not sure what is going to happen." Tears unexpectedly rolled down her cheeks, and Lynette embraced her in a tight hug.

"Do you remember what you used to tell me when I didn't get my way? You would say everything will turn out the way it is meant to. You need to have faith and believe your life will turn out the way it's supposed to."

Adriana leaned back. "How did you get so smart."

"I take after my big sister." They laughed and hugged again.

A soft knock on the door pulled the two girls apart. Wiping the tears from her face Adriana said, "Enter." The door opened and Bethany entered followed by two male servants with pales of steaming water. Lynette crawled from the bed and crossed to the wardrobe. She opened the door and searched through the dresses. After a moment she selected a gown and pulled it out. "I think this one will look lovely with your brown hair and eyes." She hung the gown on the back of the wardrobe door. "I should also get dressed for dinner. I will see you in the dining hall at eight o'clock." Then she strolled to the door and left. Adriana watched her sister leave and marveled at how the young girl she'd left behind could have turned into a young lady in just a couple months.

An hour and a half later Adriana stared at her reflection in the long mirror. Lynette had been correct; the light blue gown was the perfect dress to meet her father in. Bethany placed a kertch over her pinned up hair and secured it with diamond decorated pins, which matched her diamond earbobs and necklace.

"Oh. How beautiful. Wait, one more thing," Bethany said, hurrying to the dresser. When she returned, she held out Larid MacCormac's signet ring. "Donae forget this."

Adriana slipped the heavy ring on her finger then turned and took another glance at herself in the mirror. Although she dressed how Lady MacCormac should dress, the Mistress of Castle Corell on the outside, inside she was still her father's daughter. And her father would always think of her as his housekeeper and private secretary. She took a deep breath and let it slip out slowly. She ran her hands down the front of her gown, turned, pulled her shoulders back, and approached the door. Smiling, Bethany pulled the large wooden door open. She stepped back and curtsied.

The captain of the guards, Malcolm Haywood, stood on the other side of her door. He looked dashing in his dress kilt, white hose, and polished brogues. He bowed deeply and said, "Milady, yer a vision of loveliness this night. Ye could pass for the Queen of Scotland." He presented his arm. "May I escort ye down to dinner?"

"Thank you, Captain." Adriana smiled. She stepped out into the corridor and placed her hand on his arm. "You look very handsome in your dress kilt and fetching bonnet." He grinned that childish grin that made him appear younger than he really was. She liked the captain. He'd been nothing but gracious and respectful to her. Yes, he flirted with her, although his flirtations were harmless, done to improve her sour or melancholy moods. He was a true gentleman and had appointed himself as her guardian. She would go as far as to say that she thought of him as a brother.

"Please excuse my forwardness, milady, but ye seem

nervous. Do ye hae reason to fear ye sire? Is there something I need to know before ye present yerself to him?"

Adriana glanced at the man and chuckled. "'Tis only that I am a coward and I fear his retribution for my return."

"Yer nae a coward in my eyes, milady." He shook his head in disbelief. "Ye rode all the miles to Castle Corell alone without a maid or family member to protect ye, to marry a man who was barely clinging to life. Then ye tended his wounds and fed him. Ye kept him alive and nursed him back to health, and we all appreciate yer hard work. Ye became his lady wife and still worked beside the servants as if ye were one yourself. Ye helped with the harvest and preserving food for the winter. I think ye very brave, milady." His hand slid over hers and patted it affectionately. Adriana hesitated at his intimate caress, puzzled at his intentions. The captain stopped; and a confused expression crossed his face. Then he winked and whispered, "Come little one, yer big braw brother will guard yer back."

Adriana nodded her head and proceeded to stroll along side of him, though she still was not convinced. "Did my father describe to Cam... Laird MacCormac what his daughter looked like before your laird agreed to the alliance?"

"Well, aye. But Milaird accepted the terms. He knew the risk he was taking, that yer father might try and trick him in some way."

"I'm sure my father expressed to Laird MacCormac, that his daughter was young and beautiful. That she had blonde hair and blue eyes, correct?" She glanced up at the captain.

The young captain stared at the floor. "Aye, that's how he described ye."

"Who he described was my younger sister, Lynette." His gaze shot to hers. "I went in her place," she continued, her voice shook under his scrutiny. "She is very young, and I only married your lord because you told me his wounds were so severe, and that he was expected to die." She tightened her grip on his arm. "I couldn't let my sister go through that."

When they stopped at the top of the stone stairs, he said, "Yer strong, intelligent, and a force to be reckoned-with, milady. Ye are no coward as far as I can see. Whatever awaits ye below in the dining hall, I'm confident ye will handle with grace and ease. However, if ye fine yerself encountering a dragon, ye need only to yell and I will appear at yer side and slay him for ye."

They descended the large stone steps in silence. Adriana prayed Captain Haywood would be true to his word and stay close by her side throughout the evening. Drawing in a deep breath she crossed the threshold into the dining hall. Her father stopped talking to his man, Balfour. He stared at her. His nostrils flared; his jaw clenched with disdain as his gaze traveled the length of her. She swallowed hard. She was not sure she wanted to know his thoughts at seeing her in one of her mother's gowns.

He looked grand dressed in his purple brocade, wide-cuffed coat, matching knee-length breeches, white silk stockings, and buckle shoes. The only thing he was missing was the wide-brimmed hat he favored to wear over his long, curly black wig. Dressed like a nobleman, her father stood ready to hold court and pass judgment.

After a moment of hesitation, he bowed slightly, and proclaimed, "Lady MacCormac, what a lovely, *although expected*, surprise it was to hear you have returned home."

Her father reached out and seized her arm, leading her away from the captain's protection. Leaning close and whispered, "You surprisingly look lovely in your dead mother's dress. How does it fit, my dear, a little tight perhaps? Betrayal can make that happen sometimes."

Adriana drew in a sharp breath, paralyzed to escape his steely grip. A sneer marred his face and he growled, "You made me look the fool to MacCormac. I suspected he would tire of you and send you back to me. When exactly did he learn of your lies? What sort of retribution am I to expect because of your deception?"

His harsh words caused Adriana to flinch. She feared she would feel the strike of his fist shortly. The flames of resentment grew, and a burning flush engulfed her body. Although she wished she could flee, she straightened her spine, turned, and face her father. "You go too far, Father. You would be wise to mind what you say regarding me, Lady MacCormac, wife of Cameron MacCormac, Laird, and Chieftain of the mighty MacCormac Clan." She held his gaze until her father loosened his grip on her arm and his hand fell away.

"On the contrary, milord," the captain replied casually. He had once again appeared at her side. "Laird MacCormac sent his wife here under the protection of his soldiers since he and other warriors are searching for the band of thieves who are killing innocent farmers and raping the countryside. Once he finds them and eliminates them all, he will march upon Shealoch Castle and collect his wife."

Her father snarled and walked away. The captain snickered and winked. Turning, he pulled out a chair at the long table for her to be seated. Adriana's legs were trembling as she sank down onto the chair. She could not believe how she responded to her father's cruel hateful words. Her pride soon shriveled at the thought of Cameron marching on Shealoch Castle. Would he come to collect her, or would her father's fears become known and the mighty MacCormac would demand retribution for her deception?

"Well done milady." Captain Haywood whispered as he guided her chair closer to the table. She nodded her thanks. She knew he thought she was brave for standing up to her father and putting him in his place. She prayed that her actions today wouldn't turn on her and cause more problems for her later.

Lynette swept into the room like the queen of the castle.

"Good evening, everyone. So sorry I am late, I was in the kitchen checking on dinner," she said, waving her arms with dramatic flair. With a big smile Captain Haywood pulled out a chair for Lynette, seating her across from Adriana.

Adriana enjoyed the wonderful meal her sister had ordered in celebration of her return. The evening passed quickly due to a lively discussion on the weather, the crops, and Lynette's future. Adriana watched her father out of the corner of her eye. The lack of food he consumed, and the straight line of his lips revealed his displeasure with her. He had made it quite clear that she had publicly humiliated him with her lies and deception.

He was not a man to let one's bad behavior go unaddressed and unpunished. Glancing down the long table at his stone-faced expression she couldn't imagine what sort of punishment he was envisioning at the moment, or when he would strike.

Sixteen

C am pulled his plaid tighter around his neck. The wounds to his shoulder and leg throbbed with a never-ending pain. He'd been on the hunt for two weeks since he met with the chieftains, and he and his men always remained one day behind the murderers. It was late autumn and a chill had set in early. The constant freezing rain and strong winds drove the small army deep into the forest seeking shelter under the canopy of trees. Steam rose from their weary horse's chests and flanks, billows of white smoke puffed from their nostrils as they trudged along the narrow trail. A shiver ran up his spine, and he longed to be home in his warm bed with Angel by his side. The thought of her waiting in his chambers warmed his weary soul. But his heart ached when the sting of reality reminded him, she wasn't his and he feared that would never change.

Cam and his warriors were approaching the southern border where they had a stronger chance of running into English soldiers. If the English captured the band of killers before Cam found them, he would lose the opportunity to punish them, and protect their clans from being tracked down and slaughtered by King William.

After riding for a number of miles, they came to a clearing. Before them lay a farm which appeared to have recently been attacked. Cam cursed and spurred his horse forward. The buildings and fields had been set ablaze, and with the onset of rain, they merely smoldered, each sending streams of smokey-clouds trailing up toward the sky. A woman and a young boy picking up debris watched them approach, neither having the time, will or strength to run away. A man's dead body lay by a half-burnt building, an older man's body lay in a field.

"I am Laird MacCormac," Cam yelled as they cautiously approached. "What has happened here?" Reining in his horse a few feet from the woman, he added, "May my men and I be of service to ye?"

The boy ran behind his mother and peeked around her blood and dirt-smeared skirt. The woman nodded her head, but neither spoke. Cam and his men dismounted. Furious at the carnage they found, Cam divided his men into three groups, sending two groups out in search of some clues, anything to help locate and identify the men responsible for this senseless act. Cam, Hugh, and eight warriors stayed at the burned-out farm to help the woman and boy left behind.

They buried the woman's husband and eldest son, then the dead animals scattered about the property. Cam tempted to speak with the woman, but she wouldn't converse with him. Her eyes were empty. They held no life--no light. He witnessed an unforgettable hollowness in their depths, as if she were dead inside and merely performing her affairs.

Then he suddenly wondered if Angel and her husband were farmers. Had she sons of her own? How would she ever survive a terrible act like what had happened to this woman and her family. He had no idea where she was or if she were safe. The thought of Angel being unprotected made Cam's stomach curl and rise up into his throat. He sculked around the charred buildings, his thoughts playing-out situations where Angel was discovered and injured, or worse. Soon he found himself petting his horse, searching for any source of comfort.

Before they moved on and made camp for the night, Cam shared a portion of their provisions with the woman and her son. He informed her that they would camp close by for the night and promised to return the next morn to repair the damaged structures for her.

Cam and his men set up camp by a small stream. His men were quiet, each tending to their mounts and their own needs. Mayhap they anticipated a bath in the cool water to wash away the dirt, blood, ash, and sweat from their bodies, as much as he. He longed to wash away all thoughts of the past week except for the destruction of yesterday's attack on the small farm. He glanced down at his blood-stained hands. Would he ever be able to wash this day away? The loss the family had suffered and the sadness he had witnessed in the woman's eyes would stay with him for years. A vision of his beloved Blair invaded his mind, and he remembered how it felt to have everything you loved taken away, leaving your heart and soul exposed and raw. How one incident could quickly change a person's life forever, leaving you to wonder how you were ever expected to go on alone.

Had it been his youthfulness or his ignorance that had convinced Cam that he and Blair had a whole lifetime together. The love he had shared with her had been sweet and gentle. It was completely different than the passion he had experienced with Angel.

Angel. So mysterious and adventurous, no longer came to him. She had disappeared. Most likely returned to her husband where she felt she belonged. Cam needed to accept his plight for what it was. Angel had slipped into his life and not only healed his new injuries; she had opened old wounds and exposed the agony he'd thought was buried too deep to ever surface again. Try as he might, his heart softened at the thought of his Faceless Angel. He sighed, although he didn't know the true identity of Angel or what she looked like, he knew he would always treasure the fact that she had forced him to live again.

"What are ye so deep in thought aboot, cousin?" Hugh patted Cam's horse's hip as he drew near.

Drawing in a deep breath, Cam scratched his scruffy beard. "My mind is weary this evening." He shook his head and added, "It has wandered back to the sweet lass who nursed my wounds, and then visited my bed."

Hugh glanced around as if he expected someone to step up and intervene. Surely his cousin was not embarrassed at hearing Cam's intimate thoughts after the things they had shared over the years. Though something seemed to be gnawing at him. Crossing his arms across his chest, Cam said, "Do ye remember when I questioned ye aboot the night someone drugged me? Weel, I am still convinced ye know more aboot what was afoot that night then yer telling me."

"Aye." Hugh shuffled his feet.

"Yer answer if I recall was ye married me to Sir Alexander's daughter while I was unconscious." Cam took a step closer to Hugh. "Now, that has me wondering what one incident has to do with the other. Ye would be telling me noo what ye dinnae tell me then."

Hugh's gaze shot to the ground; his hand eased over to rest on the hilt of his sword. Then his cousin's chin rose a notch and his stare met Cam's. "I will only be telling ye the truth of it if ye place yer broadsword, dirk, and yer sghian dubh twelve paces away. And ye agree to listen to my reason," Hugh hesitantly added.

Cam eyed Hugh. Most likely, he was not going to approve *or* appreciate the man's logic, but he would listen. He needed answers. Cam walked the requested twelve paces away from his cousin. He removed his broadsword, a dirk and a pistol from his belt and placed them on the ground. Turning, he caught and held his cousin's gaze. Then reached up into his left sleeve where a leather holster held his sghian dubh. Slowly, he removed the six-inch blade and tossed it on the ground next to the other weapons. Facing his cousin, Cam placed his hands on his hips. "D'ye feel safe noo?"

Hugh gauged the distance to safety, then replied, "No, not even a wee bit." Waving his arm to one side, he instructed cam, "Move yerself away from yer weapons."

As Cam moved several steps away, he noticed their conversation had caught the attention of his other men. A couple of them were smiling and nodding their heads. The others appeared worried at what sort of game was going to be played between the two.

Cam studied his cousin who still didn't appear satisfied with the situation. He didn't know what else he could do to appease his cousin, so he crossed his arms over his chest again and waited.

Hugh still didn't appear convinced, but he cleared his throat and said, "'Tis no secret, and it wasnae anyone's intention to deceive ye."

Cam huffed a breath in disagreement.

"T'was noo known at first that the baronet had two daughters."

Not surprised at this development, Cam responded by raising one thick black brow.

"As ye been told, Lady Lynette is fair-haired with blue eyes. A sweet lass of ten and two." Hugh drew a deep breath and continued. "The eldest daughter would be Lady Adriana. A spinster at one and twenty." He nodded his head as if all was well. "When Malcolm arrived to fetch the lass Sir Alexander wasnae there. He spoke with the eldest daughter who knew of the agreement and agreed with it. In haste he informed her of the attack and how badly ye were injured. Weel," he scratched the back of his neck before continuing. "The gossip aboot the castle is that for some reason the lass took it upon herself to take her sister's place. In doing so, she accompanied Malcolm to Castle Corell and ye were married."

Cam's thoughts swirled around in his head, not quite believing what he was hearing. The gasps and chuckles from the other men sitting upon the ground watching, pulled Cam back to reality, and he said, "So, this oldest daughter, the spinster, was the one who tended my wounds and kept me alive?"

"Aye." Hugh nodded his head and took a step back.

"The spinster is my wife?" His heart pounded in his head.

Hugh took another step back, his watchful eyes never wavering from Cam's.

Cam paced back and forth between Hugh and the spectators on the ground. *Two daughters. My wife is the older sister, a spinster. Lady Adriana. It had not been a young girl who came so boldly to his bed each night, but an older spinster.* The facts lined up in his weary mind. He stopped; his gaze shot back up to Hugh's. "The spinster, Lady Adriana is my *Faceless Angel*?"

"Aye." Hugh agreed then shot an angry stare to snickers and chuckles coming from the men sitting on the grass.

"Has she been returned to her father's estate?" Cam rubbed the palm of his hands over his face. *If I am correct, we are verra close to Shealoch Castle.* He turned and faced Hugh and replied, "We must go and collect her." But suddenly he felt apprehensive and shook his head in dismay. *What evil thoughts she must be thinking about me. I must go to her as soon as possible and make this right between us. Will she ever forgive me? She must. She will.* Cam felt himself relax.

"Aye," Hugh replied, softly.

"Aye!" Cam nodded, then remembered his original question. "But I still donae understand. Who placed the potion in my brandy and how was my wife connected to that particular incident?"

Hugh coughed. Shifting his weight from one foot to another, his gaze landing on everything except Cam's face. When the man spoke, his voice wasn't much more than a whisper. "I expect she placed it there to better manage ye."

"What?" Annoyed and embarrassed, Cam scowled. Unsure of what he would do if he moved, he forced himself to stay rooted a safe distance away from his cousin.

"To...To make ye more cooperative," Hugh stammered.

Nervous laughter broke out amongst his warriors who had gathered close by to observe the spectacle. His men playfully jostled each other and pushed each other around on the ground. Cam struggled to ignore the men witnessing his humiliation. He focused his thoughts on how quickly he could reach Angel, and how heavenly it would be to have her back in his arms where she belonged.

The ground shook, the rumble of thunder increased. All of a sudden Cam and his small group of warriors were surrounded by a troop of English dragoons. Cam glanced at his weapons lying on the ground, unfortunately too far away to be of any good. His men jumped to their feet but didn't have enough time to pull their weapons.

A man with dirty, shoulder length hair and dressed in a lieutenant's uniform cleared his throat. His stormy grey eyes raked Cam from head to toe, then passed over the rest of the men before returning to Cam. He sneered at their dirty and disheveled appearance. But then he smirked, and Cam guessed the man had at last realized just who stood before him.

"Look who we have here." The lieutenant's voice dripped with arrogance. "If I'm correct, this is the murdering Scotsmen and traitor, *The Black Giant*." The man sneered at Cam.

Cam's lungs filled with air. Pulling his shoulders back he

growled, "I'm Laird Cameron MacCormac, chief of the MacCormac Clan? Who might ye be?"

"I'm Lieutenant Dunaway of His Majesty's 7th Dragoons, and you are all under arrest for treason and murder."

~

Two weeks later it had become customary for Captain Haywood to be waiting by Adriana's door when she walked out of her room, so it was not a surprise when she opened the door and found him there.

"Good morning, Captain." He bowed. She smiled at the man that she and Bethany privately referred to as her shadow. She turned and started down the corridor toward the stairs. The captain never lingered more than several feet from her side. He respected her privacy, content to wait for her to start a conversation. Loyal and quick to please, he boosted her confidence, which she especially needed now that she knew she was with child. Although he was too polite to broach the subject, she was sure he and everyone else had concluded the same.

As they approached the steps, he took her elbow and guided her down the stairs to the dining hall below where she would break her fast. Each morning, she excitedly anticipated what Mrs. Wilson had arranged for her morning meal. She devoured her food, and lately started to eat the equivalent of a small banquet between her regular meals. Although she had lost weight during her stay at Castle Corell, since returning home, she couldn't get enough to eat, and it was starting to show in her clothes. All of her gowns had become tight, forcing her to let out all of the seams.

Her life had changed tremendously over the past few months. She'd returned home as Lady MacCormac, wife to a powerful Highland Chieftain, and a mother-to-be. Her emotions jumped back and forth between being happy for the blessings bestowed on her, and sad because she would not be able to share this special time with Cameron. She still couldn't understand what she'd done to make him so angry that he demanded she be sent away without so much as a bye-your-leave.

When they reached the main floor, she heard a commotion by the arched entrance to the dining hall. Lifting her skirts, she rushed toward the men who had gathered there. She discovered a strange man dressed in an English soldier's uniform. Her father stood next to him reading a piece of paper. When she entered the room, every man turned toward her and bowed. Adriana nodded her head. "Gentlemen."

Her father's wig jiggled on his head as he shook the piece of paper at her and growled, "Your Highlander has been arrested."

Adrianna crossed to her father and reached for the letter. "Who arrested him? Where have they taken him?"

He frowned; indignant he pulled his hand away. "You've no need to know now."

"Where?" she demanded, showing as much courage as she could muster.

"They have taken him and his men to the Fort of Inverlochy in Lochaber," he said with a sneer, as if to wound her."

Adriana heard Captain Haywood clear his throat behind her and her father handed the message over.

The dispatch was from a Colonel Robert Stone from the Fort of Inverlochy. The correspondence had been addressed to her at her father's castle. Adriana glared over the top of the paper at her father, who had thought nothing of intercepting her private correspondence.

The letter informed her that her husband, Laird Cameron MacCormac and nine of his men were captured by a troop of English Dragoons. They were charged with treason with the intention of causing an uprising, murder, thieving, and destroying necessary food supplies. They had been taken to the Fort of Inverlochy to be held for trial.

Shaken by the contents of the letter, Adriana handed it to Captain Haywood, praying for his counsel. He glanced down at the letter. When he looked up his brows were pinched tight together and he said, "If they are found guilty, they will all hang."

Adriana automatically turned toward her father for his opinion, but feared he would decline any helpful assistance. He glanced around at the other men standing there and blustered before saying, "I don't have the soldiers, or the influence, to ride to Lochaber to have them freed."

Typical. She drew in a deep breath, shook her head, and sighed.

Facing her father, Adriana placed her hands on her hips and wrestled with her anger. "You may not, *Father*. But I do." She directed her attention to Captain Haywood and asked, "How many men do we have?"

Her father raised his hand as if to strike her, except Captain Haywood stepped in front of Adriana to shield her.

Captain Haywood studied her quizzically then nodded his head and replied, "Including Shealoch men, over four hundred. Excuse me, milady but ye donae suggest we take that many men to collect the Laird, do ye? It may appear as if we plan to attack the military compound."

Sir Alexander shook his head and laughed. "Do you plan to lay siege on the fort to get your husband back? Foolish girl." He straightened his black wig, then placed the palm of his hand over his heart. He glanced at the captain and added with an air of conviction, "You will not be taking any of my men with you, Captain."

The captain stepped beside Adriana. "Ye forget yerself, milord. Ye made a contract, an alliance with the chieftain of the

MacCormac clan when ye offered yer daughter to him in return for his protection."

"True." Her father sneered; the tone of his voice attested to his arrogance. "However, the alliance at the present is invalid. Worthless, due to the fact that she deceived him and tricked him into marriage."

"Trickery or not, Sir Alexander, the marriage was performed by Father Fitzgerald, witnessed by the parish and God Almighty. 'Tis lawful and binding," the captain demanded.

When her father started to bluster, the captain continued, "Ye will accompany us. Yer statement that ye offered yer daughter to Laird MacCormac in exchange for his protection is most important."

"Lady Adriana was not the daughter I promised, nor the girl Laird MacCormac expected. He will accuse me of cheating him."

"I will state my laird agreed to an unnamed daughter in this alliance." Captain Haywood took a step closer to Sir Alexander. "Ye need to trust his men will catch these murders afore they become too powerful and encouraged more rebellions." Sir Alexander nodded his head in agreement. "His desire is to keep King William from marching against Scotland," the captain replied. "His intention has always been to prevent a civil war from starting."

Adriana wrung her hands together. "Where is Lochaber? How far is it from here?"

"'Tis in the Highlands on the eastern shore of Loch Linnhe. My guess is that 'tis at least a three-days hard ride from here."

"How long will it take to get the men and supply wagons ready for such a trip?"

"Mayhap two hours, milady."

"That will be more than enough time for my father and I to ready ourselves to travel."

"Milady, are ye sure 'tis wise for ye to travel so far in yer condition?"

"I have no choice in the matter, Captain. We are the only ones who can help them. Besides, I cannot let the father of my child hang. I appreciate your concern for me. I am sure I will be comfortable in one of the wagons." When he did not appear convinced, she reached out and lightly touched his arm. Forcing a smile, she said, "All will be well. You must hurry now and make ready for our journey." When he hesitated, Adriana waved him away as if she were ushering a child out to play.

Finally, the captain turned and hastened out of the hall. Adriana sighed. Hugging her arms to herself she prayed, *"Please Lord let us reach them in time."*

Seventeen

T he heavy iron shackles around Cam's ankles hindered his steps, the chains clanking against the stone floor as he shuffled along the corridor. The irons binding his wrists and forcing his hands down, bit painfully into his skin. The young British soldier who retrieved Cam from his cell informed him that Colonel Stone wanted to see Cam in his office for questioning. They finally halted before a large wooden door. The soldier knocked twice. A deep voice bid them to enter, thus the soldier opened the door and shoved Cam inside.

Cam stumbled into the small room, coming to a halt in front of an old wooden desk. He guessed the imposing man seated behind the desk to be in his mid-fifty's. Whisps of white hair stuck out from under his powdered, military plait wig. His piercing light gray-eyed-stare indicated he could see straight into Cam's soul. After perusing Cam's appearance, Colonel Stone glanced down at a stack of papers on his desk. "Laird MacCormac." His voice rumbled from deep within his thick chest. "I understand your lands are located in the Highlands. Nevertheless, you and your troop of warriors were discovered close to the

Southern border. And may I add, within a short distance from where a farm was attacked, its fields set ablaze, and two men were murdered."

Colonel Stone's gaze shot up to meet Cam's. The chair creaked in protest as he leaned his bulky frame back and interlocked his fingers together over his chest. Even relaxed, the man's presence was intimidating, and Cam wondered how he would fair at the hilt of a sword—as an opponent.

"Can you explain to me how you and your men came to be covered in fresh blood and soot?"

"We were searching for the band of killers, hoping to find them 'afore they crossed into the Lowlands." He omitted his anticipations of finding these men and doling out *his own* form of Highland justice for their deeds. "I hae dispatched two other troops, one to the east and one to the west, while we headed south. This gang managed to stay mere hours ahead of us.

We followed the smell of smoke to the farm where we found fields on fire and a man, and his son murdered. My men and I tended to the fields and buried the dead. We promised to return the next morn to help the farmer's wife and young son repair their buildings."

Colonel Stone's skepticism was quite clear as he listened to Laird MacCormac's statement. Once again, he assessed Cam's disheveled blood-stained appearance. The colonel stood, when he straightened to his full height, he was only a couple of inches shorter than Cam. Stone strolled across the small room; his hands clasped behind his back as he studied the floorboards. A hopeless feeling washed over Cam. The overwhelming evidence pointed to him and his men. It was not going to be easy to change the man's mind. But he had to, his men's lives depended on him convincing Colonel Stone of their innocence.

"Colonel..." Cam started. As he stepped forward, the guard pressed a heavy hand on his shoulder, reminding him just where he was.

Stone shook his head then turned and faced Cam. "I am sorry, Laird MacCormac, but the murders and fires all started in the north and moved south. And with the evidence connected to your arrest..." He trailed off as he moved to the window and glanced out. Without turning he said, "I will review what you have told me this day, however, it does not bode well for you or your men. You may return him to his cell, Davis."

Cam stared at the back of the man's head. He fought to control his anger and frustration. It would do none of them any good if he tore these men in half. Any violence on his part would only make he and his men look all the more guilty.

The soldier called Davis grabbed Cam by the arm and ushered him out the door and back down the corridor. Once they reached the cell, the guard unlocked the metal door and pushed Cam inside. His cousin Hugh watched from the same spot he had occupied for the last week. The small windowless space smelled of urine, sweat, and human waste. The thin layer of straw covering the cold, damp, stone floor did little to cushion his fall.

Cam swore quietly as he landed next to Hugh with a hard thud. He did not want his men in the surrounding cells to hear his suffering. His wrists were sore, cut, and bleeding from the tight irons. They were all filthy and were given hardly enough food or water to survive. Although it appeared futile, he felt it crucial to somehow reassure his men to have faith, that "The Almighty" would not condemn them to die for deeds they had not committed. Though, the sentry's condemning words from the day they arrived invaded his mind. The tall lanky lieutenant stated that even with a trial, they all were going to hang for their crimes against the King. The burden of disappointment pressed heavily against his heart. He'd failed the Highland clans. All he could do now was pray a civil war would not break out, causing the deaths of more innocent people.

Cam sighed. There was only one thing that could keep him

from giving up. He struggled to scoot back and lean against the wall. "Tell me about her, what she looks like," he murmured to his cousin sitting next to him.

Hugh scratched his head, and after a moment without any sentiment, "She's tall for a woman."

"Aye." Cam closed his eyes and nodded his head. "I would hae guessed her to be so. And the color of her hair and her eyes?"

"They're brown."

"Is she bonnie? What do ye think of her?"

Hugh snickered and settled against the wall. "Och. She is too skinny and bossy for me. I like a woman with a little tallow on her bones. One that donae cluck none-stop like an old hen or strives to be the farmyard rooster."

They both laughed, and Cam remembered how Angel had taken liberties to instruct him while they were in bed together.

"I hae to say I dinnae trust her at first," Hugh continued in a more serious tone. "But she gained my respect and the house-holds after we witnessed how she took charge and diligently tended ye and ye wounds." Hugh readjusted his position. "She wasnae going to sit by and watch ye die for sure. She spooned broth into ye mouth day and night." He nodded his head. "Malcolm speaks highly of Lady Adriana. Says she never complained the whole time they crossed the Highlands to Castle Corell. And they rode hard to reach ye thinking ye were going to die. He said she also offered to help with the cooking and even told stories to entertain the men, took their minds off worrying about ye."

"How does she occupy her time since I recovered? Does she hide in her room or is she giving orders in the kitchen?" His mirth turned to sadness. He wished they were home at Castle Corell together. He would let her take over the castle if that is what she wished. "Where has she been hiding? I never spotted a lady in the great hall."

Elbowing Cam in the side, Hugh laughed. "Her Ladyship has walked right past ye in the hall. She has even filled ye mug. She dresses like a house maid and spends her time weeding the gardens and picking vegetables. She seems to like helping in the kitchen with the overseeing and preparation of each meal."

Although Cam was frustrated when he learned that she had been in the hall, and he hadn't known it, Hugh continued to glorify and praise his wife's strengths and bravery.

Cam crossed his arms upon his bent knees, then leaned forward and placed his forehead on his arms. "I still cannae understand why she wouldnae tell me who she was when she came to my chambers each night. Why she felt the need to keep her identity a secret?"

Hugh stammered then asked, "Who did she tell ye she was?"

"There's the problem," he glanced at his cousin. "She wouldnae tell me who she was."

He remembered the night he asked her if she was married and if her husband was a MacCormac. He shook his head in disgust. He had even asked if her husband was unwilling to be a proper husband to her. Well, he'd proven he wasn't a proper husband. Hell, he'd even sent her away. But why hadn't she told him right then that she was his wife? What was she hiding from him?

Cam's attention was drawn away from his restless thoughts when he heard Hugh chuckle. "What do ye think is so humorous, cousin?"

Hugh's deep chest rumbled with laughter, and he said, "Poor thing dinnae keen the whole castle knew she crept into yer room each night. To my understanding, Aunt Moira expressed 'twas her duty as Lady MacCormac to get with child afore ye died." The big man's shoulders shook as he chuckled.

Cam stared at Hugh, then asked, "And just how was she to

accomplish that with my injuries and the fact I was unconscious?"

Hugh turned toward Cam and gave him a lop-sided grin. "In that lies the mystery as to how our little mouse, Auntie Moira, would know how to make a mon's sword...unyielding."

When he realized what his cousin was referring to Cam's mouth fell open. "Ye donae mean to say, she told the lass..."

Hugh's eyes sparked with mischief as he nodded his head. "With detailed instructions... I was informed by a reliable source." After his declaration, Hugh coughed then cleared his throat.

Both men roared with laughter.

When their laughter subsided, Cam thought about Angel and smiled. It didn't seem possible that his brave wife Lady Adriana had all along been his Faceless Angel. Cam marveled at all the things she had endured in such a brief period of time. He wished he could meet her, have time to get to know her. He wanted to thank her for everything she did to save his life. A sharp pain deep in his chest stung with the thought of how insulted she must have felt when he rejected her and sent her away. And now with the turn of events, it didn't look as if he would be able to say how sorry he was, or even see her beautiful face before he was hanged. Until that moment, Cam hadn't considered what was going to happen to his beloved Faceless Angel.

～

The wagon bounced over what felt like fist-sized rocks and Adriana's back felt each one. By the time their cavalcade finally reached Fort Inverlochy, her head throbbed and the pain in her lower back felt as if she had been beaten by the Smithy. Needless to say, she was in no mood to listen to her father's constant complaints.

When they stopped, Captain Haywood appeared at Lady Adriana's side and helped her down from the wagon. She nodded her thanks, then proceeded to brush the dust from her skirts. She hoped her appearance wouldn't show how long and difficult the journey from her father's estate truly had been. She needed to use the fact that she was English and her position as Lady MacCormac to persuade the warden to release her husband and his men.

"I swear they deliberately make these roads too rough to traverse," Sir Alexander whined as he gingerly climbed down from his horse.

The sound of her father's whiny voice set Adriana's teeth on edge, and she winced. If he continued to complain she would have no teeth left by the time she returned home. Her father limped toward her. When he stopped at her side, she placed her palm on his arm and squeezed tightly. He balked and tried to move away but she yanked him close to her side and said, "You will not say a disparaging word against Laird MacCormac or do anything to jeopardize his chances for release. For if you do, you will live out the rest of your miserable days in a cold, dark dungeon in the Highlands. Do you understand me, Father?"

Her father winced and tried to jerk his arm away. She held fast, he grimaced and nodded his head in agreement with her terms. Adriana loosened her hold, drew in a deep breath and they strolled toward the small timber fort on the River Nevis. They entered through a wooded door. One could not help but notice the fort appeared as well under construction. The passageway was dark and dusty, the offensive odor that danced in the air caused the contents of Adriana's stomach to curdle like spoiled milk forgotten in a butter churn.

Male voices came from an opened door down the hall. Lifting her skirts and squaring her shoulders, Adriana marched toward the entrance. An older gentleman with a thick white mustache sat behind a large wooden desk. The young soldier who seemed puzzled at her sudden appearance stood in front of the desk. Their conversation stopped as Adriana strolled into the room. The man behind the desk started to rise, but she waved him back to his seat.

"Excuse me, gentlemen," she said as the two stared at her in wide-eyed silence. "My name is Lady Adriana of Clan MacCormac." She raised a haughty brow at the young man who rapidly stepped back a couple of strides so she could approach the desk. She reached out her gloved hand where earlier, she had placed Cameron's signet ring on the middle finger of her right hand. "I understand there has been a misunderstanding." The man started to stand, then paused, and said, "With your permission, Lady Adriana."

"Yes, of course." She waved her hand in the air as if shooing a fly. Panic boiled just below the surface, and she thought she was going to faint dead away at any moment. The man captured her hand and kissed her knuckles.

"I am Colonel Robert Stone. I am commander here. This," he said, gesturing to the formidable looking soldier, "is Lieutenant Dunaway of His Majesty's 7th Dragoons."

Sir Alexander stepped forward and reached his hand out to the Colonel. "Good day to you, Sir. I am Sir Alexander Boyd of Shealochen. This is my daughter, Lady Adriana, and Captain of the Guards, Captain Haywood."

The Colonel reached for Sir Alexander's hand. The men all took turns shaking each other's hands and nodding their heads. It was all very civilized, like a regular after-church-social-time, which caused Adriana's heart to pound. Her head throbbed, and she thought for sure she was going to be sick.

Straightening her spine, she gathered her courage and said, "Gentlemen, if you are finished, might we continue? I assure you my business will not take long."

"Yes, of course," Colonel Stone said, bobbing his head. "How may I be of service to you, Lady Adriana?"

"As I stated," she said, pinning the colonel with an icy stare. "An error seems to have transpired involving my husband, Laird Cameron MacCormac." Adriana handed him the letter she'd received from him at her father's estate. She fingered the large diamond necklace she'd fastened around her neck moments before they arrived.

Lowering the piece of paper, the Colonel glanced at the young lieutenant then came back to her. "I am sorry, Lady Adriana, but all the prisoners have yet to be interviewed. You must understand that we have a strict process, which needs to be conducted before a prisoner is declared innocent or guilty of their crimes."

Adriana turned to the young soldier. "Lieutenant, are you the ardent soldier who arrested my husband and his men?"

The stern-faced lieutenant bowed, then replied, "Yes, My Lady. My patrol came upon them mere kilometers from the farm which had been attacked. Your husband and his men had not yet even washed the blood from their clothes."

Although she felt a jolt at the lieutenant's statement, she continued. "Mayhap, were there any survivors of this attack?"

"Yes, a woman and her son survived the raid." The young lieutenant stood as straight as a tree during her inquiry.

Adriana removed one of her diamond earbobs, smiled sweetly at the colonel then refastened the bob to her ear. "One thing more, if you don't mind, Colonel Stone." She treated the men with the sweetest smile she could muster. "This woman who survived this brutal attack, has she identified my husband and his men as her attackers? As the men who slayed her loved ones?"

"No. Not as of yet." He then shifted his weight from one foot to the other.

Adriana turned to face the Colonel. "Is she here to listen to and witness Liard MacCormac's and each of his men's interviews?" When the colonel appeared uncomfortable, she continued. "Well, then, will she be brought here, and herself interviewed?"

"As you can see My Lady, we are currently reconstructing the fort," Colonel Stone said. "We do not have lodgings here to accommodate anyone other than our soldiers. King William demands the new fort completed as soon as possible, and with winter quickly approaching..."

A young soldier with a bad complexion appeared at the door with a note. The colonel seemed pleased with the interruption as he ushered the boy forward and took the folded piece of paper. After reading the short message, the colonel exchanged glances with the Lieutenant. He appeared flustered. He cleared his throat and what looked to be a forced smile appeared on his face. She wondered how it had taken this long for a guard to notice fifty mounted Highland warriors, and three hundred, foot soldiers, gathering in the large field next to the fort.

When the colonel glanced up from his note, he was pale and agitated. Adriana pressed a hand against the cluster of diamonds resting impressively against her breast. She leaned slightly forward as if to whisper something for his ears only. When Colonel Stone leaned in, Adriana whispered, "The extent of the clans who pay allegiants to *The MacCormac* are enormous. It would be too terrifying to be in the Highlands if my father had not made an alliance with Laird MacCormac...and I hadn't married him." She offered up the sweetest smile.

The colonel straightened and viewed the papers strewed across his desk. After a few moments, his gaze met hers and he said, "I feel there is no need to do any further interviews." He clasped his hands behind his back and continued in a slow methodical tone. "After interviewing Laird MacCormac earlier today, and giving his testimony a lot of consideration, I believe there is no need for further investigation or for a trial. Laird MacCormac's reputation is well respected."

Adriana offered her hand. The colonel bowed low and

kissed her knuckles. "Oh, thank you Colonel Stone, you are too kind." Not waiting for his response, she turned and said, "Father, Captain Haywood, shall we? Oh, Colonel," she twisted back around to face the older man again and amiably added, "I am sure it won't take very long to release my husband and his men. With your permission, we shall make camp here and wait for them? Thank you. You have been most helpful."

Sir Alexander, Captain Haywood and Lady Adriana slowly exited the old fort. Adriana drew in a cleansing breath as they strolled toward her waiting warriors. She never thought she would be so happy to crawl back onto that wagon, but she needed to sit down before she collapsed.

"I've never in my life," her father started, only to be cut off by Captain Haywood. "You were magnificent, Milady."

"I think I am going to be ill," she replied, pressing a hand to her stomach, and closing her eyes.

"Let's get ye to the wagon." Captain Haywood cupped Adriana's elbow and guided her toward the wagon. "Yes. Let us get back on the road," Sir Alexander said, heading for his horse.

Captain Haywood shook his head at her father and said, "'Tis a wonderful thing ye've done here today. There will be legends told about this day, praising yer bravery for confronting Colonel Hill and the young lieutenant."

Smiling, she placed her palm on his arm, and he helped her up onto the wagon next to Bethany. He glanced up, but his grin quickly faded when she said, "Take one of the wagons filled with supplies, then escort Laird MacCormac and his men back to Corell Castle. I will return to Shealoch with my father." The captain frowned at hearing her plan. "Malcolm," she said, covering his hand with hers. "I promise I will be fine. My father would not dare try to mistreat me after today."

The driver crawled up onto the wagon, collected the reins, and asked, "Are ye ready, milady?"

"Yes, driver." There was a commotion by the entrance of

the old fort. Adriana glanced up. Several men walked out into the sunlight. There stood Laird MacCormac, blocking the bright sun with his hand. He stared at her as the wagon jerked forward.

Eighteen

The shackles were removed from Cam's wrists and ankles and without explanation he and his men were released and escorted out of the old fort. Cam rubbed his sore wrists as he walked out into the bright sunshine. He shielded his eyes against the sun's glare and immediately assessed the situation. He could hear his men express their pleasure at being freed as each one exited the old fort behind him. Squinting, Cam turned his attention toward a large gathering of his armed warriors. He watched Sir Alexander mount his horse, then his gaze was drawn to his cousin Malcolm who was standing next to a wagon talking to a lady.

That must be Angel...Lady Adriana. So struck by her beauty, his breath caught in his throat. She looked so very regal dressed in a gold traveling gown, which she filled out quite nicely. He could not help but notice that her breasts were large and round, and close to overflowing her bodice. He remembered her breasts had been small, barely filling his palm, and now her breast appeared much larger. The realization that she might be with child hit him like a bucket of chilly water, causing him to stagger backwards a step. When? And by whom?

Then she turned her head, and her gaze found his. Her steely brown eyes held him spellbound. Cam felt weak and he almost dropped to his knees. She was the loveliest creature he had ever seen. If only he were closer so he could observe every little detail. She was far enough away that he could not ascertain her expression. The moment lasted only a second, but when he took a step toward her, she quickly glanced away. He stopped. Had she been disgusted by his ragged appearance? It had been weeks since he had bathed, shaved, or had fresh clothes to don. He must bring to mind the likes of a beggar. Cam groaned. As if punched in the stomach, his shoulders slumped forward, and his arms dropped to his sides. He wasn't worthy of her attention let alone her love or respect, especially after sending her away.

When Cam glanced up and witnessed his wife and cousin exchange intimate smiles, his self-pity quickly turned to anger. Malcolm helped her onto the wagon. Once she was properly seated, she leaned forward, touched his arm, and spoke softly to him.

Malcolm nodded his head, turned, and instructed two of Cam's men, who quickly walked off to do his bidding. He then turned and walked toward Cam. He appeared very comfortable in his laird's role. It would not end well for Malcolm if he'd been the one dreaming of taking Cam's place as chieftain—and more. Hugh and the rest of his men closed in around Cam.

"What do ye think she could hae said to the colonel to acquire our release?" Hugh asked.

Cam shook his head, not knowing how to answer Hugh's question. Although he had no answer as to how their release had been arranged, Cam had a feeling Malcolm played the role of confidant and advisor to his Lady-wife, Lady Adriana.

A broad smile crossed Malcolm's face as he drew closer to Cam. Malcolm bowed to Cam, clasped his arm then pulled him in for a hug. "'Tis wonderful to see ye all. I feared we wouldnae make the trip here in time to save ye." Malcolm greeted each of the men, when he turned back to Cam, Cam growled, "What is she doing here? 'Tis too dangerous for her to travel so far."

His cousin clasped his shoulder and said, "A wagon loaded with food, water, and blankets awaits to take ye all back to Corell Castle." Malcolm pointed to the wagon and the large group of warriors waiting to escort them. The men scurried to the wagon, crawled in, and opened the baskets of food. Walking past Malcolm, Cam stated, "I shall ride." Hugh echoed his request as he followed Cam. They were given food and water, and three horses were quickly brought forward.

Malcolm rode to Cam's right, Hugh to his left. They rode in silence the first day. There were many questions Cam wanted to ask Malcolm, but one in particular practically blinded him. Did he think Angel would come back to him? Cam had not missed how Malcolm behaved around Angel and he didn't like it. Was there something between them and if so, what did it mean.

Fear whispered in his ear that the child could be Malcolm's. If that were true, his cousin would feel the edge of his sword.

The wagon lumbered along the stone covered dirt road. Adriana's father persisted to talk none-stop to the poor men riding beside him, taking all the credit for getting Cam and his men released. As he commented on how bad the imprisoned men looked, Adriana felt sick. She had been shocked when Cam walked out of the fort encrusted in a layer of mud. There appeared to be new bruises on his cheek and arm, and a large cut on his chin. All these weeks she'd longed to see him again. Wishing for a chance to talk with him. Ask him why he pushed her away after all the time they had spent together as husband and wife.

She sighed. There was truly no need for explanations. He no longer wanted her. So, she had fought against her instinct to run to him and attend to his injuries. Instead, she forced herself to stay seated in the wagon.

Then she realized this was the first time he had seen her. Self-consciously she stroked her hands over her wind-blown hair, tucking loose strands back into place. She must look terrible. She attempted to brush the dust from her wrinkled skirts. But then her hand shot up to the old scar that ran along side of her face. Had he been close enough to see it? Her fingers skimmed over the rough, raised edge. No, he'd been too far away to see the disfiguring mark. It no longer mattered if he saw it now or not. There was only one thing she needed to concern herself with him seeing. The baby. Had he noticed the weight she'd gained since returning home? Would he figure out that she was with child, that she carried his heir? Would he come for the baby once it was born? She placed a protective hand over the small rise in her belly.

The baby was hers until its birth, then he would take it away...but only if he could find it.

Nineteen

C am leaned back in the chair and stared through the grate at the dancing red, orange, and yellow flames. He'd spent a good portion of the day in the library working on a stack of overdue correspondence and his body ached from sitting and no physical activity. He had hoped the paperwork would have demand all his attention and kept him too busy to think about his wife and her condition. Although a brilliant idea, the plan hadn't taken hold. Like a dog with a great bone, he couldn't put the exchange he had witnessed between Angel and his cousin Malcolm out of his mind. And now, since he returned to Corell Castle, whenever he encountered Malcolm, he wanted to confront the man about their true relationship. Except deep in his soul, Cam wasn't sure he wanted to know the truth. His temples throbbed.

A soft knock came on the library door. "Come in," Cam called.

His steward poked his head around the thick wooden door and said, "Milaird, I hate to disturb ye, but if ye hae a moment I do wish to speak with ye on a couple of important issues."

"Aye, Mr. Pembroke, ye may enter."

Good, a distraction was just what he needed.

The timid man slowly approached the large old desk, which had been in the same position in the library for as long as Cam could remember.

"What do ye wish from me," Cam inquired, staring up into the man's milky-gray eyes.

"Weel, I do wonder aboot this year's crops. What yer thoughts are concerning how the fields fared with the amount of rain we have received this summer. And now with the fires claiming the field by the river and the one east of the large meadow."

Cam scratched his new growth of beard and noticed the older man's empty hands. "Bring me all the reports from the crofters as soon as ye receive them and we'll inspect them."

"Aye, Milaird." The man nodded his head then added, "And I'm wondering if ye hae any idea what the upcoming market prices on grain and cattle might be this season?"

Cam had an idea what the prices were going to be, except his concerns lay with the poor crofters and the loss of animals and crops. His aspirations were in catching the band of raiders before they killed again or caused more damage to the remaining fields. As far as the rain, it had been a much-needed blessing, that helped extinguish many of the fires. The notion of how much damage the rain could possibly cause the lower fields had never crossed his mind.

There came another knock at his door, and before Cam could reply the door swung open. Maddy the cook stood with her fists perched on her ample hips. The front of her apron, waistcoat, and face, appeared to be covered in finely milled flour and small twigs and leaves of fresh herbs stuck out from her hair. "Milaird," she said, marching into the room. "'Tis sorry I am for busting in on ye, but I cannae take this any longer."

Not sure he wanted to know what her problem was other than an obvious unpleasant incident with some bread flour,

Cam sighed and asked, "What might ye be trying to tell me, lassie?" He knew by calling the older woman, *lassie*, the endearment would take the starch out of her underskirts.

Maddy, who was nearly as round as she was tall, closed her eyes and exhaled a long breath. When she opened them, they twinkled with mischief, and she grinned. "I am sorry milaird."

"Aye. I know ye are. Just speak what's on yer mind."

"I am happy to watch over the castle when yer gone, and I am sorry for yer troubles, milaird. But now that yer back... The work, 'tis too much for me along with my regular daily duties. I have added extra lads in the kitchen, but as ye can see," she flapped her arms down to her sides and sent up a cloud of white powder all around her, "Isnae going weel," she added with a slight tilt of her head.

Cam rubbed his hand down over his mustache and beard hoping to wipe away the grin he felt forthcoming. Maddy had been the castles' cook for many years and she held a special spot in his heart. He would be most unhappy if she became so dismayed that she left the castle.

"When might Lady Adriana or Lady Moira be returning," she asked, interrupting his thoughts.

The pounding in Cam's head intensified, traveling from his temples down and around to the back of his neck. Closing his eyes, he rolled his head hoping to relieve the building tension.

"I can make do for a while milaird... I will inquire in the village if there be a woman interested in helping me." Maddy stood unmoving waiting for his answer. He doubted Angel would ever return to him after the way she had recoiled from him at the fort. Waiting patiently for his response, Maddy swiped the back of her hand across the tip of her nose. What answer could he give her when he had none for himself?

Another knock sounded upon Cam's door. Without waiting for permission to enter, the door swung open, and Malcolm hastened up to Cam's desk. Cam straightened in his chair and glowered at his cousin and growled, "What do ye want?" Wringing her hands before her, Maddy gave a quick curtsy and backed out of the room, Mr. Pembrook scurried out behind her and quietly closed the door.

Malcolm stood straight, feet together, his arms stiff at his sides in a military manner. He stared straight ahead at the wall just to the left of Cam's head.

"What 'tis the meaning of forcing yer way in here without my permission to enter, Captain Haywood? Do ye hae important news to report to yer Laird and Chieftain?"

His cousin's nostrils flared as he drew in a deep breath. He exhaled and said, "I hae no news aboot the raiders to report today. I am here to inform ye within the hour a small troop of soldiers and I will be departing for Shealoch Castle."

"And now, ye no longer require *my* approval to take *my* warriors from *my* castle?"

Malcolm's back appeared to stiffen even more. "'Tis urgent that I return to Shealoch Castle straightaway, milaird."

"Oh. Aye. And what might ye be thinking 'tis so important ye feel 'tis necessary for ye to be there and not here where ye belong," Cam growled. He knew who waited for his cousin along the south border. Cam told himself he could not fetch Lady Adriana because he'd been away for so long, there were important matters here that needed his immediate attention. Not that he feared being rejected by her a second time. The taste of failure and self-doubt were bitter on his tongue, enraging him. Cam came to his feet, leaned forward, and slammed his palms down on the desk. The loud bang exploded like a pistol shot. "And what might I ask—makes ye feel the need to run off to Shealoch Castle?" He glared at Malcolm, daring his cousin to speak his wife's name.

Malcolm shifted his weight from one foot to the other, then cleared his throat and finally spoke. "My presence is required... o protect Lady Adriana, milaird."

"Protect her from whom or what?" Cam asked, leaning further over the desk toward the man. What sort of danger might befall his wife?

"From her father." Malcolm pinned Cam with a glare. "Sir Alexander possesses a sharp tongue and a fierce hand."

The severity of Malcolm's words brought Cam up straight. Why hadn't she spoken to him about this? Had she done things to displease the baronet? Had she been a troubled and unruly child? "Captain Haywood, this is not yer assignment, so why do ye feel obligated to protect her?"

"She is my Laird's Lady wife. A guardian should be at her side at all times to protect her from any and all forms of danger."

They stared at each other for several moments. Cam knew his cousin well enough to know that Malcolm held honor and responsibility to the clan above all else. And if he could not be there to protect his wife, then he would have sent Malcolm.

As if reading his thoughts, Malcolm bowed, turned, and left the library. Cam crossed to the hearth and stared into the flames. His head fought to ignore the pain deep in his chest. She was not just his *Lady wife*, she was Angel. His brave, beautiful, and passionate, Faceless Angel.

Cam made his way down to the great hall in hopes of finding Hugh with an updated report from his patrols, but the hall was empty. He sulked over the fact that Angel had ridden all the way to Fort Inverlochy to save his life and have him released from prison, to then just turn her back on him and ride away without a word.

Storming out of the hall, the lad Kinny who did not appear to be paying attention to where he was going, ran into Cam. Although the lad had seen to Cam's needs and wounds when he returned, he had not been friendly or personable like he had before Cam sent Angel away.

Grabbing the boy by the arms, Cam asked, "So, do ye have a

bee in yer bonnet today, lad? What has got ye rushing around and avoiding me?" He knew the lad was missing his mistress.

Kinny stopped and stared at Cam. "Nay, milaird." Not waiting for a response, Kinny bowed and stormed off.

"What's got him so upset?" Hugh inquired from behind Cam.

"Och, like everyone else around here, the lad's missing his mistress." He threw his hands up into the air and added, "The whole damn place is carrying on and morning as if the lass were dead."

"Aye. I hae overheard the servants saying much the same. Are ye fixing to fetch her back?"

"The lass made her choice when she rode away and returned to her father's estate." Cam shot Hugh a knowing glance. "She doesna want me or to be here. Besides Malcolm has appointed himself her protector. I would think he has already left."

Hugh's long dark hair brushed across his shoulders as he shook his head. "Hae ye asked yer lady wife *what* she wants? 'Tis obvious ye would like the lass to come back to ye."

Cam crossed to the window and glanced out; his mind filled with the vision of Angel and the moment she'd spotted him. Then the image of Malcolm's hands touching her as he helped her up onto the wagon. Another image entered his mind, of Cam running his cousin through with his broadsword.

Mayhap he should retrieve the lass and bring her back. Surely, she would come willingly. Once she returned and was at his side where she belonged, life at Corell Castle would be restored to its well-ordered routine.

Adriana stood before the bank of windows in her mother's old chambers, which she now called her own. The lovely morning sky was painted in streaks of soft pink, purple, yellow, and orange, which harmonized with the white fluffy clouds. She could see for miles across the flat terrain of her father's land. Though it was a picturesque sunrise, she missed the rolling hills and scotch pines, which stood tall and proud in the distance from Castle Corell.

Wrapping her arms around herself for more comfort than warmth, her conversation with Malcolm the previous day reiterated in her head. When she had heard he had returned, she'd gone straight to him to find out how Laird MacCormac was faring. She worried he hadn't been eating enough and had been working himself too hard since he'd returned home. Plus, she agonized over his wounds and if they were being tended to and healing properly. Although Malcolm had reassured her Laird MacCormac was progressing well, she couldn't help fretting about him. He had appeared so thin and battered when he walked out of the fort, it tore at her heart. It had taken all of her restraint not to go to him, comfort him and tend to his wounds. But she hadn't felt ready to let him see her face or know she carried his heir. When she saw the look in his eyes, that revealed he'd noted the extra weight she'd put on, a shiver slithered up her spine.

He knows I am with child.

A knock sounded on her door and Bethany entered the chambers carrying a small tray.

"Good morning. I am pleased yer up and looking so well." Bethany placed the tray on the table. Adriana glanced at the plate filled with fruit, warm, crusted buttered bread, and a small bowl of porridge. Her stomach tightened at the thought of eating only to run to her chamber pot and cast it back up.

Bethany crossed to Adriana and took her hand in hers. "Ye are feeling well—are ye not, milady?"

Adriana forced a smile. "I'm concerned about the baby and how everything will change yet again after it's born."

"All will be fine milady. I will be here to help ye when 'tis time for the birthing, and here afterwords for anything ye might need. Bethany patted Adriana's hand. "All will be weel. Laird MacCormac will come to his senses and arrive to take ye and the baby home."

She feared that after he saw her face, the only reason he would want her to return with him was because he knew she was carrying his heir. But what would happen to her after the child was born. Would he send her away, cast her out or... kill her.

Adriana's hand went protectively to her belly. "That's the part the worries me the most."

Twenty

After camping for the night in the nearby woods, Cam, two hundred of his elite warriors, and their traveling party, approached Shealoch Castle. A lone sentry sounded a horn with one long low tone, announcing their arrival.

Cam and Hugh, accompanied by young Kinny who insisted he come along to attend his laird, led two dozen horsemen carrying flags representing Corell Castle and Clan MacCormac, through the main gate. The rest of his warriors remained mounted and awaited further instructions outside the wall. The walled-in structure appeared more like a large manor house with one tower attached to the original keep, than a castle.

The surprised expressions on the people milling around and working in the bailey reinforced Cam's suspicion that they were not expecting him. He was both anxious and leery about finally coming face to face with Angel for the first time, in the light of day. If only he had been close enough to see her face the day, she and Sir Alexander arrived at the fort to speak to the colonel on his behalf. He had dreamed of being able to gaze upon her loveliness since the night he awoke and found her sensually perched upon him. With her standing over by the wagon, she had been too far away for him to see her face clearly or comprehend her expression. And when she abruptly turned from him and rode away with her father and his men, it was clear she didn't want anything other than see him, and his men freed.

He anticipated her return to Corell Castle, except she'd chosen to stay away. Unable to accept his loss, Cam chose to go and reclaim her. Who was going to stop him and two hundred warriors from retrieving his wife and taking her back to where she belonged?

A tall thin man, Cam guessed to be in his forties with broad shoulders and gray hair strolled out of a building toward him. One side of the older man's mouth hiked up in a lopsided grin. Several young lads raced forward to attend to the horses. "Laird MacCormac," the man said, holding Cam's gaze. "I am Captain Balfour. Captain Haywood said you wouldn't be far behind him."

Cam dismounted, as did Hugh and Kinny. Turning, Cam handed Kinny his reins, wherein, he watched Kinny hand them off to the waiting lads. Cam inhaled deeply and scanned the area with a mixture of curiosity and suspicion. He realized he didn't like the idea that they had expected his appearance. His cousin Malcolm was due for a talking to, amongst other things.

Captain Balfour gestured toward the keep. "Follow me. Sir Alexander has been anticipating your arrival." When he turned to follow the captain, Cam noticed Hugh shaking his head. Turning further, he found Kinny was right on his heels. The boy's head twisted from one side to the other, taking in as much of his surroundings as he could. If Cam stopped abruptly, the lad no doubt would ride right up on him.

Weel, the lad wanted adventure. He just may end up with more than he'd gambled for.

Captain Balfour led the trio into a great hall where he spoke to a servant who hurried off to do his bidding. Cam turned to find Hugh and Kinny taking in the magnificent hall, like himself. Although the great hall at Corell Castle was much larger and held an immense collection of ancient weapons, this hall had beautiful tapestries hung on the stone walls, clean stone floors, a warm wood fire roared in the huge hearth, and all the tables appeared to be rather new.

"Jesus, Mary and Joseph," Kinny exclaimed barely above a whisper.

Clearing his throat, Cam murmured, "Donnae be so obvious lad."

Kinny snapped his gaping mouth shut and sank down onto a bench by a long table.

Cam turned his attention back to Captain Balfour, who stood stately with a glint of pride in his eyes. A serving lad appeared with a tray and offered them each a glass of brandy. Balfour gestured toward a table and said, "Please be seated. Sir Alexander will join us momentarily." Cam and Hugh settled on the bench across from Kinny, and Balfour sat at the end of the table. Cam wondered as to why the baronet would greet them when it was Lady Adriana he wished to see. He opened his mouth to voice his request when a vision appeared in the archway. The lass was fashioned in a day dress of burnt orange, goldenrod, and chestnut brown. Her flaxen hair was stylishly pulled up onto her head with several curls hanging down to frame her beautiful face. With her sky-blue eyes and dove white skin, she was a vision of loveliness. Cam assumed her to be the daughter that had been promised to him.

They all shot to their feet.

Kinny coughed on his brandy and stepped backwards, almost falling over the bench. Cam reached across the table, grabbed him by the scruff of the neck, and held him up.

Hugh muttered, "Jesus, Mary and Joseph."

Cam agreed with his cousin's comment, yet replied, "Donnae be so obvious...*lad*."

Her smile was pure sunshine. She floated into the room, stopping in front of Cam, and curtsied. "Lord MacCormac. You are most welcome to Shealoch Castle. It is so very nice to finally meet you."

Balfour stepped forward. Lord MacCormac it is my pleasure to present Lady Lynette, the jewel of Shealoch Castle."

Cam bowed his head. "'Tis verra nice to make yer acquaintance, Lady Lynette. Ye are truly a rare gem. Yer sire must be quite pleased with ye." Someone cleared his throat behind him. Cam suppressed a grin and stepped to the side. "May I introduce my cousin Hugh MacCormac." As Hugh bowed and voiced his pleasure in meeting the girl, out of the corner of his eye, Cam caught the tall gangly carrot head standing behind him. When Lady Lynette faced Cam once again, he said, "And this is... My man." Speechless, the poor lad's face reddened, and after a moment he came to his senses and bowed.

Cam stepped away from Lady Lynette and the others who were now vying for her attention. He rubbed at the sudden ache on the back of his neck. Had Angel been told that he had arrived? What if she refused to see him? Resting his hand on the hilt of his sword, Cam returned to his glass of brandy on the table and finished it off. The situation could easily turn ugly if he wasn't informed presently as to his wife's whereabouts. His glass clanked hard against the table when he set it back down. He swiped his arm across his mouth. Cam rounded the table to face Captain Balfour, ready to order the man to fetch Angel and bring her to him. But then, an unmistakable laugh came from the corridor, and he turned. She entered the hall on Malcolm's arm, and her laughter died the moment she spotted him.

He could not breathe. Could not even move, for her presence was so overwhelming. Hypnotized by her intense stare Cam gazed into large round brown eyes. Her brown hair was fashioned off to one side of her face and pulled back and he could almost feel the long curls flowing through his fingers like silk ribbons. She was striking in the light pink and ruby day dress, with her large breasts threatening to overflow the close-fitting bodice. He did not like the way she clung to Malcolm's side like a frightened child. He wanted to rush to her, take her in his arms, except she appeared skittish, and he feared she might turn and fly away.

Pulling himself together, Cam slowly strolled across the room and prayed he would not distress her. He stopped in front of Angel, nodded his head, and said, "Lady Adriana."

"Lord MacCormac." The sound of her sweet voice caused every little hair on his body to stand on end.

"Might I speak with ye in private, milady?"

Hesitantly, Angel glanced up at Malcolm. He patted her hand and released her. She turned and led Cam out of the great hall. Her familiar scent engulfed him as they crossed the hall and entered a small, more private chamber. Cam closed the door.

Angel drifted further into the quaint little sitting room, trying to put as much distance between them as she could. When she turned to face him, she raised her chin with the slightest hint of defiance. With the light coming in through the large windows, she knew the moment that he had noticed the old scar that ran along the right side of her face. His brow pulled together with concern. He reached out his hand, but before he could touch her, she sidestepped out of reach. Twirling away, she traced the mark with her fingertips.

"Does it still bother ye," he asked, coming to her side.

"No. It is really nothing for you to worry about. It happened a long time ago. What might I help you with my lord."

"I am here to thank ye for whatever ye did and said that prevented my men and I from hanging. T'was quite surprise when I learned we were pardoned and free to go. Then when I walked out of the fort, I saw ye and yer father and the many men ye brought with ye. Yer a smart lass, ye are."

Angel nodded her head and smiled slightly. "When the shocking news from Colonial Stone arrived stating that you were arrested for murder and treason, I knew it was absurd. We had to do something to get you and your men released."

"Weel, I'm pleased to have such a resourceful and clever wife." When she looked away, he added, "I have come to bring ye back to Corell Castle where ye belong, lass." She wrung her hands, then moved away from him. "I feel it would be best for ye and..." He stammered. "If ye were settled... Where ye will be safe and weel looked after afore the cold and snow comes."

She contemplated his words before she turned and wandered over to the fireplace.

"Ye will be better taken care of at Corell Castle than ye would be here under yer father's care. Yer sister is welcome to accompany ye if ye wished it."

At the mention of her sister, Adriana faced him and smiled. "Truly, Lynette may come with us back to Corell Castle?"

"Whoever ye want. If ye need to bring extra servants, ye may. Whatever ye wish—Angel."

When she heard his endearment for her, she froze. What did it mean? Did he want her as a wife, even after he had seen her face? "Thank you, my lord," she said just above a whisper.

"Ye may call me Cameron when we are alone," he said, stepping toward her. "I will camp with my men outside the main gate tonight. We will leave tomorrow when ye hae finished packing."

She nodded her head, "Thank you, Cameron."

Cam followed his wife back across the hall. He took immense joy in knowing he had made her happy when he'd called her Angel. Her blush even matched her gown. She was so lovely. He had almost gathered her in his arms. He needed to feel for himself that she and her baby were all right.

Although, he wondered as to why she did not mention she was with child. She also kept moving away from him as if he had laid an unkind hand on her. Malcolm had mentioned her father had a cruel and heavy hand. The mere thought of Sir Alexander laying a hand on Angel sent him into an internal rage. He drew in a deep breath then released it slowly. All would be well once they returned to the Highland. Still, they had much to discuss.

~

Adriana paced around her bedchambers in Corell Castle. Since arriving, Lynette and Penny had taken to investigating the oldest parts of the castle, and Adriana hadn't seen much of either of them.

Her husband, Cameron on the other hand, had dismissed Captain Haywood as her bodyguard, sending him out with the other soldiers on patrol. Adriana didn't mind though; the man had become overly protective of her. Cameron had replaced Malcolm with himself, which hadn't been much change relating to her privacy. He turned out to be even more vigilant than the captain.

Everything had changed this time. Before, when she first arrived, her main concern had been to tend to her husband's wounds, and to help in the kitchen and gardens. But now, the maids and Maddy the cook, must have guessed she was with child because they were all fussing over her and treating her as if she were a royal visitor. Maddy even went as far as to personally come to Adriana's room to inquire what she would like to eat, which was nice, but the older woman no longer welcomed her help in the kitchen or in the gardens.

The sun gleamed in the sky, and she longed to be outside, to take a walk around the inner bailey. She knew Cameron loomed on the other side of her door, and perhaps he would escort her on her stroll. Being close to him still overwhelmed and intimidated her.

On their return trip to Corell Castle, he exhibited his duties as Laird MacCormac. With his hair loose around his shoulders, his face shadowed in dark whiskers, and astride his enormous destroyer, the legend of the Black Giant came to life. He rode the line and roared orders to his men. He oversaw the supply wagons, and periodically stopped by her wagon to check on her wellbeing. His men respectfully did his bidding and their journey commenced smoothly, allowing them to arrive in a timely manner. Speaking with him in the daylight seemed very strange. For some reason she had more confidence lying in his arms in the dark than standing next to him in the daylight where he could see her scar and judge her.

She crossed to the window and glanced out over the inner bailey. Her thoughts drifted back to the day before when the sound of several horns in the distance announced their arrival at Corell Castle. When the wagon she'd been placed upon entered the main gate, she noticed that the riders who entered before them had dismounted and were now lined up on either side of the road along with many of the other castle inhabitants. The bailey had grown eerily silent. As her wagon passed the women curtsied, the MacCormac men and warriors, bowed. At the time, she had thought everyone's behavior was a reaction to their laird's return, but after the way she was being treated, she wondered if the strange attention hadn't been for her.

Adriana's attention was drawn to the people below as they hurried around the bailey setting up tables and stacking piles of sticks and logs. Everyone seemed jovial as if they anxiously anticipated some type of party. Whatever the celebration, it was warm enough outside for her to enjoy a stroll around the inner bailey. Drawing in a deep breath, Adriana grabbed her shawl, opened the door, and strolled out into the cool corridor. Her husband stood partially leaning against the wall, his arms crossed over his wide chest. His long black mane was pulled back and tied, he had even taken the time to shave his face and neck that morning.

He raised one bushy black brow. "I wondered if ye were planning to hide out in yer chambers all day," he murmured. His low smooth voice caressed her, sending little shivers up her spine.

She pulled her wrap tighter around her shoulders, and said, "There is no need for you to wait by my door. I am sure you are kept informed of my every movement." She started toward the steps.

He stepped up beside her. "Ye are correct. My staff does keep me informed of what goes on in my absence."

"How convenient for you." She shot him a sideways glance. "I will save them the trouble of reporting my behavior to you this morning. I plan on meandering around the inner bailey. That is with your permission, my lord."

Both black brows rose as he tilted his head to the side and observed her. "Ye do not need my permission, lass. My concern is for yer safety. Until the band of murderers are caught, 'tis not safe for ye to roam around unescorted. So, I will stroll along with ye... With yer permission, milady."

She sighed and continued to walk. Did he expect she would flee? Where could she go? He slowed his long stride to match hers as they walked. She felt intimidated by his presence. Her greatest fear was what the future held for her. Would he let her stay here in Corell Castle after she gave birth or would he send her away?

They met two young maids carrying wash pails in the corridor. Though the girls were in a hurry, they stopped and curtsied, then rushed off. "Everyone in the castle is preparing for Hogmanay," Cam said. "'Tis a tradition which takes place the last week of the year. It includes cleaning the castle from top to bottom."

Adriana had heard of the Highland tradition, though she did not know much about it. "Everyone is also required to pay their debts before 'the bells' sound at midnight on the last day of the year," he continued. "This permits everyone to start the new year fresh and clear of debt." They descended the stone stairs to the main floor, and she wondered what would happen to a poor soul who could not pay off his debts. As they approached the large wooden door that led outside, she turned to ask him, but before she could, he said, "There is another very important tradition. 'Tis called the 'First Foot'." He pulled the heavy wooden door open and held it allowing her to walk through it. "To ensure good luck, a dark-haired mon, like myself," he smiled and winked, "offering gifts of coal, salt, and whisky ought to be the first to enter yer hoose after midnight."

Adriana turned her head toward him. "What happens if the first person to enter is not a dark-haired man, but perhaps a woman?"

"Och." He frowned seriously and rubbed his jaw. "A woman, ye say? Ah, that could cause all sorts of terrible problems for the poor mon of the hoose." He grinned and winked again. Was he flirting with her? She turned away and hurried outside and into the bright sunshine and cool crisp air, which worked as a balm to her aching spirit.

To the right, smoke from a spit swirled up toward the sky and she caught the scent of a succulent pig roasting. A mixture of odors from the ale house, forge, and others she could not name filled the air. It was glorious. "Thank you for permitting me to leave the keep," she said still avoiding his gaze. "Being in the fresh air and in the bright sun is a wonderful gift."

"Ye are not chilled, then?" he asked.

"Oh no. I love being outside. I used to walk the grounds at Shealoch each day. It seemed the gardens always needed something trimmed, picked, or turned over."

"Ye enjoy gardening?"

"Oh, yes. But since I have returned here, Maddy will not let me out into the gardens." The instant the words left her mouth she wished them back. Stopping, Adriana turned to face him. "Oh, milord, I did not mean to speak unkindly. Maddy does mean well."

He smiled down at her, a strange expression on his face. "I will speak with her so that she will let ye do as ye wish, but only if ye promise to be careful and not over tax yerself."

"Thank you, milord."

"Cameron," he said, softly.

"Cameron," she repeated and grinned. "I do appreciate that. And I promise to be most cautious."

He nodded his head in agreement, then offered his arm. Adriana studied him for a moment, before sliding her hand under his elbow. They walked by the ale house; chickens pecked the ground for bugs and at crusts of bread someone had thrown out for them. As he guided her around a huge tree, he said, "When my grandfather was a lad, he planted this tree. 'Tis a caorunn tree," he said with a hard 'k' sound. "'Tis said it will bring ye bad luck if ye chop it down."

She didn't comment, she wasn't sure if he was teasing her.

He added, "'Tis a symbol of great strength and protection."

"Well, Corell Castle and its people have great strength, and they are well protected here. So, your statement must be true."

His chest rose with pride. Then he said, "Would ye join me this evening, Angel, to watch the bonfires?"

They paused at the bottom step to the keep. She glanced up into his dark eyes. She had prayed for them to go back to the way they were before he'd sent her away. It thrilled her that he wanted to be with her, but she had so many misgivings about their relationship. But then she heard herself say, yes.

"Very good," he said, taking her by the elbow, he helped her up the steps into the keep. "Ye must rest now, for ye will be needing yer strength. The celebration can go on weel into the morning hours."

Instantly, she was nervous. What would she do if he wanted to be alone with her? She no longer had the body of a girl, but that of a woman with child. Then she remembered Penny saying that men were not bothered by their wife being with child, that some even enjoyed it. Cameron departed at the entry to the great hall, saying he looked forward to the evening.

Adriana's mind filled with questions as she climbed the stairs to her chambers. She wondered why he had not mentioned his baby or her scar. And he hadn't revealed his reason for sending her back to her father. Would he explain everything to her this evening when they were alone? Or could his friendliness be a ploy to gain her trust, only to be disposed of after his child is born?

Twenty-One

C am stood by Hugh next to a small bonfire in front of the ale house. He took a long drink from his mug, and then stared into the flames. Earlier that afternoon after their walk, Cam had posted Kinny outside of Angel's door, but when he questioned the lad later, he reported she had never ventured from her room. Was she avoiding him? Would she present herself for the evening's Hogmanay festivities as she had promised?

Did she fear he would punish her for carrying a child that wasn't his? He hadn't the time to dwell on that misfortune. What mattered most was that the child was a MacCormac, and Cam would continue to rule and hold the clan together. He'd already decided if she agreed to return to him as his lady wife, he would accept the child and raise it as his heir. He had no other choice; he didn't want the clan to divide and fight against each other to choose the next chieftain. Cam needed to find a way to convince Angel to come back to him as his lady wife and mistress of his keep. But how the Bloody Hell was he supposed to do that?

"'Tis there something wrong with yer ale," Hugh asked, sniffing his own mug, then taking a cautious sip. "Mine is fine."

Cam glanced down at his half empty mug, and growled, "Nae, 'tis fine."

"Then why do ye make such a face, as if ye spotted a toad in yer ale?"

"Och, I've a notion my lady wife doesna wish to remain married to me. I fear she wishes to be with another."

Scratching his head, Hugh glanced around then asked, "What do ye propose to do? Mayhap we should hunt this mon down and beat him till he sees the mistake he's made."

Cam shook his head. He wished he knew how he could transform their lives back to when she openly came to him as his loving faceless angel. She had saved him from certain death and had given him back his life. Now he couldn't live without her. "I am not sure what I should do." Cam collected his thoughts and glanced up at his cousin.

Over Hugh's shoulder he saw Angel and her sister exit the keep and start down the steps. She looked regal in a dark green cloak, the white fur trim around her hood framed her lovely face. Hugh's gaze followed Cam's. They both stared. Then, as if out of nowhere, Kinny bounded up the steps and produced a modest bouquet of freshly cut flowers, likely from the conservatory. He nodded and presented Lynette with the flowers. The lass grinned shyly and accepted the bouquet. She turned and spoke briefly to her sister then sailed away on Kinny's arm.

Angel stood alone on the steps and gazed out over the scene before her. She clasped her hands together and glanced around as if pondering whether to proceed down the last step or return inside to the safety of her bedchamber.

He watched her rake her teeth over her lower lip. The pure innocence of the act triggered a response from, what had she called it, 'wee willie'? "Looks like ye should be taking lessons on how to woo yer lass back, from the long-legged, red-headed-one," Hugh remarked. He snickered, slapped Cam on the back and shuffled away.

Cam banged his mug down on the table. He gnashed his teeth and growled like an angry dog. From under the huge caorunn tree he formulated his strategy on how to approach his lady. Not wanting to miss an opportunity to be alone with her, he traipsed across the bailey. Damn, why hadn't *he* thought to bring her flowers? The thought crossed his mind even though he knew the answer. Although years had passed, he still avoided passing by Blair's favorite area of the castle. He approached Angel, who stood on the last step which brought her almost eye level to him. Cam stopped in front of her. He had longed for a moment like this. He'd wanted to gaze into those eyes and read her thoughts, her dreams, and her desires, except what he saw in those big round brown eyes right now was uncertainty.

Tilting his head somewhat, he said, "Good evening, milady." He presented his hand to help her down the last step.

"Good evening, milord." She placed her gloved hand in his and took that last step.

"Ye look lovely. Are ye certain yer dressed warm enough? Even though 'tis not as damp as most years, there is still a chill in the air this evening."

She smiled shyly, opened her cape to reveal her heavy gray wool skirt, then lifted her hem and showed him her walking boots. "I think I will be comfortable, but if I get chilled, I will stand closer to the fire."

Nodding, he offered his arm, and she slipped her hand around it. Cam placed his hand over hers and steered her along the worn path. A strong sense of pride and contentment washed over him with her by his side. He hadn't realized how lost and incomplete he'd been before she entered his life. He never thought to feel this way again. "I hope ye've been feeling weel." He glanced down at her stomach, then rebuked himself and hoped she hadn't noticed.

"I followed your advice and took a long nap this afternoon so I would be refreshed for this evening."

"Good, lass. Ye must be hungry then. Do ye wish something to eat or drink." They strolled around the inner bailey amongst the others who were celebrating Hogmanay. People stepped aside, smiled, and bowed and curtsied as they approached. After a moment Cam slid her hand down his arm intending to hold it in his. Except Angel gently pulled her hand away. She lowered her hood and clutched her hands before her.

Caught off guard by her beauty, Cam cleared his throat and stopped next to a table. "Would ye care for a cup of mulled wine or ale, Angel?"

She shot him a surprised stare, paused for a moment, then nodded her head. "Mulled wine, please."

He was handed a large mug of ale and a small cup of mulled wine. Smiling, he handed her the warm cup. "Thank you, milord."

"I thought we agreed ye would call me Cameron in private."

Glancing around at the many people who scurried about, she giggled. "I do not consider our surroundings exactly *private*, milord." She sipped her wine, her gaze never leaving his.

The sound of her amusement was heavenly to Cam. It was a sound he feared he would never hear again. "It gives me great joy, lass, to hear yer laugh again."

She turned away shyly and returned to their walk. "I have a gift for ye," Cam said, reaching her side in one long stride. Angel stopped and stared at him. "'Tis not on my person, but in yer bed chambers." Her eyes widened and her cheeks turned delightfully red. Was it caused by the warm, mulled wine or the thought of them alone together, in her bed chambers? He feared by the look of panic on Angel's face that she might take flight, leaving him forever. "'Tis my mum's harp. The one in yer room. I would like for it to be truly yers. The lovely toons ye play, 'tis as if a true angel held the blessed instrument in its hands. No one has ever made the harp sound more heavenly then ye do."

She stared as if in disbelief for a moment. "Thank you, milord. It is a gracious gift indeed. I will treasure it for as long... Forever." She bestowed a sweet smile upon him, then said, "earlier today I witnessed another group of soldiers leaving the keep. Will they be gone long?"

"Aye. Each time one group returns, another is sent out to replace them." Had her interest and concern been genuinely for his people, or had she only been inquiring about her lover, Malcolm? The thought of Angel's attention going to his cousin instead of himself aggravated him. He'd been a blithering fool for thinking he could persuade her to consider coming back to him. He shouldn't be surprised that she favored Malcolm. His cousin was younger, with no visible scars, pleasing enough to look upon, and had better manners than most.

Obviously, she hadn't been pleased with the husband, she herself had schemed to wed. She hadn't wasted any time in changing his appearance. She'd chopped off his hair and shaved his face, she had also seen the many scars his body possessed. Had her plan been to get with his child, and if that hadn't happened, she'd find another to fulfill her wish? Did she intend to pass the child off as his heir? She must not have realized he would figure out her scheme.

Uproarious laughter surrounded them, though Cam no longer felt inclined to celebrate. He steered Angel back toward the steps leading up into the keep. "'Tis late and growing colder. Best ye go inside and find yer bed."

"Oh! Yes." She glanced up at him, yet Cam glanced away. "Good evening to you then, milord." He watched as she turned and climbed the wide stone steps.

"Yer stroll with yer lady wife went weel?" Hugh asked, coming up next to Cam and clasping him on the shoulder. "Though ye look as if ye could use a mug of ale."

"'Tis something much stronger than ale I'm afraid I'm needing," Cam murmured as he let Hugh drag him into the midst of the crowd. His cousin could easily persuade him into fighting someone now.

'Tis fruitless to keep dogging her trail, and time I join in the search for the band of killers no matter how long it takes.

Adriana awoke like every other morning with Cameron on her mind. Rolling onto her side she punched her pillow and shoved it back under her head. Why did her husband have to be so confounding? The night before he openly teased, and flirted with her, acting as if he still desired her. They weren't used to speaking to each other out in the open, but she had hoped he would have at least explained why he sent her away only to drag her back. He had never even asked how she was feeling or about his child. Didn't he care about his heir? Most of all, she had wanted to ask what was going to happen to her after the baby was born, and if she would be sent away once again. Except before she had a chance, something had changed his mood. He had deposited her at the bottom of the steps, and as if she were a child, sent her off to bed.

It wasn't hard to understand his reason for sending her away in the first place, he didn't want a wife. A lover yes, but not a wife. Was he wanting her to come back to his bed? To be honest, the thought had crossed her mind. She missed the time she lay in his arms and sharing his warmth on the cold, rainy nights. Now that she could feel the baby move, she wanted to share this special time with him.

She sat up and swung her legs over the edge of the huge bed. Her belly bulged out and she placed her hands over it. "You are growing bigger with each day," she said, rubbing it gently. The baby moved, it felt like fluttering wings as it repositioned itself.

If she had figured correctly, it wouldn't be long before the child arrived. She sighed. There were going to be a lot of long, uncomfortable, lonely nights ahead.

Standing, Adriana slipped on her heavy robe and slippers, crossed to the hearth, and placed a few pieces of wood over the glowing coals. She watched as the fire roared back to life. Moving backwards like a horse hooking to a cart she settled into a high-backed chair and closed her eyes, hoping for a little break from reality. However, it wasn't long before she recalled how considerate and attentive Cam had been in the beginning the night before. He had even gifted her his mother's harp. She paused and wondered, but why? Did he expect she would play soft melodies for him each night like his beloved Blair had years ago? Furthermore, if he didn't love or care for her and wasn't planning to keep her as his wife, she wasn't going to concede to offering any marital benefits, including playing sweet melodies for him. A riot of emotions tossed around in her head, yet the one that seemed to always find its way to the top of the list was fear. She still had no idea of what was to come of her after her baby was born. She lay awake each night wondering if she and Lynette should pack what they truly needed and leave. She didn't want to return to her father, but where could they go? Adriana concluded that she needed to formulate a plan to escape, during the light of day when her head appeared clearer.

There was a knock on her door, it opened, and Bethany entered carrying a tray with Adriana's breakfast. Bethany wore a peculiar, almost mischievous grin as she ambled to Adriana and set the tray down on the table before her.

"What are you about today, Bethany?" Adriana asked warily. "The last time I saw that expression on your face, we nearly poisoned my husband with your foolish potion we placed in his brandy."

"It's nothing quite that exciting I'm afraid. But I do have a surprise for ye, milady."

Adriana rolled her eyes. "Is this a good surprise, or I'm I going to regret ever hearing it."

"Aye! I am sure ye will like this news." She settled into the other chair next to the table. Adriana welcomed Bethany's kindness from the moment they met. They had become fast friends when she had first arrived, and she highly valued that friendship.

After taking a sip of her tea, Adriana set the cup down and placed her hands on her lap. "Alright, what is this big surprise you have for me."

The woman's face lit up when she grinned. "When I was cleaning the rooms in this wing in preparation for Hogmanay, I came across the nursery. 'Tis verra close, just down at the far end of this corridor. I was told no one was allowed to enter the chamber since Lady Blair's passing. I know ye don't have much for yer baby, and ye hae not said yer husband has given ye permission to enter the nursery yet, but I think we could sneak in, take a few things that yer going to need, and be back to ye room without anyone ever knowing."

"Oh, we can't do that." Adriana's giggle came out slightly apprehensive. "Besides, I have made a few sleeping gowns and nappies for the baby from some of my older clothes, and even fashioned the bottom drawer to one of the wardrobes as a bed for the baby. I don't think the baby is going to need much more than that for a few months."

Bethany shook her head. "The wee one's going to need more than a few gowns and nappies." She crossed to the bed and began to fuss with the covers. "What's more, I'm sure yer aware that the laird and a large troop of soldiers left the castle at dawn on patrol, which means yer are free to move aboot the castle without a guard dogging yer heels." She fluffed the pillows and arranged them neatly on the bed. "I was told they were laden with supplies and not expected back for weeks."

Adriana wondered at the woman's words. Why hadn't he

mentioned last night that he was going to accompany his men this morning. Especially if he planned to be away for such a long period of time.

While she ate, and Bethany helped her dress and fashion her hair, Adriana recalled how Cameron's mood had changed when she had mentioned watching a patrol leave yesterday morning. If he had planned to leave so soon, why hadn't he mentioned it to her then? The fact he hadn't offered anything from the nursery to her, and he neglected to escort her back to her bedchamber the night before, reinforced her belief that he did not consider her his wife. Her main concern at this time was to come up with a plan on how to keep herself, the baby, and Lynette safe.

Cam pulled his plaid tight around his neck as his horse trekked across the rough highland landscape. The constant drizzle which had plagued them all morning, had turned to sleet. When they changed directions and headed west, gusts of wind blew the sharp shards against his face. There was no need to turn around, he knew his men were just as miserable as he. They'd marched out of Corell Castle four days ago, and the weather had been wretched every moment of their journey. Forced to sleep on the cold wet ground made old injuries ache and every man grouchy. His men were half frozen and tired, they wanted to return to their warm homes and their loving families. A knot twisted in his belly. Unlike them Cam had no loving family waiting to welcome him home.

Like a man afflicted with sickness, Cam's every waking moments since he'd left Angel at the bottom of the steps were dominated with thoughts of Blair and their baby or Angel and hers. He constantly tormented himself wondering if there was even the slightest chance his wife's baby could be his own. His desire for her to resume her place by his side as his lady wife, and for her child to be raised as his heir, had vanished when she drew her hand from his, then inquired about her lover.

As hard as it was to accept, he realized the honorable thing to do would be to release her. Let her go and be happy with the man she loved.

Twenty-Two

Adriana laid awake most of the night worried about what the future held for her and her unborn child. Where would they go, and what would she need to keep the baby safe and well cared for? The nursery Bethany had mentioned crept into her thoughts and stuck there. She tossed and turned with the desire to investigate Corell's nursery. She tried to tell herself it was from curiosity or boredom, but she knew deep down it most likely stemmed from genuine panic, and her desperation to have what she might need with her for when the baby came, and she was forced to flee.

Her bedchambers felt like a prison cell as she paced around the room, waiting for Bethany to arrive with her morning meal. When she finally entered, Adriana rushed to her. After her friend put her tray down, Adriana grabbed her hands and said, "I have been thinking about the nursery you told me of, and I would like for you to take me there."

Bethany squeezed her hands and grinned. "'Tis not far from here, in the newer portion of the castle, which has nice glass windows." Taking her by the hand, Bethany scurried toward the door.

They hastened down the empty corridor. Adriana prayed they wouldn't run into anyone who she felt she would have to explain what they were about. They both giggled as they hurried along, like two lasses hiding from their governess. As they turned a corner, they met Lynette, and the girl's face lit up with a wide smile. "I was just coming to visit with you. Where are you two off to in such a hurry?"

The three women stood in the corridor. Adriana wasn't sure if she should tell her sister where they were going, but then Bethany said, "Come with us, we could use yer help. Ye can guard the door and let us know if anyone is coming."

Adriana planned to take only a couple of items that she was sure no one would ever notice were missing. She glanced over at her sister. Maybe she shouldn't take anything. What would Lynette think of her for stealing from Laird MacCormac?

"This is it," Bethany whispered, checking their surroundings before pushing down on the door's iron latch. The door opened and as Bethany positioned Lynette out in the corridor, Adriana snuck into the dark room. The room smelled of dust, mold, and old wood. A streak of light peaked out from behind a curtain, drawing Adriana's attention. Each footstep kicked up a layer of dust and left her tiny footprints on the carpet. She pulled the dark blue velvet drapes back and bright sunshine flooded the large space. Tiny specks of dust danced in the sun's rays like little fairies. Crossing to another set of curtains, she drew them back, letting more light into the room, then moved on to the last set of windows. Except, the third set of curtains when pulled back revealed a small chamber with a narrow bed, a wardrobe, a small cabinet, and a charming metal crib. Adriana turned in a circle taking in the enormity of the space. The curtained-in area was obviously set up for the family's nurse or nanny.

There were two sets of huge bookcases in opposite corners of the room, their shelves cluttered with books and toys. The bottom shelf of one of the bookcases was set up with a small stable and a collection of tiny carved wood horses, cows, sheep, goats, and several dogs. Two wooden swords, the blades and tips worn down, proved they must have been the favorite toys of two young lads. A wooden boat with a ripped sail lay on the floor next to a large wooden horse on wheels. A low round table with four chairs had been placed in front of one of the bookcases, which reminded her of the table in the nursery at Shealoch where she and Lynette had played for hours. She wondered how many children had lived and played in this chamber, and how magical it must have been.

To her left, against the wall were two narrow beds, a small table positioned perfectly between them. Then she noticed a lone rocking chair under a window, with its own table placed next to it. The spot seemed very cozy and so inviting even though a thick layer of dust covered everything. She strolled across the room to inspect the beautiful tapestries that covered the walls. One was a colorful summer scene by a lovely lake, the other tapestry was of a field of cows. Adriana turned and surveyed the chambers and envisioned the area cleaned and polished as it should be. Putting the chambers back in order would be the perfect distraction she needed to occupy her time before she, Lynette, and the baby left. Adriana hurried over to the closest window and opened it. Sneezing, she said, "This place needs a good cleaning." She turned to Bethany and added, "The curtains need to come down and be washed. The rugs need to be taken outside for a good beating."

Bethany's gaze traveled around the chambers. "It will be a huge undertaking. All of the furniture will need to be moved. Just think how delightful it will be when we hae finished. Ye and yer child will share many wonderful hours together in here."

Adriana wished that were true, yet she didn't share her misgivings. Although Bethany had been a good friend to her, she had a husband and so she needed to stay here with him. Penny, her sister's maid, also had a husband. Neither would be informed of her plans to leave Corell Castle.

"I'm sure you can find two strong men who could help us." Adriana said, rubbing her belly. "Two who can be trusted not to mention any of this to anyone else, though." Adriana walked over to the small cabinet next to the crib. Inside were two piles of nappies and a neatly folded stack of sleeping gowns. She brushed the palms of her hands together to remove the lingering dust. "If I were to take anything, it would have to be washed," she said mostly to herself.

Then she noticed a blue wooden rattle. Picking it up she examined it and could tell before the handle had been pounded into the round main part, the hollow part had been filled with tiny seeds or pebbles. After someone fit the pieces together, the whole thing had been painted blue. Whoever fashioned the baby toy put a lot of time and love into making it. She wondered if Cameron had made it for the poor baby he had lost. The rattle would have been a wonderful gift from a father to his child. Although she would have liked to have the rattle, she decided against taking it. The less she had to carry when they left, the better.

Bethany shushed her. She put her finger to her lips and frowned. Lifting the hem of her skirt, Adriana scurried over to the door and listened. She heard voices, her sister wasn't alone in the corridor. "It's Kinny," she mouthed to Bethany. She heard him ask Lynette what she was doing there.

Her sister replied, "I must have taken a wrong turn some-where. I was trying to find the east tower again. I wanted another look at the scenery. I didn't get much of a chance to view the landscape the other day when you took me up there." Adriana heard him laugh, and then he offered to show her the way. The corridor went quiet. Adriana and Bethany stared at each other, their mouths dropping open. "I cannot believe she went off alone with him like that," Adriana said.

"Weel, ye know a lass will do what she must to protect her sister." Bethany smirked, then winked. The reminder of what she had done for Lynette made Adriana blush. Her sister was growing up. Just so it wasn't too fast.

Adriana, Bethany, and Lynette spent the next week discreetly cleaning the nursery. They cleaned, as if she and the baby would occupy the space, yet Adriana continued to form a plan for when it would be best to leave, and just how they could slip away from the castle without being seen.

Cam and his men had stayed away much longer than he'd expected. It had been weeks since the morning he'd rode out of the main gate; the morning he'd left Adriana and his future behind.

He and his men covered much of the Highlands, but there had been no sign of the raiders and Cam prayed they had stopped. Deep in his soul he wanted to catch them himself, to dole out his own brand of justice for putting many of the clans at risk of suffering King William's wrath. He split the men up into three troops and sent two troops out in opposite directions, and soon the killing, looting, and burning began again. Each time they drew close to the killers, they vanished.

It was the middle of the night when Cam and his half-froze men rode through the main gates and into the bailey of Corell Castle. His body ached and he couldn't remember the last time he'd eaten.

After Cam soaked his sore, tattered body in a hot bath and had eaten his fill, he crawled into his large bed, but couldn't sleep. His past haunted him, and his future eluded him. With a bottle of brandy in his hand he roamed the cold dark corridors like an ill-fated, ancient spirit. Soon he found himself in the nursery. Although he'd experienced both joy and pain in this chamber over his lifetime, generally he'd felt surrounded by his family and their love here. The musty air had disappeared, and cool, fresh air filled the space. He crossed the room, lit only by the glow of the moon through the drape-less windows, to where a window stood open. He set his bottle on the table, closed the window, then settled into the old rocking chair. The old chair creaked as he leaned back and rocked. Closing his eyes, he relaxed and felt content for the first time in weeks.

A faint clanking of metal sounded in the silence awakening Cam. He opened his eyes as a ghostly figure in a white gown holding a candle before her, quietly entered the chambers. He wondered why his body hadn't tensed. Had he passed in his sleep? Could this be a spirit from his past come to collect him? The way he felt at the moment he wouldn't have minded. He kept an eye on the tall slender spirit, her long dark wavey hair hung to her rounded hips. She floated across the room to the cabinet next to the metal crib, set her candle down, and picked something up from the top.

"Do ye haunt my castle like a disenchanted ghost with each twilight, lass?"

He heard her gasp. She jumped to the side and spun around to face him, bumping into the cabinet causing something to fall and hit the floor. She stood with one hand pressed against her throat, the other protectively against her belly. Afraid she may have hurt herself, Cam jumped up and rushed to her side. "Are ye hurt lass?" He reached out to take her elbow to steady her, but her rounded belly, which had appeared to have grown considerably since he'd left, stood between them. "What are ye doing here," he asked, knowing his request sounded more like a growl than a question.

She drew in a ragged breath. "Oh! Cameron, you frightened me. I didn't think anyone would be here."

He reached out and took her trembling hand in his. "Come, lass." He led her back to the rocking chair. "Sit here," he said, gesturing to the chair. She resembled a cornered hare, moments before the dogs caught up with it. "What's the matter lass, are ye afraid of me?" When she didn't reply, he said, "Ye needn't be. I willnae hurt ye." She still didn't appear convinced, so Cam knelt before her and offered a slight smile. "What were ye looking for?"

Her eyes were still large and round, but she said, "I am sorry I came in here without your permission. I only took what I needed for when the baby is born." She raked her teeth over her lower lip in a way which stirred his loins. Then she said, "Except, tonight I couldn't sleep. I admired the little blue rattle and couldn't get it out of my mind, so I came back for it. I didn't think anyone would miss it." She looked as if she might cry. Cam got to his feet, walked over by the crib, and picked the rattle up off the floor. He held the tiny thing in his hand. Memories of his past washed over him, and his heart twisted with a dull ache. Returning to Angel, he knelt again and handed her the rattle.

"As mistress and my lady wife, the castle and everything in it is yers. Ye are free to roam around and explore any portion of the castle ye wish."

She held the rattle as if it were the most precious thing. "Thank you. Do you know who made this rattle, it's quite lovely."

Cam was happy the chamber was dark, for he feared he blushed for the first time since he was a lad. "I made it years ago for my son."

"Oh." Her lips formed a perfect, little, kissable circle. "Then you must keep it." She handed the baby toy back to him.

"No." He held the palm of his hand up. "'Tis yers now. For yer child." His words ripped at his heart. He struggled to breathe. Cam stood, strolled to the window, and glanced out into the darkness, hoping to find the right words to express his emotions. Emotions he couldn't even name. After a moment he said, "Tell me who cleaned this chambers?" When she didn't readily answer, he turned and glanced down at her. Her eyes were closed, and she clutched the rattle to her chest. Had he been too gruff? Softer he said, "I hope ye did not clean this large room by yerself, lass." Her gaze shot up to his. "Tell me who helped ye?" When she shook her head as if to say, 'no'. Cam laughed. She would not betray her friends in fear he may punish them. "Never fear lass, I shall not ask ye again to name yer cohorts. Ye can add that to all yer other secrets." Grabbing his bottle of brandy, Cam strolled over to the nurse's bed and sat down. He drank deeply.

"If we are going to share secrets, milord," she said softly. "Then why were you sitting here, by yourself, in the middle of the night, in the dark?"

Cam glanced at her. She seemed to have more confidence the further away he was from her. "Over the years I hae found myself in this room imagining how different my life would be if my wife and son would hae both lived." At first, he had longed for what he had lost, then for the missed opportunity to be a husband and father. When he had finally come to terms with the way his life was going to be, it was turned upside down when an unknown enemy attempted to kill him. Upon awakening and not knowing who he could trust, he finds this woman, a nameless stranger, in his arms making love to him. Suddenly, his life had more secrets than the Bishops and Cardinals combined.

"Tell me about her. What she was like." Angel's soft voice cut through his thoughts, bringing him back to reality.

He set the bottle on the bedside table. "Blair... She was sweet. She loved to spend hours in her flower gardens and the solarium. She would ride across the fields with the sun on her face, laughing all the while." He smiled when he noticed the rocking chair rocking back and forth. "Blair was young and so tiny I could hae put her in my pocket." Angel smiled and continued to rock. "Her hair was as black as a raven's wing. She had mysterious eyes; they were the color of the sea when a storm was brewing." He chuckled. "But the lass was verra gentle."

"How young were you when you wed?"

"Weel, let me think, he said, scratching his chin. "I must have been three and twenty, and Blair was six and ten." Suddenly Cam felt very tired, so he laid back against the pillows. He sighed as a picture of Blair, large with child danced in his mind. "She had been verra excited when she learned she was going to hae my child. And the days and nights for months were good. Then one hot night in August all our dreams and plans were destroyed." His life had ended. The room spun once; Cam felt like he was floating on his back in the river. He'd had enough brandy for the night. He struggled, but worked his way until he was sitting up on the edge of the bed. It felt much better to have both of his feet on the floor. Glancing over at Angel, he saw her wipe away a tear on her cheek. "Tell me, Lady Adriana, why did ye take yer sister's place and return with my men when there was a strong chance that I was going to die?"

She gave a helpless little laugh. "I don't know where to start."

"Start at the beginning."

She placed the rattle on the table and rose to her feet, then turned toward the window. "I'm afraid it's not that easy." The room grew quiet and after a few moments he thought she wasn't going to say anything else. Then unexpectedly, she said, "One day I overheard my father telling one of his men that he wasn't going to let me marry. That no man had offered for me, and no man ever would."

"Why would he say such a thing?"

"Because of my scar... I was too ugly. No man would ever

want me for his wife. That my father planned on keeping me. I was to work as his housekeeper as my punishment."

"Punishment for what? What could ye hae done to warrant that strong a punishment?"

"Retribution for my mother's death."

"How did yer mum die, lass?" Cam crawled slowly off the bed, not wanting to spook her in fear she may stop and not continue.

"My mother and I had gone to the river to swim. She crawled onto the bank and yelled for me to come out of the water, but I wanted to stay. Suddenly, I was caught in the current and I couldn't make it back to the shore. My mother came out to get me but was caught by the current herself and pulled under. I was able to grab a hold of a floating tree branch, which scratched my face, but I wasn't strong enough to go after her. I couldn't help her." Angel started to weep.

Cam walked up behind her, placing his hands on her shoulders; he gently turned her around to face him. He brushed the hair away from her cheek and gazed into her beautiful amber eyes. He wanted to hold her in his arms and kiss her. Hopefully, alleviate years of sadness and torment, yet he knew it wouldn't be that easy.

Glancing up at him she said, "I wasn't strong enough to save her. I was little, only eight years old." She started to sob.

Cam pulled her into his arms, struck anew by her beauty and lush curves. "It wasn't yer fault, Angel. Ye would never hae been able to pull her to shore."

"My father holds me responsible for my mother's death. At first, he beat me, but would never give me a reason why. As I got older, he ignored me or treated me not much more than a servant. He informed me of the alliance he'd made with you for protection, and that you would accept Lynette as payment. But then your men came to collect Lynette, and they said that you were going to die." She leaned back and glanced up at him, blinking back her tears. "It was the perfect opportunity for me to get away from my father. Plus, it gave Lynette a chance for a love match someday."

"Ye could hae let me die once we were wed. Ye would hae had the security of clan MacCormac to protect ye from yer father."

"Oh. No." Her expression showed that her feelings were genuine. "I could never have done that. I couldn't save my mother, so I swore to you on the night of our wedding, I would do whatever I could to save your life."

"Yer bravery made ye take yer sister's place, marry me, then tend to my wounds and save my life."

Angel shook her head. "I wish I *were* brave. If I were, I would have stood up for myself, stood up to my father."

"Angel, why did ye come to me each night? Why would ye not show yerself to me, or tell me who ye were?"

She turned her head and tried to turn away from him. He didn't release her. He would never let her turn away from him again. She paused, then said, "When you didn't die, I knew I needed to get pregnant as soon as possible. I feared if you saw my face, learned I wasn't the young and beautiful girl my father had promised, you would send me away or..." She raked her lower lip with her teeth before glancing back up to him. "Have me murdered. I couldn't risk showing myself to you or tell you we were married."

Tilting back his head, Cam laughed. "Ye are the bravest lass I hae ever heard of. Blair was never strong, or brave like ye. She could hae never left her family, rode across country to marry a man she dinnae know, who was about to die. Then marry him, heal him, and give him back his life. Then ye gathered not only one army of warriors, but two and marched into a military encampment, face Colonel Robert Stone and demanded the release of me and my men."

He gazed into her eyes. "Ye are my brave and beautiful Angel." He lowered his head and kissed her.

His lips were first soft and tender, but the pressure increased as his passion grew. Adriana had waited a long time to be held in his arms like this again. Kissed with a promise of what their life could be. Nonetheless, he hadn't revealed why he sent her away, or what his plans were for her after the child's birth. That small corner in her heart warned her to be weary of his motives. Did she dare presume he could one day feel the same love for her as he'd had for Blair?

Adriana's rapid heartbeat thumped in her ears, and her mind ran through the possibilities of what might happen between them if she stayed versus what could happen to her if she left. Would she be allowed to be a mother or merely a nursemaid to her child? Did he desire her as his bride, or would he treat her as an unwanted wife once again? Was he truly sincere? Could she trust him?

"I missed having ye in my arms and warming my bed at night, lass. Ye belong to me, and I'll never let ye out of my sight. Ye will never leave Corell Castle again." She stared up into his eyes. Her urge to run must have shown on her face. Cameron's thick black brows drew together as he intently watched her. If she stayed, she would be staking her life on his idea of affection. His words of caring for her sounded more like ownership, which made the risk too high.

Adriana stepped back; her hands placed protectively on her stomach. "I'm sorry. I must go." She prayed he didn't notice the tears filling her eyes as she turned away from him and fled from the chamber.

Twenty-Three

C am heard loud voices and laughter coming from the great hall as he trudged down the corridor. Entering, he found his ex-brother-in-law, Rory Murdock and his men sitting at a low table, eating from trenchers piled high with meat, cheese, and bread, and drinking ale. Rory rose when he spotted Cam. Cam nodded to the man and walked on by. He was in no mood to listen to the man's whining today.

As of late, Angel took to avoiding him by staying in her room playing her harp. It had been weeks since the night he'd kissed her in the nursery. A kiss filled with such passion he'd been afraid he might burst into flames with longing for her. He meant to tell her he didn't care that the baby wasn't his. He loved her and was willing to claim the baby as his own, but she had rushed out of the room before he could explain. He'd wanted to go after her, except her reaction to their kiss proved her feelings lay somewhere else.

He thought of the last few months and wished things had transpired differently. After leaving her home and all that she knew, she had been left alone and vulnerable in this strange castle. While he lay helpless on death's door. Malcolm had been strong and available. He'd been ready to step in for Cam as Laird, and as husband. How could she not have fallen for him? Cam regretfully resigned to the fact that Adriana had chosen Malcolm over him. He would stand by her choice, however, the thought of living without her by his side made him physically ill. How would he ever let his angel go?

That morning when Kinny had brought the message to him stating Hugh and his men were mounted and ready to leave, the lad had had declared that the castle was abuzz with the preparation for the forthcoming MacCormac heir. Cam exited his chambers with a sour taste upon his tongue. Servants scurried past him in the corridor, bobbing quick curtsies and rushing off. It seemed every person in the castle was avoiding *his* needs and had taken to getting ready for Angel's baby's arrival, which wasn't for another few weeks.

Distracted with his thoughts of Angel, and what the future held for them, Cam was startled when Rory unexpectedly appeared at his side. Cam turned to face the man. A disgusting odor accompanied the filthy and ragged appearance of Rory Murdock. "Och, Murdock, hae ye and yer men taken to bedding down with the pigs?" Cam took a step back from the man. "Ye smell like a three-day-old gut-pile." Cam knew he'd pushed his men hard, but this was disgusting even for Rory.

Rory snarled, "My men and I aspire to ride to Edinburgh for some lively entertainment." A roar came from the table, where his men filled their faces with Cam's food and ale.

"'Tis not safe for ye to go noo. The king's dragoons yearn to capture a party of Highlanders. Ye'd all be arrested and imprisoned as traitors."

"My men and I hae needs, MacCormac. We hae worked hard for ye, and we desire an array of assorted amusements." Rory offered a sneering grin, which revealed his stained and decaying teeth. His men raised their mugs and roared a resounding cheer to emphasize their agreement with their leader's request.

Cam shifted his weight from one foot to the other and released a loud sigh. Arguing with Murdock was going to make him late for his meeting with three other clan leaders. The lairds were gathering to discuss their spring seeding programs, damage done to the arable and pastoral lands, and who would need to buy or trade seed before spring planting. "'Tis not a good time to go trapesing off to Edinburgh. Ye must stay close to the castle."

Rory took a step closer and hissed between his teeth, "A proper *Chieftain* would see to his men's needs afore his own."

Cam had avoided his ex-brother-in-law over the past five years since his sister's death, yet Cam knew the time would come when the man's true feelings for him would surface. Rory had blamed Cam for Blair's and his nephew's deaths. Except, Rory was no longer a lad of ten and eight, and Cam had an inkling Rory longed to take over as chief of Clan MacCormac. Cam felt the hilt of his sword under his hand as he stared down at Rory. "Ye best mind yer feral tongue lad whilst ye still hae one." He pushed passed Rory and headed for the archway leading to the corridor.

∽

Adriana entered the great hall just as Cam approached her. "Milord," she said, stepping out in front of him. "I would speak with you, if I may."

He glanced at her briefly. "I hae no time noo, lass." Taken aback by his response, Adriana stared after him as he charged out of the keep through the large wooden doors. She had wanted Cam to walk with her around the bailey so she could explain her behavior and apologize for running out of the nursery the way she did. There were still things they needed to discuss. Most importantly, she needed to know what his intentions were toward her once his heir was born. Would he treat her as his lady wife? Several heavily armed men brush passed her, forcing her back against the wall to avoid getting trampled. The man who appeared to be the leader of the troop sneered down at her as he passed by, the rest of the troop ignored her.

Pulling her shawl up over her shoulders, Adriana decided to walk by herself. She ventured down the steps and across the inner bailey. The sun on her face and the fresh air felt marvelous after being locked up inside all winter. Roaming around the corridors of the castle wasn't quite the same as being able to be outside. She'd been out a couple of times over the past few months, but Kinny had always escorted her. She was restless, and today was a perfect day to get out and stretch her legs. The bright sun and warm air had melted any remaining snow, so she wasn't afraid she might slip and fall. Since she couldn't speak to Cameron, her thoughts turned to finding other ways to calm her nerves. The smells of springtime, clover, freshly turned soil, reminded her of the wildflowers she'd picked as a child. It would be lovely to find some and bring a little springtime back inside with her.

Soldiers on horseback and boys with carts piled high with wood passed by without a acknowledging her. The women tended the gardens, and others milling around the inner bailey took no notice of her either. They acted as if she were already gone. Maybe they didn't want an English woman living there and wouldn't mind if their chieftain sent her away after his heir was born. Adriana scanned her surroundings. It seemed to be the perfect time to ascertain a way for her, Lynette, and the baby to escape without being noticed.

Adriana passed through the gate to the outer bailey. Men were practicing in the training ring, three men stood by the smithy's shop, and there was a man and two boys hanging fresh candles. Adriana lumbered along to the main gate. The guard's hard expression softened as she drew closer. "Good day," she said, approaching him. "I wish to go outside the wall and pick some flowers." She pressed a hand to her belly and rubbed her back with her other hand. The guard glanced around. "I won't be long," she promised. He nodded and let her pass.

Once outside the gate, Adriana spotted a patch of purple and white flowers along the wall. She waddled over to a patch of alliums and anemones. Bending low, she picked several. Off in the distance she spotted yellow gorse bushes and a field of heather, but they were too far for her to make it there and back without some help. Adriana picked an armful of purple and white flowers and wished she had thought to bring a basket with her. A washer woman, burdened with a heavy basket came along. Bobbing her head she said, "Good morning to ye milady."

"Good morning. Isn't it a wonderful day," Adriana replied as she lifted the bouquet to her nose and breathed in the flower's heavenly scent.

"If ye be wanting more flowers, mistress," the woman said, "I saw bluebells along the trail to the river." The woman pointed to a narrow trail leading to the west.

"Oh, you are very kind. Thank you so much." Clutching the flowers to her side, Adriana lifted her skirts and headed in the direction the woman had indicated. Not wanting to roam too far from the castle, Adriana hoped she would come across the flowers soon. The trail was rough. Careful not to trip over rocks or raised roots, she took her time, cautiously watching where she placed each foot.

When she heard voices, she glanced up to find a group of warriors walking toward her on the trail leading their horses. One of the men in front was the man she'd seen arguing with her husband in the great hall. His brows were low over his intense gaze, his lips pressed close together. His wide stride was going to bring him straight to her, which frightened her. Obviously, he was still quite upset with his laird. The group stopped directly in front of her, making no move to walk around her. Apprehensive, Adriana turned around to head back to the gate but found the men surrounding her. Glancing at each of the men, she realized none of them looked familiar. Although she didn't know all her husband's men, she expected to recognize one of them. Returning her gaze to the leader she smiled and said, "Oh. Excuse me. I'll step aside so you can pass." When she started to move, the man seized her arm. He swiftly lifted her up onto his horse then stepped up behind her. Adriana panicked, and tried to scream, but a hand covered her mouth and stifled her cries. The other men had mounted their horses. The group turned and galloped across the field away from the castle. Adriana held her belly and prayed she wouldn't fall. A fall from this high up would probably kill both her and her baby. She needed to stay calm and figure out a way to escape this madman.

Twenty-Four

Cam and his men rode back through the main gate to Corell Castle, looking forward to their evening meal. The meeting with neighboring clan chiefs had taken only a few hours, and he was pleased with how much was accomplished in the short period of time. The larger clans had an abundance of various grains and livestock available to sell or trade to those hit hardest by the raiders. He felt confident there would even be sufficient grain to haul and sell in Edinburgh after harvest.

He rode through the outer bailey, stopping his mount when he reached the gate to the inner bailey. "Milord! Milord!" Cam turned to find a distraught Lynette running toward him causing his heart to sink to the pit of his stomach. He leaped from his horse and grabbed her as she flung herself into his arms.

"What has happened, lass?"

"She's gone," the girl cried. Her body trembled as she clung to him.

"What the devil..." He thrust the girl back and glanced down into her tearful eyes. "What are ye going on aboot?"

"We've searched everywhere, and we can't find Adriana." Lynette cried. "I enlisted the servants in the search, but it has been over an hour, and no one has found her yet."

Malcolm and Hugh appeared at Cam's side. "What has happened?" Malcolm asked.

Turning to Hugh, Cam said, "Check with the guard at the main gate to see if he saw Lady Adriana adventure outside of the main gate earlier." Hugh nodded, swung up onto his horse's back and raced across the outer bailey to the main gate.

He regarded the weeping child clinging to his sleeves. In a gentle voice he said, "Lynette, calm yerself. Go back inside the keep and continue to search for yer sister. Hae the servants check each chamber again, and the storerooms below. Do ye understand lass?" Lynette nodded, but before she turned to leave, Cam added, "We weel find her. I give ye my word." The girl nodded again, turned, and raced off toward the keep.

When Cam turned back around, he found a crowd had gathered. He strode to the middle of the group and yelled, "Has anyone seen Lady Adriana in the baileys or walk out of the main gate earlier?" Just then Hugh returned but didn't dismount. Cam's gaze locked with his cousin's, and Hugh announced, "The guard confirmed that Lady Adriana walked out the gate. She said she wouldn't be long, so when he returned from his midday meal and he didn't see her come back, he figured she had returned whilst he ate."

A hunched over washer woman appeared at Cam's side. "Milaird, her Ladyship was picking flowers outside of the gate alongside the wall. I told her there were more flowers along the river trail. The last I saw she was heading in the direction of that trail. That be aboot two hours ago."

Nodding his head, Cam leaped upon his horse and galloped across the outer bailey and out through the gate. He spurred his horse, urging him to go faster. He prayed he would find Angel well. That she had lost track of time or fallen asleep under a tree. Except he'd fought too many battles to mistake the horrific feeling of dread in his heart at the moment.

As he approached the river trail, Cam reined in his horse and came to a stop. A pile of white and purple flowers lay wilted and discarded upon the ground. Horse hoof prints covered the area. Cam's attention was drawn to the sound of pounding hoofs. When he turned, he found he'd been followed by twenty-some of his warriors. Not waiting to explain, and convinced Angel had been captured, he tore off in the direction the hoof prints set out. Cam tracked the other horses quite a few miles before coming to a small clearing. He spotted a group of twenty-five to thirty men on horseback along the edge of the forest.

When the horsemen turned to face them, one man held a woman before him. Cam couldn't see the man's face, but he recognized Angel's golden overdress and white kertch she wore over her hair. A growl started low in his belly, boiled, and became a roar as it escaped his throat. Cam pulled his sword, his horse reared, and they charged forward. His men followed him across the field toward the waiting soldiers. As they drew closer the man holding Angel suddenly pushed her off his horse and charged forward. Cam watched his pregnant wife hit the ground. His stare shot back to the horseman. He wasn't surprised to see it had been Rory Murdock hiding behind her. Cam rode straight for his ex-brother-in-law, ramming his horse into the side of Murdock's horse as the coward attempted to turn away.

Murdock fell from his horse, scrambled to his feet, and withdrew his sword. Cam leaped from his horse, drawing his own sword. He was bathed in anger and hatred. Metal struck metal with a deafening clank. "If ye feel ye need to confess yer sins Murdock, ye hae one minute to do so before I run ye through."

Rory snarled. "Ye hae been unable to catch me, least kill me.

Ye are no longer worthy of being chieftain of the MacCormacs."

"What did ye expect to gain by burning fields and killing defenseless farmers?" Men were fighting all around them. Several already lie lifeless on the ground.

"When ye married my sister, I tried to kill ye and take over as chieftain of the clan, but ye got her with child, so I altered my plans. Then they both died, which left me with nothing."

Cam changed his position hoping to see how Angel faired, but Murdock kept pressing forward and Cam didn't dare turn his attention away from the man.

"How fitting it would have been if His Majesty's soldiers would have hung you for my deeds. Although it weel give me great pleasure to dispense of ye here and noo." All of a sudden Murdock charged forward. Cam blocked the man's blow with his sword, then pulled his sghian duhn and slipped it between Murdock's ribs. The man stared into Cam's eyes in disbelief before falling to the ground dead.

Cam glanced around and found all of Murdock's men's lifeless bloody bodies lying at the feet of his own men. Though his men where covered in dirt, sweat and blood, their adrenalin was still high, and they awaited their laird's next command. Frantic to learn if Angel was hurt, Cam turned and found Malcolm kneeling down, holding her protectively in his arms. Cam's first instinct was to run his cousin through. One more dead body wouldn't be hard to explain. Before he made his move, Malcolm whispered something to Adriana. She nodded her head, and by the time Cam reached her side, Malcolm had helped her to her feet. Adriana glanced up at Cam, her eyes filled with distress.

"Are ye well, lass? Do ye think ye can ride back to the castle?"

She favored him with shy smile and replied, "Yes, milord. I am unharmed, I think I can make it back."

"I will carry ye to my horse." He glanced over her head to Malcolm to see if the man was going to protest or not. When Malcolm didn't object, Cam scooped her up into his arms. Everything could have easily turned out differently. He thanked the Lord for keeping Angel safe as he carried her toward his horse.

The sound of approaching horses drew everyone's attention. An English patrol of dragoons charged toward them. Cam's men, covered in the blood of their attackers, stood at the ready, waiting for their laird's instructions.

The soldiers pulled their horses to a stop and curiously assessed the battlefield and the recently demised. "We meet again, Laird MacCormac."

"Ah, Lieutenant Dunaway. I'm afraid yer too late." Still holding his wife in his arms, Cam gestured with his head to the dead lying on the ground. "My men and I hae found and dispatched the gang of murdering thieves. Ye may collect what's left of them if yer interested." He stood Angel on the ground next to him.

The lieutenant surveyed the numerous bodies on the ground before him. "It would seem you have made my life considerably easier." His gaze went to Angel. "Lady MacCormac." He nodded his head respectfully. "What is your involvement in all of this? I pray you are not injured in any way?"

Cam pointed to the lifeless body of Rory Murdock. "Murdock captured my Lady wife, earlier this day and we tracked them this far.

"Murdock charged forward and attacked my husband and his men," Angel said, her chin coming up defiantly.

Cam wrapped his arm around her shoulder and pulled her to his side. "As ye can see, lieutenant it dinnae fair weel for them."

The lieutenant shook his head. "You are a lucky man, Laird

MacCormac to have the brave and beautiful Lady MacCormac to stand up for you once again, and for your wife."

Cam grinned at the lieutenant, and thought yes, he was very lucky. Turning to face his men, Cam pulled his sword and raised it to the sky, and declared, "To the brave and beautiful Lady MacCormac."

Cam's men raised their swords and shouted, "To the brave and beautiful Lady MacCormac!" Alarmed, the horses the lieutenant and his soldiers were riding frantically danced in circles. Cam smiled down at Angel, and she chuckled.

Bethany, Penny, Lynette and even Maddy had made it a point to visit Adriana every couple of hours over the next three days. They all fussed over her making sure she was as comfortable as possible.

A knock sounded on Adriana's door. "Come in," she said, pulling the bed covers up and over her belly. Cam entered, then laughed as he drew a pillow out from behind his back and tossed it onto the bed next to her. "Here, I thought ye might need another pillow to help ye get comfortable." They both laughed.

"This is a little ridiculous I know, but I am quite comfortable," she said, taking his pillow and placing it amongst the many others surrounding her on the bed.

"Hae ye been able to get any rest today or has yer three guard dogs at ye door been making too much noise so ye cannae sleep?"

Adriana chuckled at his accurate description of Malcolm, Hugh, and Kinny, who had taken it upon themselves to search and question each person who tries to approach her door. "They made such a fuss over the tray of food Maddy brought me, that the poor woman almost dropped the whole thing on the floor." She giggled when she saw him chuckle, then added, "Needless to say, she banded all three of them from the kitchen for a week." It was wonderful to see her husband grin.

"I am not sure if I can get them to leave ye unattended," he said, "but I can try."

"Thank you, but they are quite entertaining to listen to. Especially, since Lady Moira and her brother arrived. I think she might be the only one who can actually control those three."

He paced around the room as if there was much on his mind. Adriana struggled to be patient, waiting for him to tell her what was truly bothering him. Patient was all she could be right then. She had been tucked in so tight in her bed that she couldn't have crawled out and forced him to speak if she had wanted to. When he finally spoke, his words surprised her. "I dinnae sleep at all last night," he said, rubbing the back of his neck. "I worried aboot both ye and the child. 'Tis relieved I am that yer both weel, lass."

"I understand your concern. I'm sure you're worried because of what happened with Blair and your son."

He winced at her words, then said, "Lass, if ye want yer freedom, I'll let ye and yer child go."

Adriana couldn't believe what she was hearing. Was he wanting her to leave again? When he turned to leave, Adriana reached out her hand as if to grab his sleeve. "Wait! Why would you say such a thing?"

"I love ye, lass. And if that is what would make ye happy..." He looked dejected and her heart ached for him. "Ye deserve to have what ye wish, Angel. Ye deserve to be with the mon ye love." He took her hand in his and rubbed his thumb over her palm. "I don't care if the child isnae mine. If it 'tis a boy, it would still be my heir. Someday he will be named chieftain of the MacCormac Clan."

Adriana watched as an array of emotions flashed across her husband's face. All this time had he thought the child was someone else's? Whose? "I *am* with the one I love, Cameron." When he gave her a confused look, she squeezed his hand and added, "The child is your child. Who did you imagine the father to be?"

"I donae know." His gaze fell to the floor. "I'm afraid with all the time ye spent with Malcolm, and how close ye two are..."

"Malcolm?" She pulled him closer to her. "Even though you were unconscious when we married and then you sent me away, I have faithfully honored my vows to you."

He watched her attentively, then said, "The only reason I sent ye away, was because I thought ye were yer sister, a mere child. If I had known ye were my Faceless Angel, I wouldnae hae sent ye back to yer father."

She ran her teeth over her lower lip as her eyes welled up with tears. "Before I knew I was carrying your heir, I couldn't take the risk that once you saw my face you wouldn't be disappointed and reject me." Her father had lied to her so many times, then with how Cam had treated her, she wondered if she would ever be able to trust a man ever again.

"Disappointed, never, lass. I wouldnae be standing here if it wasn't for ye." He knelt on the bed and brushed a light kiss upon her lips. That wasn't enough for Adriana though. She wrapped her arms around his neck and pulled him down upon the bed next to her and deepened the kiss.

Later that night Adriana was restless. Her lower back ached something fierce, but it was hard to know just how to relieve the pain. What she really wanted was to get out of bed and walk around. She pushed the covers back and scooted to the edge of the bed. "Bethany! Penny! Are either of you out there," she yelled.

The door opened and both women hurried into the room and to her side. "What can we do for ye milady? Do ye need to get up," Bethany asked, reaching for her arm.

"What I need is to get out of this bed and walk. I am stir-crazy from doing nothing but sitting."

Penny grinned. "You feel like getting up and walking? Are you having pains in your belly or lower back?"

"Isn't that what I just said to you," Adriana snapped, unlike herself.

"I'll stay with her while you go and send for the midwife," Penny said to Bethany. "It may take hours before the baby arrives, but then it might not. Better to have the midwife close by in case the baby gets anxious to make an appearance."

Bethany turned to Adriana as if asking for permission. Adriana nodded her head then moaned as another pain struck her lower back. She squeezed Penny's hand and yelled, "Yes. Go. And hurry." Though Bethany was already gone.

Penny's smile was reassuring when she said, "Lie on your side, milady and I'll rub your back. That should make your discomfort bearable." Penny helped her to lie back and then roll onto her side. The woman's hands worked magic on her lower back as she rubbed them in a circle. Adriana moaned with appreciation.

Once the midwife came Adriana lost track of time and reality. It seemed like she pushed for hours before the baby finally arrived. The gray-haired midwife wore a worried expression as she whispered instructions to Penny as she took the baby away. Adriana stretched her neck trying to see around the woman to her baby lying on the table by the fire.

"What is wrong? Is there something wrong?"

≈

Cam paced the corridor. No one would let him into Angel's bedchamber or tell him anything about the baby. Something was wrong. He was going to lose both his wife and child again. The thought twisted his insides until he felt he would retch. He approached the door where Kinny stood like a stone statue. The lad glared at him until Cam turned and moved away. Someday the skinny long-legged lad was going to prove himself a fearsome warrior.

Placing his palms against the stone wall, Cam drew in several deep breaths, hoping to calm himself. If something had happened, someone would have come out to inform him. What would he do if he lost them? That couldn't happen. He spun around when he heard the door to his wife's bedchambers open. When Bethany came out, Cam rushed passed Kinny into the room. He glanced at Angel, saw her distressed expression and tears, and hurried over to the midwife's side. "The babe," he asked, reaching for the child.

"Milaird," the midwife said huddled over the babe. "He isnae ready to meet his parents yet."

"Has he come to early? Will he be alright?"

"Aye, he may hae come a little early, but he will be fine. Give me a few minutes more to prepare him."

"A son!" he exclaimed, then turned toward Angel. She was propped up in the bed weeping. Cam hurried to her side and took her hand in his. "How are ye lass? Donae cry, our son 'tis fine. He is strong and brave like his mother. Everything is going to be fine."

Angel nodded yet continued to cry. "What are ye so upset about?"

"I don't know," she replied, staring up at him with tear-filled eyes. "It is silly, but I worry you will stop loving me?"

Cam held her hand, then reached out and traced the scar on her face with his finger and smiled. "That will never happen. A person who receives their scars due to bravery has earned the right to display them proudly. Donae ever hide this. 'Tis who ye are, love." He leaned forward and gently kissed her lips. "There is only one way to prove that I will always love ye. That my love is true." He raised her hand and kissed her palm. "Will ye marry me, Lady Adriana?"

Adriana laughed as she wiped away her tears. "We are already married, Cameron."

"Aye, but I owe ye a proper wedding. And I would like to be awake for it this time." He kissed her again, then whispered, "We never had a proper wedding night, either." He pulled her into his arms and kissed her with all his heart, promising a long life together.

J uly weddings could be unpredictable, but no more so than the couple getting married. The Highland spirits had whipped together a magical day, with a cloudless sky and a cool mountain breeze, which smelled of fresh heather.

Laird Cameron MacCormac, dressed in his finest kilt stood at the altar next to Father Fitzgerald in the small kirk. His hands damp with sweat as he waited as patiently as he could for his love to arrive.

The benches in the kirk were all filled, and more people lined the stone walls around the small interior. People who couldn't fit inside the little stone kirk meandered outside, some already celebrating the blessed event with mugs of ale and wine.

Cam's gaze floated over their friends and family who had gathered to join in the celebration of the birth of their son and to witness their marriage. Sir Alexander was seated next to Aunt Moira on the first bench right in front. They looked too friendly to him as they gazed at each other with silly smiles on their faces. No sillier than Lynette and Kinny who sat next to them. Bethany and her husband Big Alec were seated in the second row next to Penny and Mr. and Mrs. Wilson. Malcolm and Hugh were most likely out in the bailey already celebrating. Earlier, Cam had overheard them arguing on what the little laird should be named. Cam's father's name was William and he had mentioned he would like to name his son after the lad's grandsire. He received a strange look from his cousins who then informed him their next laird was to be named after each of them. Cam had turned and walked away, leaving the two to their arguing.

When Cam didn't think he could take waiting much longer, there she was. A vision dressed in a silver and gold gown, which hung off her shoulders. She held a bouquet of white, yellow, and pink roses, that matched the ones laced through her brown curls piled high upon her head.

Lady Adriana smiled shyly as she glided up the aisle. Everyone disappeared when her eyes met his. She joined him at the altar, standing by his side as Father Fitzgerald read from the bible. When the vows were finally finished, and they were once again married, Cameron turned to Angel and said, "I've loved ye from the moment ye held my soul in yer wee hands. And I will always love my beautiful, and so verra brave, Angel." He pulled her against him for a kiss.

Angel smirked, and with a Scottish brogue whispered, "And I love ye, my little laird."

A roar erupted from outside the kirk. Hundreds of warriors who had gathered around to celebrate this glorious day raised their swords to the sky and yelled, "To the brave and beautiful, Lady MacCormac."

THE END

**Don't miss out on your next favorite book!
Join the Melange Books mailing list at**
www.melange-books.com/mail.html

~

THANK YOU FOR READING

~

Did you enjoy this book?

We invite you to leave a review at your favorite book site, such as Goodreads, Amazon, Barnes & Noble, etc.

DID YOU KNOW THAT LEAVING A REVIEW...

- Helps other readers find books they may enjoy.
- Gives you a chance to let your voice be heard.
- Gives authors recognition for their hard work.
- Doesn't have to be long. A sentence or two about why you liked the book will do.

About the Author

The saying, "You can take the girl out of the country, but you can't take the country out of the girl" describes this author. She likes to herd cattle on horseback in Montana, snowmobile in Wyoming, garden and write romance novels. Her tales stem from a combination of past experiences and a lot of wishful thinking. The women in her novels are country girls, who find themselves in strange predicaments with men, who definitely have the makings of true heroes.

LuAnn has been writing since 1996 but has been dreaming up wild adventures her whole life. She resides in east central Minnesota.

Lfnies1@yahoo.com
www.luannnies.com

Also by LuAnn Nies

WITH SATIN ROMANCE

MacCormac Warriors Trilogy

Faceless Angel

Novels

Shadow Trail

Catrina's Cowboy

Freeing Abigail

JoAnna's Rescue

Bearly Christmas Darling

Entitled